promise me
you

ALSO BY MARINA ADAIR

Nashville Heights series

Promise Me You

The Eastons

Chasing I Do
Drive Me Mad
Betting on Us

Sequoia Lake series

It Started with a Kiss
Every Little Kiss

Heroes of St. Helena series

Need You for Keeps
Need You for Always
Need You for Mine

St. Helena Vineyard series

Kissing Under the Mistletoe
Summer in Napa
Autumn in the Vineyard
Be Mine Forever
From the Moment We Met

Sugar, Georgia series

Sugar's Twice as Sweet
Sugar on Top
A Taste of Sugar

promise me
you

MARINA ADAIR

Montlake
Romance

This is a work of fiction. Names, characters, organizations, places, events, and incidents are either products of the author's imagination or are used fictitiously.

Text copyright © 2018 by Marina Adair
All rights reserved.

No part of this book may be reproduced, or stored in a retrieval system, or transmitted in any form or by any means, electronic, mechanical, photocopying, recording, or otherwise, without express written permission of the publisher.

Published by Montlake Romance, Seattle

www.apub.com

Amazon, the Amazon logo, and Montlake Romance are trademarks of Amazon.com, Inc., or its affiliates.

ISBN-13: 9781503903548
ISBN-10: 1503903540

Cover design by Letitia Hasser

Cover photography by Mackenzie Kessler

Printed in the United States of America

To Joan Swan, for the hours of plotting and replotting and the years of friendship and unconditional support. Without you this book would never have been. Thank you for being such a warm and grounding influence in my life.

NEWSLETTER

Get the inside scoop on upcoming appearances, giveaways, book releases, and all things Marina Adair delivered right to your inbox! Don't wait—visit www.marinaadair.com/newsletter to sign up today!

XOXO,

Marina Adair

CHAPTER 1

If this was what marital bliss felt like, then the only boyfriend Mackenzie Hart would ever commit to would be battery operated.

It wasn't so much that some guy had spilled his beer down the front of her overpriced dress. Or even the fact that she was two shots into the night and the rehearsal dinner still hadn't started. Nope, what had Mackenzie flipping the universe the big one was that the only man she'd ever wanted to have and to hold was about to marry someone else.

"Ball and chain locked and loaded," Cash Kane said from behind the bar, a big-ass grin on his face. "I can't believe my cousin's actually getting hitched tomorrow."

Neither could Mackenzie.

"Next there'll be a mess of kids, and our band will go by way of the Diaper Genie," Paul, the band's bass player, slurred, making it obvious that he had drowned one too many sorrows.

There wasn't enough alcohol in the world to numb Mackenzie's pain.

Ever since Hunter Kane, local musician and legendary ladies' man, had announced his shocking engagement to one of Nashville's biggest debutantes, the band had been scared. Scared that his new wife would grow tired of the long stretches on the road, scared that she'd convince him to go solo—like their label had been pushing for—and scared because they all knew damn well that without their front man, the Hunter Kane Band was going nowhere fast.

Mackenzie was scared too. So scared she hadn't slept in weeks. Her headaches were coming more frequently, until her vision became so blurry she couldn't drive a car without the fear of running into something—or someone.

Over the past few years, Hunter had gone from friend to writing partner, and eventually he'd become the man who taught her it was okay to trust. He was the only person in the world who really got her—looked past her hang-ups and saw the woman she could become.

Sadly, at the moment, the only thing she was in danger of becoming was sick.

"Well, at least he'll have a hell of a honeymoon. I know it's wrong to covet your bro's woman, but man, oh man," Paul said with a long look at Hadley, who stood under the twinkle-lit gazebo with Hunter, slowly swaying to the live band.

"They should have saved the money and stayed home for all the sightseeing they're going to do," the drummer, Quinn, joked. "Hundred bucks says they don't see anything besides the hotel room ceiling."

"Two hundred, they never even make it to the bed." Paul reached into his pocket for his wallet.

Quinn gave the bride-to-be another slow once-over and shook his head. "Three hundred, he doesn't even get her out of her dress." Bills hit the bar top, and he looked at Mackenzie. "You in?"

Mackenzie rolled her eyes. "And listen to you try to mansplain how to get a woman out of her wedding dress? No thanks."

The guys laughed.

Mackenzie didn't. She was too busy trying not to picture Hadley in her wedding dress. And she sure as hell didn't want to picture Hunter getting her out of it.

Nope, she wasn't in a betting mood. Not tonight.

Because tonight symbolized the end of her dreams for love, family, and children. Tonight marked the end of her dreams period. For Mackenzie, Hunter was it. Problem was, his dreams lay in the perfect poise and beauty of the woman dancing in his arms.

From her vantage point at the bar, Mackenzie was able to see the bride's slim back, her delicate sheath dress trailing to the floor.

Hadley Clemonte was tall and elegant, her glossy golden curls spilling over her shoulders and onto the white silk of her dress. Her eyes brimmed with emotion, and her smile spoke of a woman about to be married. Her unwavering poise showcased her family's deep and moneyed roots. Her confident nature spoke volumes about the benefit a supportive and wonderful family offered.

Hadley was stunning, cultured, perfectly feminine, a real southern belle. Four things Mackenzie could never be.

"One more," she said, waving her empty glass in the air.

Brody Kane, the band's agent, walked up to the bar, his deep blue eyes going soft with concern. The familiar expression made her heart flinch, as thousands of memories washed through her. Even though Brody and Hunter were cousins, they were often mistaken for brothers. And the look in his eyes was so similar to Hunter's it was difficult to swallow. So she shifted her gaze to the bottles lining the back of the bar.

"What?" she said. "It's a wedding celebration. Look, I'm even wearing a dress." She lifted her light orange dress, which Hadley had handpicked and Mackenzie was sure was the epitome of fashion. "The color is 'cantaloupe whimsy' and it has no straps, so Hadley used some kind of sticky tape to hold it up. Tape, Brody. I deserve another shot."

Brody lifted his hand to order another round, then took the stool next to her. "Or you could tell Hunter how you feel rather than just walk out that door and disappear."

"You mean walk up to him and say, 'Hey, I got you the silver chafing dish off the registry, which I'm sure will come in handy on the tour bus. Oh, and by the way, I know you're about to get married in front of five hundred of your closest friends, family, and journalists, but I think I like you. Check Yes or No.'"

Brody's expression was one of gentle understanding. "Or how about, 'I know you think of me as a friend, but my feelings for you have changed. I thought you should know, because palling 'round with you hurts. A lot. And it's making our working relationship really difficult on me.'"

She shook her head.

Today wasn't about her. Or the band. It was about Hunter. This marriage was the right move for him. Hadley was well spoken and sophisticated and would be the perfect wife for his booming career. Also, she wasn't staring down a future full of boundaries and limitations like Mackenzie was.

Hunter's career was on course to go the distance. He deserved a partner up to the challenge. Most of Mackenzie's life had *been* a challenge, and that said nothing of how squirrelly it was about to become. What she needed was a safe place to recover.

A quiet place to regroup.

"Tonight, at the rehearsal, when Pastor John said, 'Speak now or forever hold your peace,' by not speaking up, I nonverbally verbally agreed to the silence-forever clause. And I take nonverbal verbal agreements seriously." She sent Brody a pretty convincing smile. "You, as my agent, should know these things."

Brody rested a hand on hers, and she forced herself to remain still, to suppress her surprise at the unexpected contact. "What I know is that you have two choices: either say something or walk. Both will tear you up, but the not knowing . . . that's what will haunt you forever. Trust me."

Mackenzie did trust Brody. It was why she'd confided in him about her situation. That, and he was morally obligated as her agent to keep her secrets. Even from his biggest client, and relative, Hunter.

"I'll be all right," she assured him. "I just need some time."

All Mackenzie knew about love was sacrifice. As the only child of a single mom, she'd learned it was easier to say she was all right, even if she wasn't. As an adult, she'd learned to just keep smiling when things got rough. But nothing about this moment was ever going to be all right.

She could tell Hunter she was finally over her mom's death and ready for a relationship.

But that would be a lie. And Mackenzie had promised never to lie to herself again. Even for love. She'd done that once and lost her mom—the single most important person in her world. She'd only recently gained the strength to find closure, leaving behind the binding web of guilt and heartache. Only to discover that the universe had a sick sense of humor and the heartache was just beginning. At least for her, and she refused to burden Hunter with that.

It might not seem like it now, but this change was for the best—for everyone involved.

"What's one more haunt to keep me company?" Mackenzie picked up her shot and, with a salute, downed it, then stood.

She'd known what needed to happen when she'd RSVPed to the rehearsal. Without a backward glance, she moved toward the door. In her attempt to go unnoticed, she knocked over a barstool and, unaccustomed to wearing anything higher than cowgirl boots, stumbled into something strong, solid, and body-meltingly warm.

"Where are you sneaking off to, Trouble?" Hunter asked, and that low, gravelly southern drawl that made him a superstar rolled right through her.

"I don't sneak," she said, refusing to meet his gaze, since his BS meter was always dialed to interrogation setting.

"I know sneaking when I see it. And you're sneaking. Out of my rehearsal dinner."

"I'm not sneaking," she said, looking at his hands. His big, masculine, almost-married hands that had grabbed her waist to keep her from falling. "And for your information, I was looking for the ladies' room."

"The ladies' room is behind you. And the exit, which you were making a beeline for, would be in front of you. Just past the rose garden, the horde of guests waiting for supper, and your pride."

"Fine," she admitted. "I was sneaking."

"I know." He sounded *so* smug. "You always look like you're two seconds from crying when you're contemplating something illegal."

She snorted. "Leaving a dinner at which you aren't obligated to pick up the tab is hardly illegal."

"It is when my fiancée thinks my best friend hates her," he said quietly.

Well, isn't that just great?

"I don't hate Hadley," she said, looking up and—*oh God*, how was she ever going to say goodbye when those warm blue eyes of his drew her in.

They were deep and bright, and the color of a gentle rolling sea. So mesmerizing she was actually standing in a poufy dress in the middle of a wedding rehearsal, waxing poetic.

She needed to get a grip.

"Then what's going on?" he asked. "You bailed on the last few weeks of the tour, you cut out of the bachelor weekend early, and you've been avoiding us all night."

You. I've been avoiding you.

"Jesus, Hunter, I help you write songs. That's it." Her throat closed, because after tonight she wouldn't even be able to do that. "So when we wrapped on the last song for the album, I decided it was time to come home."

Just because Hunter treated her as if she were a full-fledged member of the band, it didn't make it so.

"As for the bachelor weekend, I cut out two days early," she added.

"It was a three-day trip."

"The guys were talking about going to a strip club. I don't do strippers."

"That's a shame." His eyes roamed down her body, slowly coming to a stop at her heels. "Because you in those shoes with a stripper would have made for one hell of a bachelor party."

Even though she knew he was teasing her, an unwelcome but all too familiar heat surged through her body. When it reached her cheeks, she smacked him in the chest, averting his attention.

Unrequited love sucked—but not nearly as much as it would if he learned about her feelings the night before his wedding. She smacked him again.

"Ow," he said. "And I don't do strippers either." She rolled her eyes. "Okay, well, just that one time in Tuscaloosa, but she was in grad school and liked Merle Haggard, and we dated for almost a month." Which before Hadley would have been considered a serious relationship for Hunter. "Plus, I'm not that guy anymore. I'm getting married tomorrow, and my best friend won't even give me one dance before she cuts tail."

"Brody is your best friend."

"He isn't wearing a dancing dress."

Hunter's fingers slowly slid around to her lower back and pulled her farther into his grasp, his strength enveloping her. She'd relied on it, and after her recent diagnosis, she needed it with a desperation that consumed her. That was the excuse she gave herself for allowing her head to fall gently against his chest, resting there.

"One dance with the girl who knows my every move," he whispered. "That's all I'm asking for."

One last dance, she told herself.

Mackenzie breathed in his scent—yummy male with a punch of high-octane testosterone, and a sweetness that was addictive. The last time he'd held her like this was the night her mother had died. Hunter

7

had brought her to his place, given her a shoulder to cry on, and promised her he'd be with her every step of the way.

Her mother's death had been the most painful experience of Mackenzie's life. Even more heartbreaking than watching the funny, bright woman she admired slowly lose her sight and her independence.

Her mother's blindness had defined both of their lives. For Susan it had meant the end of an accomplished career as a professor of photography at the local university. For Mackenzie it had meant becoming her mom's eyes to the outside world.

A job that, had Mackenzie taken it more seriously, could have stopped her mother from stepping into the crosswalk.

Could have, should have, would have. The story of Mackenzie's life.

"I don't feel much like dancing," she said, stepping back. "I just came to tell you how happy I am for you and that you deserve every ounce of love that comes your way." She looked into those blue pools. "You're a good man."

He studied her long and hard, until she felt the tears she'd been holding back start to surface.

"You look pale. Is it another migraine?" If only he knew how far off the mark he was. "What did the doctor say?"

"That in a short time everything will be normal," she lied, and the dread she'd been carrying since her diagnosis slammed hard in the pit of her stomach. This would be the last time she'd ever see Hunter's face or watch his eyes darken with emotion.

And this would be the last time she'd ever be able to look up at the man who owned her heart.

"Does it hurt now?" He cupped her cheek.

His hand felt smooth and comforting, while the calluses on his musician's fingers made tiny shivers scatter across her bare skin. She swallowed several times before she spoke, praying she wouldn't sound as fragile as she felt. Because Mackenzie didn't do fragile. And Hunter knew that.

"My head's fine," she said.

She couldn't feel anything over the aching in her heart. Hunter's genuine concern only made it worse. No one cared for her like he did, and now that he was getting married, taking care of her would be inappropriate.

She'd always known that Hunter could never be hers. But now it was a fact.

The weeks that followed the announcement of his engagement had dragged by, and her grief had turned to a dull longing. Hanging in the background of her every breath was the constant reminder of the changes that would surely come. And losing Hunter wasn't the only change headed her way.

Gone would be the closeness they shared, the comfortable silent moments and the pee-your-pants-laughing ones. The ones that were so intense no words were needed to express their awesomeness.

But a ring was in play. And in less than twenty-four hours, vows were to be exchanged. This had to be goodbye.

"I hate to cut out early, but I can't do this right now," she said.

"Okay, let's grab a seat," he said, already looking for a place to put her. "I'll get you a drink."

He slid his palms down her bare arms and took her hands, offering comfort and understanding. But he didn't understand. And all of a sudden it became imperative that he did.

"Not the dancing, Hunter. *This*." She gestured back and forth between them to encompass the enormity of her words. "I can't do this right now." Her voice broke. "I have to go."

"Whoa, don't cry. Give me a minute, and I'll just grab Brody's keys and drive you home."

"You can't leave," she said, horrified. "It's *your* rehearsal dinner."

"But driving at night is bad for a migraine."

And staying here for one more moment would be bad for her heart. The weight of her decision was all-consuming. Her chest tightened to the point of agony, and the bile that had been churning in her stomach for the past six weeks burned the back of her throat.

She didn't have any destination in mind. Only knew that she had to get out. Spread her wings one last time before she settled into her new future—so that Hunter could hold on to his.

"I'll be fine." She'd weathered storms rougher than this. "Be happy, Hunter."

With one last glance, to put every nuance of his face to memory, Mackenzie turned to walk through the rose garden, the pungent fragrance stinging her nose, the weight of the night clinging to her skin.

Being with Hunter was like music without sheets—no restrictions or limitations. Just easy, natural, freeing. He embodied a sense of peace and weightlessness that had given her hope to dream when she'd desperately needed something to hold on to.

It was the same gift she was determined to give him in return. Which was why she had to say goodbye.

CHAPTER 2

Three years later . . .

There was not enough alcohol in the bar to ease the growing pressure. Hunter Kane's chest felt as if it was going to explode right there in front of his cousins, and not a single one of them would do a damn thing. Other than tell him this was his own fault.

The sorry-as-shit part was that they'd be right.

Hunter had been sitting on his ass for the last year, waiting for inspiration to walk back into his life. But since he'd let her walk right out without a fight, he wasn't holding his breath.

"Come on, Brody," Hunter said to his oldest cousin. "You make it sound like I'm asking you to get me a meeting with Johnny Cash."

"That would be a hell of a lot easier, because what you are asking is beyond impossible," Brody said, not even trying to hide his piss-poor attitude. Hunter assumed it was partly from the predictability of the conversation—one they'd had many times recently—but mostly because it was well past last call.

"You're my agent," Hunter pointed out. "By definition your job is to make the impossible possible when it comes to ensuring the band's happiness and continued success."

At that moment Hunter's needs included a meeting with the most sought-after songwriting team in country music. He'd made this particular request so many times over the past year he'd lost track, but each one ended with the same disappointing result.

Two years ago, Hunter Kane had been a singing sensation headed toward living-legend status. There wasn't a person he couldn't get a meeting with. Even the president of the United States had knocked back a few stouts with the front man behind the Hunter Kane Band, who'd been deemed the greatest thing to hit country music since Garth Brooks and Keith Urban.

Then they'd released their fourth album. And what a clusterfuck that had been. With their lead songwriter MIA, the label had paired him up with a team of writers who'd put an end to Hunter Kane Band's trendsetting sound. While the album had contained two number-one hits, both written by the elusive Mack and Muttley, it was considered a commercial flop.

A mistake Hunter would never make again.

Which was why Mack and Muttley's continued rejection lit a fire under Hunter's ass, making him more determined than ever to lock down a meeting.

"No, *your* agent works in that big office three blocks over," Brody said. "He has a fancy schedule that is carefully managed by his amazing assistant, Raydeen. You should call her. Set something up."

Hunter looked at his watch. "And wake her? Big Daddy raised us better than that," he said, referring to Brody's father, who had stepped up to raise Hunter when his own father turned out to be ill-tempered for the job. "I mean, what kind of asshole calls someone at two fifteen in the morning on a work night?"

"The same kind of asshole who pulls his cousin from a warm bed to come down here and hold his hand." Brody dropped his hand on top of Hunter's—hard. Then squeezed with enough force to fracture a few bones. "Now, if we're done here, I'd like to go back home to my wife, who's hopefully still awake in that nice warm bed that I left."

"Your wife told me I could call any time. Those were Savannah's exact words." Hunter shrugged. "Who am I to argue with a pretty lady?"

"Jesus." Brody ran a hand down his face. "And you wonder why you're divorced."

Hunter didn't have to wonder. He knew exactly why he was divorced. He simply wasn't cut out for marriage. Period.

Whatever that elusive trait was that allowed his uncle and cousins to love so freely had clearly skipped Hunter's branch on the family tree. Oh, he loved his family and his music so fiercely he was often paralyzed with its power. But when it came to letting other people into his heart, he seemed to be more of a hard-ass like his father than he wanted to admit. So when Hadley wanted out less than a year into the marriage, he hadn't fought her on a thing.

He'd taken her around the world, bought her a dream house in one of the most prestigious areas in Nashville, and showered her with all kinds of things. Sadly, in the end, after the success and the touring and the insane hours, the divorce was probably the nicest thing he'd ever given her.

"How are you doing with that?" Brody asked, his voice softening with genuine concern.

Hunter knew by *that* they were no longer talking about the divorce, but Hadley's new marriage. "Good. She seems happy and genuinely in love. Chet is a good guy, stable, works a suit job with a membership at the country club. She deserves that."

She was also expecting her first child. A difficult reality for Hunter to swallow, since she'd made it clear that parenthood wasn't a role she had interest in pursuing. Apparently, she'd meant with him.

Hunter loved kids, wanted a few of his own someday, when he had the time to devote to being a great dad. But he worked too damn much.

A side effect of being responsible for so many people. It wasn't just about his own success. He had bandmates, roadies, a whole team of people and their families whose financial security depended on Hunter's ability to go the distance. To settle this standoff between the label and his bandmates.

The band refused to record songs that the label picked, the label tossed out every song Hunter sent over, and if he didn't find some way to get everyone on the same page, the band was going to miss their studio time. End result: the album would suffer.

He wasn't sure how he'd been appointed the savior of the fucking universe. Last he'd checked, he'd handed in his cape the day Hadley asked him for a divorce. Yet here he was, sitting in his uncle's bar, sucking down a beer, trying to get another runaway horse back in the corral.

Only this time he was man enough to admit that he needed help.

"What did Mack and Muttley say?" Hunter asked.

"Same as before: a regretful no," Brody said without an ounce of regret in his tone.

"That's it?"

"Yup. That's it."

Hunter rested his weight on his arms and leaned over the tabletop to make sure Brody could see the whites of his eyes. It wasn't a lack of effort on his cousin's part that had gotten them here. In fact, Brody was one of the hardest-working agents in Nashville—his roster of exclusive clients proved that. He just had a hard time thinking outside the box.

If there was one thing Hunter had learned on his road to success, it was that there was always more than one way to sweet-talk a deal, and it usually involved skill, persistence, a couple of cigars, and a whole lot of alcohol.

"Afraid that answer won't do. This meeting needs to happen, and it needs to happen this week."

His career depended on it. If he didn't hand over new material for the next album, his label was going to lock him in a room with another set of shitty writers. The band would freak. The songs would suck. So the only way he was going to please all parties involved was to submit the perfect batch of songs.

The tricky thing about perfection—it killed creativity.

"The label gave you a list of qualified writers," Brody pointed out. "You scared them all off."

"Having a YouTube channel doesn't make you qualified."

"Cody Kelly has more than ten million followers."

"He's nineteen," Hunter said. "With peach fuzz for a beard. If the kid can't keep a proper beard, he can't fucking write with me."

Brody leaned back and let out a frustrated breath.

Right there with you, cuz.

Hunter had studied the industry, identified the patterns that made some bands a mere flash while others held on for the long haul. Only a select few made it to the coveted icon status. The Hunter Kane Band was going to be one of them.

And fucking peach fuzz wasn't going to get them there.

Not that Hunter cared about the fame or money—he was neck-deep in both and threatening to go under. What he needed was the artistic freedom to write songs that connected—songs like he'd had at the beginning of his career.

Hunter wasn't just a musician. He was a writer, and he was at a point in his music where he would either lose momentum and fizzle into obscurity or move on to become more than just another industry fluke. In order for him to do that, he needed to try something new. Which was where the writing talents of Mack and Muttley came in.

Hunter scanned the iconic bar's walls. Big Daddy's was one of Nashville's oldest honky-tonks and the first venue Hunter had ever played. He took in the gold and platinum records, which hung beneath the neon MASON JARS ARE AS FANCY AS WE GET sign and next to an old photo of the bar. The records were his, but the picture was of his uncle, taken the night he'd opened the honky-tonk in the late seventies. The gleam of pride and joy in Big Daddy's eyes made swallowing hard.

That was the kind of man Hunter wanted to be. Big Daddy had been the hardest-working man Hunter had ever known. He'd given 100 percent of himself to this bar but never compromised time with the family and never gave up the fight to make his dream come true.

It had been only six months since Big Daddy had passed, but the loss was so fresh Hunter could taste it. That's why he loved coming to Big Daddy's: his uncle was in every brick and bar top.

Hunter remembered the summer he'd spent with his uncle and cousins resanding all five thousand square feet of original wood floors to earn enough cash to buy his first guitar. Mostly, though, he remembered the day Big Daddy took out a loan against the bar to fund Hunter's demo tape.

Big Daddy hadn't had a lot of money, but he'd been rich in love and faith. Enough so that he'd been willing to put his bar on the line to help Hunter reach his dreams. Even though Hunter wasn't his kid.

That demo tape had taken him from playing opening gigs for no-name acts in small towns around the south to landing a record deal with one of the biggest labels on the planet. And now the Hunter Kane Band played stadiums and arenas all over the country. Sometimes as the opening act, sometimes as the headliner, but always to a sold-out crowd.

It wasn't the loan that had made the difference. Big Daddy's unwavering belief that Hunter could be more than his old man had given Hunter the singular focus he needed to push ahead in an industry designed to hold performers back. Hunter was determined to live up to the opportunity his uncle had provided.

He had the fame and a growing collection of platinum albums, but every day, every song, was starting to feel the same. Hunter wanted to create something deeper, more textured—a journey that his uncle would have chosen. One that challenged his talent as much as his character.

Hunter knew in his gut that this next album would help him find that feeling of fulfillment missing in his life and his work of late. He just had to finish writing it.

Releasing a sigh, he dropped his head against the seat back. "The band won't record any more crossover fluffy crap. And if we come out with another album like the last one, there won't *be* a band. I want the long career, not the flash and fizzle." Hunter paused. "If we do this right, we can position the band in a unique spot to go the distance, just like Mackenzie and I mapped out."

Hunter felt his chest tighten.

After all this time, saying her name still brought on a rush of longing and pain so intense it was physical. He was at the exact place in his career they'd planned for, fought for, and dreamed about, but she was no longer a part of that dream. Hadn't been since the rehearsal dinner.

The memory of that night made him glance down at his ringless finger. After a moment, Hunter forced himself to focus and close off the part of his mind that always carried so much pain.

"The band isn't willing to work with just any writer, we're looking to work with the *perfect* writers for this album. No more of this mix-and-match BS like last time. Which, I don't need to remind you, nearly ruined us."

"Give up the tampons and stop being so emotional about everything. You know the cycle: once you stop overthinking and get to work, you'll write hit after hit regardless of the writing partners."

It wasn't going to work. Period.

Hunter had tried everything to get his swag back, but the only hits he'd recorded weren't his. And he didn't want to spend his career singing other people's stories. He wanted to tell his own. At least, that's what he'd told Brody. In truth, he wasn't sure what he wanted anymore. He just knew that he would find it with these songwriters.

"Mack and Muttley are my only choice. I won't work on this album with anyone else."

"Be prepared to be disappointed. Because they are at the top of their game and extremely particular on who *they* choose to work with. And they can," Brody said. "They were named by *Rolling Stone* the best songwriters of the year. Not to mention the most reclusive. I've accepted a trailer full of GRAMMYs and CMAs on their behalf. And guess what? They choose to go it alone."

Hunter understood what Brody was saying. No one even knew what this duo looked like. They were like the Sia of country music.

No one, that was, except his take-no-prisoners agent and favorite cousin, Brody Kane, who was still rattling off all the reasons Hunter's plan wouldn't work.

"They didn't show up to the Country Music Awards. Turned down the *Tonight Show*. What makes you think they'd meet with you?"

"Because for me to make it to the next level, I *need* them. It's like they write the things I need to get out but can't quite put into words or chords. Every time they give me a song, it's the perfect song at the perfect time in my career."

At the perfect time in my life.

Brody leaned back in his chair and really considered Hunter's plea. "They already give you first options on all their best material. Believe me. I see every song before anyone else. They write those songs specifically for you and no one else. I had five top artists bidding on the last set they wrote. Mack and Muttley flat-out refused to consider anyone else, said it could only be you. They were your last three number ones, by the way. What more do you want?"

Hunter braced one leg on the opposite knee, laced his fingers behind his head, and dropped the bomb that was sure to send Brody into one of his anxiety-driven meltdowns, including pacing, ranting, nuclear-strength heartburn, and finally ending with Hunter getting his way.

"I want to cowrite the entire album with them. All fourteen songs. The three of us locked in a studio till it's done kind of situation."

Brody snorted. "Good luck with that."

"I'm serious."

"So am I." Brody rolled his eyes so hard Hunter thought his cousin would fall off his chair. "I get that people pretty much do whatever you ask. I know I do. Half the time I do what you want before you know you want it. Cash is right. This has all gone to your head, turned you into some fucking diva," Brody said, and Hunter laughed.

"Cash drinks craft beer. It doesn't get more diva than that."

"He also outweighs you by thirty pounds," Cash said from the other side of the bar.

"You could be Garth Brooks for all I care," Brody said. "Mack and Muttley do not—I repeat, *do not*—work with artists."

"They'll work with me," Hunter said.

Hunter's laid-back confidence had allowed him to win over even the stodgiest of people in the industry. He might not have met these guys, but he knew the type. Unlike LA, Nashville attracted good old boys who would rather throw back a few brews while sitting around in jeans and T-shirts playing cards than entertain some self-serving ego of an artist.

Good thing, for all involved, Hunter was as easygoing as one could get. He'd bring a couple of six-packs, a fifth of Jack, and his old six string. By the end of the night, there'd be chords and contracts.

"And why is that?"

A slow, smug grin spread across Hunter's face. "First off, because you know I'm right. Second, you represent both parties involved, so it'll be easy to set up the meeting." He leaned forward, resting his elbows on the bar top. "And did I mention I think I'm comin' down with the flu? Might just have to retract that babysitting offer for next weekend."

Brody's jaw tightened, and the vein in his forehead darkened, exposing an elevated heart rate. He blinked several times, probably listening to the sound of his sex life coming to a tragic ending. "You know how much this trip means to Savannah."

"What I know is that my niece, angel that she is, has taken to sleeping in your bed. If I remember correctly, right smack-dab in the middle of you and your sexy wife. Seems like a full bed makes for lonely nights."

Brody ran a hand down his face. "Don't even get me started. Now Caroline says she wants a dog for her birthday. One of those little fluffy accessories that shit in your car and piss on your boots."

Hunter smiled. He knew exactly the kind of dog his niece wanted. Had shared a bed with one for three years. "Wait until you catch it watching you have sex." He let loose a low whistle, and Brody sagged. "What you need is some much-needed alone time with that lovely wife of yours."

Caroline was almost four and having a hard time adjusting to life without Big Daddy.

They all were.

Cash had cut back his tattoo business to part-time so he could help keep the bar going, Brody had taken over booking the local talent, and their youngest brother, Wade, was dealing with all the legal issues. So if Caroline asked for Hunter to babysit, then he'd babysit.

That didn't mean he wouldn't give Brody a hard time about it first.

"It's been five months. Five months! Do you have any idea how long that is for a man who shares his bed with a smoking-hot wife?"

Once upon a time, Hunter had had his own smoking-hot wife, and sharing a bed with Hadley had been beyond fun. Too bad they'd never been in the same place enough to play tangled-sheets tag all that often.

"I just want one night full of foreplay followed by mind-blowing sex, but my daughter is the human equivalent of the walls of Jericho. My hands are blistered, for Christ's sake," Brody admitted.

"Sounds like your teen years all over again," Hunter joked, almost feeling sorry for the guy.

Almost.

Because not only did Brody have a smoking-hot wife, an adorable daughter, the dream career, and the fucking white picket fence—he'd also found a way to make it all work. So yeah, it had been a rough few months, but his cousin was living the dream.

"She bought a bikini, man. Just for this trip. It's red and has little ties to hold it together. Little itty-bitty ties that wouldn't stand up to a slight breeze, so don't screw with me."

"Someone has to. You seem pretty hard up. If some of the stress of this album was gone, I'd probably heal in time for you two lovebirds to make it to Saint Lucia. There's this swimming hole that sits at the bottom of a clear blue waterfall, and at night it's deserted. A bathing-suit-optional kind of situation." Hunter leaned in and winked. "Just think what a couple in love, without a rug rat running around, could do with all the free time and—"

Brody ran an unsure hand over his face. "Thursday. Seven p.m."

"You serious?" Hunter smacked the bar top, disbelief fading into anticipation. "This is great. Thanks, man."

"Yeah, my pleasure," Brody said drily, and Hunter ignored the eat-shit-and-die expression that went along with it.

"Where do you want to meet? Here? My house?"

"God no," Brody said, looking as if he was rethinking the whole thing.

"Your office is pretty private. We can always meet there. Neutral territory."

"That might work," he said. "Seven o'clock."

"I'll be there."

Brody looked as if he'd rather be anywhere *but* his office on Thursday. "My staff will be gone for the night, so don't come expecting food or pampering. I'll get you a face-to-face, but the rest is up to you. No matter what happens, you take Caroline." Brody's grin went smug. "The entire weekend. Two nights and three days. Take it or leave it."

Hunter considered the extra few nights of babysitting and decided the trade was well worth it. Caroline was more mature than he was and acted like a monster only when she didn't get her way. Not a problem when Uncle Hunter was around.

In Hunter's world, ladies always got their way.

Realization sunk in that the last step was finally in motion. Suddenly, he felt like a kid who'd just got his first six string.

CHAPTER 3

"Now you're just being stubborn."

"If I were a man, you'd call it assertiveness," Mackenzie said, but it was clear that Brody wasn't buying it.

Nope, Brody and his weird Spidey sense were zeroing in on the embarrassing fact that the only thing Mackenzie was being was a big fat chicken. She was one question away from sprouting wings and taking flight, but she was okay with that. Everyone was allowed a fear or two.

Mackenzie's was facing her past.

And by past she meant anyone who knew her *before*. And, okay, by anyone she specifically meant Hunter Kane. Admitting one's problem was the first step in overcoming it, and she was in no rush to take the second step. "I need more time."

"How much more time are we talking?" Brody asked.

"Maybe a few more months." Or never. Never worked for her.

"I can bring it up in a few months, or you'll be ready in a few months?" Brody asked, and *damn*, he was catching on to her strategy. "I only ask because a few months ago, you said you needed a few more months. And, well, here we are."

"Now you're just being pushy," Mackenzie said.

"If I were a woman, you'd call it communicating," he said and had a point.

Mackenzie had clearly communicated her wishes when it came to Hunter. Although her answer remained the same, Brody felt the need to readdress the situation, in case hell had finally frozen over. There might be a few snowflakes on the distant horizon, but they wouldn't stick long enough to change her mind. Not right then anyway.

The only reason she was still sitting in his office was because Brody was the closest friend she had left, and she'd promised to hear him out before disappointing him—yet again.

And damn, if that wasn't her second greatest fear.

"You can't avoid him forever."

"I'm not avoiding him," she pointed out. "I just don't see the need to rush into an awkward face-to-face."

Brody's tone turned gentle, sympathetic enough to have Mackenzie shifting in her seat. "It's been a year since the divorce. Three since disappearing."

Nashville was a big city. Surely, she could make it another few years. If she were really determined, she could make it a full decade. Because it had also been three years since the doctor visit that had derailed her life.

Since she'd learned that her mother's blindness was also hereditary. And since Mackenzie's life had spiraled out of control. She had been a rising writer in the music industry, creating songs that were paving her way toward success. Then the vision loss Mackenzie had experienced in her right eye became permanent and, over the following year, moved to the left, forever blurring her path.

"I finished rehab eleven months ago. I need more time to adjust."

"You walked out of rehab eleven months ago," Brody corrected.

"Right." *There is that,* she thought, reaching down to pet Muttley.

She didn't have to reach far, because Muttley was ninety-five pounds of poodle-mastiff mix who preferred to be on Mackenzie's lap. Not the typical behavior for a Seeing Eye dog. Then again, nothing about Muttley was typical. He was the size of a bear, hated loud noises, and was a three-time guide-dog-school failure. But he had heart, and that's what mattered.

"I can barely remember how many steps it is to the bathroom," she added. "I don't need to tell you how meeting with Hunter before I'm ready would set me back."

"Or maybe it will be the thing you need to move forward," Brody said. "I know the weight it will take off my chest to come clean."

"I never meant for you to be stuck in the middle."

"But I am."

"I know." And she hated that but didn't know any other way. While Mackenzie wished things could be different, her music was the only thing she dared share with Hunter right now. Anything more had the potential to take her under.

With a heavy exhale, she ruffled Muttley's ears. The sound of his wagging tail thumping the floor echoed, cutting through the ever-growing silence.

Putting her best friend in an uncomfortable position was the exact reason she'd thought long and hard before reaching out to Brody in the first place. She'd needed an agent, and he was the best. She would never want to come between family but didn't know who else to go to. It wasn't as if there were job listings for blind musician-songwriters.

Brody had vowed to do whatever he could to help, but she doubted he'd meant lying to his family when he'd made the promise.

A light disturbance in the air brushed over her cheeks, carrying a faint hint of leather, testosterone, and frustrated man. Brody rounded the desk and nudged Muttley aside. It was a big nudge, followed by an even bigger bark, because Muttley fancied himself a watchdog in a guide dog's vest.

But Brody wasn't having any of it.

"Back off, Cujo," he said, then squatted down in front of Mackenzie, resting his hands on the chair's arm. "I'm not suggesting you rekindle the relationship, but Hunter has a right to know you're okay."

The exact reason she needed more time. She *wasn't* okay. She would be, she'd make sure of it, but that day wasn't today.

She was pretty sure tomorrow wasn't either, but she knew it would come. It had to.

Mackenzie might be a runner, but she wasn't a coward.

"I have a right to my privacy," she said, smoothing her palms over her thighs. "I am sure he understands a person's right to privacy."

"And as your paid adviser, it's my job to tell you when something isn't working anymore."

He captured her hands between his, stilling her nervous habit and gently brushing his thumb over her knuckles in a familiar and brotherly manner. "Hunter wants to collaborate with you. And I think it's a great idea."

"It's a horrible idea." Fear clogged her throat, and she jerked her hands back. Before she could break contact completely, Brody tightened his grip.

"It's a great opportunity to put the past where it belongs and move forward. For everyone," he said gently. "Imagine what you two could produce."

She knew exactly what they were capable of together. Just like she knew exactly what she was capable of handling at the moment. And it wasn't being confined in a small space with the one man who could remind her of all that she'd lost.

Hell, the thought of writing with him again sent her heart into a free fall. That he wanted to work with her, had specifically asked, terrified her as much as it pleased her. That alone was enough to say no.

Over the years, she'd fought hard to forget the way his arms felt around her while they'd strummed the same guitar. The passion and emotion that had come out of their music but never translated into their relationship. She'd never let it, because she'd known since she was eighteen that she carried the mutated gene and that there was a solid chance she'd end up like her mom.

And she knew, no matter how desperately she wanted to go back, to see him, those moments could never be relived. Not without sacrificing some of the headway she'd worked so hard to claim.

Hunter was a force of nature, picking up everything in his path and taking it on the journey with him. It was what made him so successful—in business and in life.

Mackenzie had a different life now. One that didn't involve being carried anywhere. She needed to create her own path. He needed to live out his. Neither of them could do that if they refused to let go.

"It isn't going to happen."

"Savannah told me you'd say that. She also said to pass along that either you get a life that extends beyond occasional Sunday supper at our house and going to the dog park, or she was going to put you up on one of those dating sites."

"I would just move," she said, even though the thought of packing up and starting over again sounded daunting. She'd done it before—several times with her mom, then again after she was released from rehab—and hoped she'd never have to again. The last thing she needed was to let her past find her.

Or define her.

"Savannah would hunt you down and bring you home." With a quick squeeze, Brody released her hands and sat in the chair next to her. Muttley took up residence on her feet, sprawling across them. "I know the past few years have been difficult—"

"Difficult?" She laughed, because one word could never describe what she'd been through. The changes and the struggle she'd been forced to endure. And she'd done it, survived even. Then she'd written a port-folio of songs about it.

More important, she'd made steady progress. Then three months ago, she'd hit a wall. One she didn't know how to climb over without confronting her past.

"Okay, they've been hell," Brody amended. "But Jesus, Mackenzie, you've had more than a dozen Billboard hits. I get calls every day from artists wanting to work with you. And while I appreciate the spike my cool-dad factor has taken from accepting awards on your behalf, not to mention seeing Savannah in a slinky dress, this needs to stop."

"I know."

"The only time you get out is when I have papers for you to sign. And you only agree to come after-hours, when my staff has gone home."

She forced herself to breathe, then channeled her inner badass. "Only because you refuse to come to my house for our appointments. That was our deal. Read the contract if you've forgotten. You get thirty-five percent, which is virtually unheard of, by the way, and I get my anonymity."

Taking another deep breath, she called for the courage to deliver the ultimatum that, if he took it seriously, could successfully destroy what little human connection she had left. "If the arrangement is no longer working for you, and you decide you would rather terminate our agreement, then I understand."

Brody's exhale was slow and tired. "Never going to happen. We're family, and I hate upsetting you, but it kills me to see you so isolated."

"Me too," she whispered.

Brody pulled her to a stand and into his embrace. Slowly, her arms slid around his waist, and her forehead rested on his shoulder.

"I understood your need for privacy at first, but this has gone on too long. You're going to end up some old lady with only a collection of clutch purses, porcelain plates, and that dog for a bed partner."

They remained in that embrace for a time, both letting the words sink in. It wasn't often Mackenzie allowed herself the luxury of leaning on others. She had learned from her mother how easy it was to become dependent. Mackenzie would never do that to herself—or anyone else.

But for a moment, she allowed herself to be held. Let herself imagine what it would be like to not be in this all alone.

"Muttley isn't so bad," she said, rubbing her face back and forth across Brody's shoulder, wiping off the tears she knew had escaped.

"The dog snores worse than I do," Brody said with a low chuckle. "And if you want to give your songs to someone else, I know Carrie Underwood is interested in 'To Fly' and Keith Urban wants 'Friday Night.'"

She pulled back. "Those aren't available. I wrote those for Hunter." Brody was silent for a long moment, and a bead of unease began in her belly. "He doesn't want them, does he?"

The unease grew with the silence until it was a big ball in the center of her chest, twisting and tightening, suffocating her.

She amended her earlier statement because *this*, right here, was her worst fear. That Hunter would outgrow her songs or get to a point in his career where he wrote all his own stuff. If he didn't want her music anymore, then he would finally sever the last connection she had to him, the only thing that kept her writing. The constant that had pulled her through the darkest moments.

"He says unless he meets the writers behind the music, and I use the term *writers* lightly"—Mackenzie snorted at this—"then he won't record any more of their songs."

"But my song was his first number one hit. I've had at least three tracks on every one of his albums. All number ones. And these new ones are even better. They're perfect for this point in his career."

"I know that, you know that. Hell, he even knows it, but Hunter's playing hardball."

Mackenzie stepped back until her heel connected with the foot of the chair, reached for the arms, and eased herself down. "Did he even listen to the new tracks? I mean, does he know that some of the industry's biggest musicians are dying to get their hands on them?"

"He did. He does. And he doesn't care. He made it clear he won't record your songs unless he meets the writers who are able to 'put to sound what his soul sings' or some flowery artistic bullshit like that," Brody said. "You know how stubborn he can be."

Mackenzie knew better than anyone that getting Hunter Kane to change his mind once set was like steering a horse into a burning barn.

"Why change what's working?"

Writing at home gave her the comfort she needed to write and the privacy she needed to allow herself to be vulnerable. Sitting in a studio for weeks on end with the band staring at her? Asking her what had happened? Dealing with the silent pity?

No thank you. She wasn't ready for that.

"It's not working anymore, honey," Brody said gently. "Not for Hunter. And not for me."

Her stomach twisted at the idea that she might never get to write another song for Hunter, hear his voice breathe life into her music. Every word she wrote was for him, from her heart.

Only he didn't want them. Not on her terms anyway.

"Would it be so bad to see him again? To reconnect?" Brody's voice dropped, as if he wanted to lessen the impact of the conversation.

Brody had always been that way with her. She'd been nineteen with no work experience and desperate for a job to help with her mother's bills. Desperate for a life that wasn't defined by appointments, rehab therapy, or limitations.

Brody had been the one to get her a job waiting tables at his dad's bar. He knew her résumé was BS, even knew she was lying about her age, but he'd hired her anyway.

Given her a shot.

She'd worked every night shift she could, waiting for her mom to adapt to her new life, waiting for her own life to begin. It seemed as if

Mackenzie's entire life had been spent waiting. Until she'd forced her mother to take a big step—a step she wasn't ready to take.

The guilt was still suffocating and would have taken her under too, if she hadn't turned to her music. Which was how she'd met Hunter. And he'd filled her world with some of the lightness that she'd been craving.

Now everything was dark—and there was no escape.

"We both know that can't happen," she said.

"I don't see why not—"

The beep of his phone cut him off. He answered and turned his back to her. "Brody Kane here." The person on the other end said something, and then Brody said, "No, I said seven, not seven fifteen and . . . You're late . . . Uh-huh. Whatever, I'll be right down."

Brody disconnected. "That was dinner. Fried chicken and waffles. Your favorite. I have to go let the guy in, since you refuse to come during normal business hours, when the front-desk clerk is still here."

Guilt for keeping Brody from his family rolled through her. Even stronger was the comfort that warmed her chest at the idea of sharing a meal in a family-like setting, even if it was just her, Brody, and some takeout. But she couldn't afford to fall back into old patterns. Relying on others to make her world safe was a dangerous habit. "Thank you for the sweet thought, but I already ate."

"Uh-huh, and when was the last time you ate something that wasn't from a microwave?"

Well, there was that.

"Last Sunday, when you used your same guilt tactics." She stood and gathered her things. "Plus, you get to feed me next weekend at Caroline's birthday dinner."

Immediately, the crushing uncertainty that came every time she left the familiar began to build and take hold. Her breathing picked up, her hands began to sweat, and her heart pounded erratically against her breastbone.

Sensing her rising panic, Muttley pressed his body into her side, letting her know he was there. As quickly as it had come on, the unease and panic dissipated, leaving behind a feeling of serenity and autonomy.

"I'm fine for tonight," she finally said. "Plus, Savannah is probably waiting at home with supper in the oven."

Brody snorted. "She told me I'd better feed you or I was sleeping on the couch. She's afraid you'll lock yourself in a room, start writing, and remember your supper two days later."

"If Arthur ever thinks I'm working too hard, he lets himself in and force-feeds me," she said, referring to her sweet silver fox of a neighbor who had become more than a friend—he had become her self-appointed keeper. "So, thanks, supper would be fun, but—"

Brody sat her back in her seat. "Great. Make yourself comfortable. I'll be back in a sec."

Mackenzie got comfortable in the chair with a small smile. Even though her continued success demanded independence, the occasional pampering was nice. Stall tactic to talk about Hunter or not.

Her heart fluttered at the thought, which was all kinds of ridiculous. It wasn't as if she could ever escape Hunter. Nope, when you were in love with a celebrity whose personal life was plastered all over the tabloids and entertainment news shows, trying to put him in the past was difficult. Steering clear of him when you worked in the same industry, lived in the same city, and had the same agent was damn near impossible.

High five to her. Mackenzie had managed the impossible for nearly three years. Facing the impossible seemed a hell of a lot easier than sharing her secret.

Her decision to remain anonymous had never been intended to hurt anyone—it was for their protection. Hunter would have insisted on taking care of her, watching over her. It was the kind of person *he* was.

Luckily for both of them, *she* refused to be a burden to anyone.

Not to mention Mackenzie was barely dealing with her own loss. She could only imagine how Hunter would react. God, the outpouring of concern would only add to the already staggering weight.

Remembering the pain of watching the man she loved love someone else had her turning her head toward the exit.

He's single now, her heart sang. But the little voice in her head, the one who waited until she was ready to give in to hope, spoke up and reminded her that Hunter could never be hers.

It wasn't a new realization but a fact Mackenzie had accepted early in her life. And the reason behind her decision to leave three years ago.

A decision that not everyone agreed with or even understood. But not having someone to fall back on would force her to stand on her own two feet, reemerge as a stronger—healthier—person. It had taken a lot of convincing on her part, but Brody and Savannah had reluctantly supported her decision to withdraw into anonymity. It had been necessary for her healing, but she hated that she'd put Brody in the middle.

The door squeaked behind her, and Muttley let out an impressive *whoof.* An unwelcome prickle of unease raced down her spine, as the feeling of being watched sent her senses into hyperdrive.

Mackenzie jerked her head around to face the door. A faint hint of something earthy and dangerous made her breath catch.

"Who's there?"

◆ ◆ ◆

Hunter hadn't even started negotiating and already he knew it was a nonstarter. No amount of beer or shooting the shit was going to make this a successful pairing. Because his good old boys weren't boys at all.

And Brody was a fucking liar.

This meeting was with a petite brunette with bright mossy eyes. Eyes that had haunted his every thought for the past three years. She was wearing one of those long sweater dresses that clung to her body, showing off enough curves and manufactured bravado to level a guy. But it was the way she struggled to straighten those delicate shoulders, which he knew were strong enough to carry the entire world, that had his heart clenched so tight he thought he just might pass out.

All the fear and worry he'd harbored came back in full force, quickly followed by confusion and finally anger. White-hot anger that burned the back of his throat.

He was calling bullshit. On the whole thing.

Hunter had looked everywhere for Mackenzie. Spoken to friends, his family, industry connections. No one had heard from her. Leaving a giant hole in his world since that last dance.

Mackenzie had bailed on his wedding, not even bothering to show up for his big day, then did him one better and left for good.

Mackenzie hadn't just been his writing partner. She'd been like family to him. But she'd disappeared and hadn't said a fucking word.

To anyone.

Or so he'd thought.

Except there she was. Sitting in his cousin's office, looking like the answer to all his problems. Gorgeous as ever. Like nothing was amiss and he hadn't spent the past few years obsessing over what he'd done to deserve her silence.

Wondering if she was okay.

Jesus—he felt his eyes burn with relief—*she's okay.*

She was alive and well and his prayers had been answered.

He couldn't take his eyes off her. In a pair of red cowgirl boots and matching red lips, she didn't look anything like the timid coed she'd been a few years ago. Her wavy hair spilled down to the middle of her back, her hands rested on the chair as elegant as ever, and there was an inner strength that radiated from her core.

Mackenzie Hart was even more stunning than he remembered. That sensual beauty in contrast to her petite size brought out a protectiveness in him that he hadn't felt since that first time he'd seen her all those years ago at Big Daddy's.

The band had been finishing up their practice session when a pretty little waitress in a skirt that showcased one bombshell of a body came walking over.

"Last call," she'd said, her sweet Georgia drawl rolling over him like honey. "Can I get y'all anything?"

"A Lone Star," he'd said. And then, because he'd been a cocky twentysomething with a hard-on for spinners, he'd added, "And maybe a kiss."

"One Lone Star." She'd scribbled it in her little notepad—which told him she was new. Big Daddy didn't let waitresses write stuff down unless they were in training. Plus, he'd have remembered a face like hers. "Anyone else?"

"Aren't you going to even ask me where I want that kiss?" he'd asked.

"Not interested."

"You sure looked interested a few minutes ago when I was picking up my guitar." The guys had laughed, but not Mackenzie. Nope—she'd yawned. "Couldn't keep your eyes off me. Or my instrument."

"Actually, I was trying to figure out what you were doing with your hands. I mean, if you can't get the chords right, what makes me think you'd be any better with your lips?"

Hunter had redefined his type right then. Oh, he'd liked his women bold, and her bite-me attitude was right up his alley. But there was something about her melt-your-soul eyes that drew him in.

"Not only am I great with my hands," he'd said, hopping off the stage, "but these fingers here have been hailed as poetic genius."

Unlike the rest of her gender when under his scrutiny, she'd never once broken eye contact. The closer he got, the bigger she tried to make herself appear—head high and shoulders squared as if she could handle anything.

He'd leaned a hip against a booth and said, "I believe the *Nashville Tribune* wrote, 'The most skilled since Merle Travis.'"

"Merle might have had something to say about that." She'd shrugged but couldn't seem to help stealing glances at his satin vintage Les Paul Junior—a present from his dad. "Especially about those last notes."

"What the hell does that mean?"

That time when she'd smiled it had been big and real, so bright it lit up the entire room. And her eyes, those warm green eyes, had twinkled. "The last notes you played were wrong. You know, the ones going into the chorus."

"I wrote it. There's no way they're wrong."

"If you say so. I'll be back with that Lone Star."

But he hadn't wanted her to go. She was the first woman who didn't pretend that his shit didn't stink—which was exciting. And sexy as hell.

Then there was her confidence. Hell, he'd started to question his own freaking chords. "Hold up a second, Trouble. I don't want to look like an ass. Well, at least a bigger ass than I already am. Show me what you mean."

She'd shoved her notepad into the V of her top, securing it under her bra strap—her black lacy strap—and held out her hand.

He'd offered up his guitar, but when she grabbed for it, he didn't immediately let go. "What's the magic word?"

"That would be *asshole*, remember?"

He'd laughed. Cocky twentysomething Hunter knew jack shit about women. But he knew there was more to Mackenzie than a pretty face and smart mouth.

Without asking permission, she'd taken the guitar and cradled it close to her body, balancing it on her knee. Her familiarity with the instrument said she'd put in a lot of hours strumming. And when her hands glided over the strings with grace and patience, Hunter had known she'd been playing her whole life.

She'd strummed a few chords before her fingers came to rest and she closed her eyes, blocking out her audience, and transitioned effortlessly into the song he and the band had been hashing out all morning and the better part of the afternoon.

"Well, shit." Confident, sexy, *and* talented.

She'd played the entire riff from memory, chord for chord. Her beautiful voice had hummed the melody as she played the chorus then stopped, hitting him with a pair of double-barreled dimples that stirred up all kinds of trouble south of his buckle.

"See? Way too flashy," she'd said. "With your voice, you don't need to go all *American Idol*. It takes away from your talent. It would sound better like this."

Mackenzie played a more complex combination of notes that called for rooted singing. Her version ended up landing them their first paying gig at a bar by the university.

The unexpected connection that hummed between them that night had been so intense and so right it was unlike anything he'd ever felt before. Then he'd discovered she was nineteen—a little too young for his twenty-eight-year-old self—and put her firmly in the friend zone. And by the time Mackenzie was old enough to be an option, she was so ingrained in the band and such an important person in his life he was afraid to go there.

Hunter didn't have the greatest track record when it came to women. And he didn't want to risk screwing things up and losing her. Only she'd left anyway.

But she was back. And that chemistry he'd done his best to ignore over the years? Yup. That was back too. A blast of heat strong enough to take him out at the knees.

Lust wasn't the only emotion humming through his veins. There was plenty of anger and frustration pumping, a lethal combination that had him dialed to *shit just got real.*

Hunter knew Mackenzie was a loner. Had learned that she'd rather go it alone than rely on anyone else. One of the many cruel lessons life had taught her early on. So yes, he understood her obsessive need for independence. But to disappear on him when all he'd ever done was care for her?

Yeah, there was a serious come-to-Jesus meeting headed their way. It wouldn't be fun, but Hunter needed answers. Long-overdue answers.

He stepped past the threshold into the office, and Mackenzie whipped around. Placing a startled hand on the back of the chair, she rose and faced him.

Hunter put on what he hoped came across as a fancy-meeting-you-here smile but didn't bother to hide any of the worry or heartache she'd caused. Those green pools hit his, and not an ounce of recognition registered on her face. No regret, no shame, not a single glimmer of apology was aimed his way.

Nope, she stood there, arms at her sides, shoulders back, eyes wide with confusion. As if *she* was the offended party.

And, okay, those wide eyes weren't aimed at him, per se. It was more like she was staring off into space. Collecting her thoughts for some BS explanation or whatever. So Hunter crossed his arms too, determined that *she* would be the one to do the explaining.

"Brody?" she asked. "Is that you?"

Hunter didn't know what pissed him off more. That she was still playing some fucking game or that in less than six-tenths of a second her sweet drawl settled right in his chest.

He was about to tell her that he wasn't pussy enough to be confused with Brody when Mackenzie took a hesitant step forward, her foot catching on the leg of the chair. For a solid heartbeat, he froze as she stumbled. Her second step wasn't much better, and she pitched forward, thrusting her hands in front of her to break what would have been an epic fall.

Only she didn't fall. Before Hunter could move, a dog shot out from behind the chair and placed itself under her, maneuvering his big body into the perfect position and bracing himself like he'd done this a million times before. Even more shockingly, Mackenzie grabbed on to the dog's back and avoided toppling over.

She let out a frustrated breath, then straightened. With her eyes closed and her cheeks flushed with embarrassment, Mackenzie reached down to pat the enormous dog, who was anchored to her side. The furry savior was also wearing a leather harness with a green vest.

The dog's eyes locked on to Hunter's—friendly but fiercely protective. The same expression Hunter had worn whenever *he'd* been around Mackenzie.

"That was close," she said with a self-conscious laugh, her hand on her heart and her breathing labored. "You're a good boy, Muttley."

For a solid heartbeat, everything stilled. It was as if a freight train were coming straight at him. He could feel the floor vibrate, smell the truth as it careened right into his chest.

Then it stopped. A full stop. His breathing, his heart, his anger. It all stopped and refocused with a single thought. Mackenzie couldn't see his anger or his worry.

Mackenzie couldn't see a fucking thing.

CHAPTER 4

"Why the hell didn't you tell me?" Hunter barked as he pushed through the front door of Big Daddy's.

It was the question he should have asked Mackenzie ten minutes ago, back in that office. Only, instead, he'd run like the hounds of hell were on his ass and hadn't stopped until he was good and pissed.

Sixteen flights and a few uphill blocks left ample time for the anger and frustration to reach dangerous levels. Thankfully, the perfect target sat at the end of the bar, sipping from a frosty mug and wearing a shit-eating grin.

"Aren't you a ray of sunshine." Brody pulled from his beer, as if Hunter's world hadn't just been flipped on its fucking head. "I take it the talk went well?"

Hunter didn't answer. Didn't need to. Because there weren't enough words in the English language to sum up exactly how many different levels of fucked-up that meeting had been. Which worked for Hunter, since the kind of come-to-Jesus meeting he desperately needed had little to do with words and more to do with action.

Some swift *fist* action—right to Brody's face.

And three years of lies and complete bullshit packed one hell of a punch.

Brody's head flew back, the impact knocking him off the barstool and onto his ass, splashing beer onto the bar top and a few nearby patrons.

Brody righted himself and wiped at the blood trickling from his nose with his shirtsleeve. "What the hell?"

"My thoughts exactly, bro." Hunter grabbed Brody by the shirt, their faces so close he could feel his cousin's heart pounding with adrenaline.

"Hey, thanks, Brody," Brody said in his best Hunter imitation. "I can't believe you put your entire career on the line by violating a binding confidentiality agreement with one of your biggest clients. I mean, that bonehead move could lead to a lawsuit that could ruin you. So thanks for doing me a solid, *bro*."

"Thanks?" He shoved Brody into the wall hard enough to send a few platinum records crashing to the ground. "Three years and you said not one word."

"Whoa, not cool," Cash said, looking at the spectacle they were making. As the oldest Kane cousin and the owner of their dad's bar, Cash didn't like people making a mess in his place. And because Cash was six-foot-three and 220 pounds of tattooed hothead, most people knew better than to try. "You know Big Daddy's rules. No one fights in here except the owner. And that would be me."

"Special circumstances," Hunter said, his eyes never leaving Brody's, his fists still bunched in his cousin's starched shirt.

"Is this about the time Brody got all hormonal over Savannah and shoved you into the gym locker and hurt your little man feelings?" Cash asked with a grin.

Brody sent Cash an eat-shit-and-die look. Hunter kept his eyes locked on his target. "Something like that."

Cash let out a big, irritated sigh, as if he were the one whose whole world had been flipped upside down. "Fine, but you know the rules. No blood on the customers, so take it elsewhere."

"You really want to do this, Hunter?" Brody asked.

"Yup."

"Beating the shit out of me won't fix things."

"Nope. But it'll make me feel a hell of a lot better." And right then Hunter needed to feel something other than this ache of betrayal.

Without a word, Brody shoved Hunter back, then wiped the blood off his lip. He headed through the bar, nodding and smiling at startled customers, not stopping until they were in the back office.

Hunter did his best to keep himself in check until they were behind closed doors.

"You already got in one shot," Brody said, slamming the door. "Now you're going for two, and that's just greedy." Brody underscored his last statement with a quick advance and sharp right cross to Hunter's jaw.

Jesus. Did his cousin have titanium knuckles?

Hunter's adrenaline pumped hard, making him feel like a freaking gladiator and helping him rebound from the blow faster than expected. He rushed Brody, lifting them both up off their feet and toppling them over the desk. The impact was enough to rock both their worlds, but neither missed a beat.

Fists flying and arms jabbing, each fought for the dominant position. They tumbled over and over, finally landing with Brody on top, his fist cocked back and ready to deliver another blow when a bucket of ice-cold water rained down over them.

Gasping, they both looked up to find Wade. Brody's younger brother stood in a starched suit and tie worthy of dinner with their mom, Vivian Kane, an empty ice bucket in his hand. The look he shot their way said he was having dinner with Aunt Viv, and they'd interrupted it.

"You ladies finished? Or would you like to take it to the alley out back?" Wade said in that southern gentleman's tone that always pissed Hunter off.

When neither moved, Wade dabbed the corner of his mouth with the cloth napkin he'd carried in with him. "Or I can go get Mom and tell her you broke Dad's favorite beer mug. The one they got on their honeymoon. We're having dinner with some of Dad's friends in the back room. Your call."

Both men looked at the chipped mug and swore.

With one last shove, Brody rolled off Hunter, and they sat up.

Wade set down the bucket and walked to the bar fridge beneath the desk. He fished out two cold beers, tossing one to Brody and the other to Hunter—hitting him square in the gut.

Hunter grunted. "What was that for?"

"Being an ass."

"What about him?" Hunter pointed to Brody, who was leaning back against the wall, holding the can to his eyebrow.

"He'll get his when his wife sees that black eye. Now, if you'll excuse me, I need to head back to dinner. Sheriff Bradly was telling Mom about his new proposal to promote positive police and citizen engagement. Which will come in handy when he busts in and arrests you for being stupid and disorderly." Wade didn't wait for a response and instead slammed the door as he left, causing a framed family photo to fall to the floor.

Hunter looked around at the disaster of an office. Files strewn across the floor, overturned alcohol cases, a smear of scarlet on the white leather chair Cash had brought in when he took over running the bar. The room looked like a crime scene.

"Always hated that chair," Brody said.

"Right. What kind of man buys white leather?"

"The kind who drinks imported espresso in one of those dainty little cups Cash keeps in the top drawer," Brody said with a laugh, then grimaced as he touched his split lip. "I should call Mackenzie, beg for her not to fire me." He eyed Hunter. "Again."

"Don't start crying like a little girl. You're out of the woods." Hunter touched his rib, which hurt like hell and immediately sobered. "At least with her. Me, I'm still weighing my options."

"Fire me. It would make my life so much easier," Brody said, standing. "But I'm still going to go check on her, make sure she's okay."

"She's okay." Hunter wasn't so sure he'd ever be. Just picturing her sitting there, staring blindly at the door frame, brought a fresh dose of emotion. This time it felt a hell of a lot closer to guilt than the anger he'd been clinging to. "She didn't even know I was there."

"Wait. What?" Brody spun around, his face hardened with anger. "You just left her sitting there? Jesus." He pulled his keys from his pocket and headed for the door. "She won't know where I went and—"

"I didn't leave her there," Hunter cut him off. "I'm not a complete asshole." Not that his family would agree. Otherwise they wouldn't be in this situation. "I ran into your assistant in the lobby on the way out. Told her there was some mix-up with the dinner and you'd be back in a little while. Raydeen said she'd keep Mackenzie company until you got back. So you've got a few minutes to explain to me what the fuck is going on." A rough laugh escaped, and Hunter's chest caved painfully in on itself. "You at least owe me that."

"The only thing I owe you is another black eye." Brody's words were softened by the fact that he collapsed in the chair and rested his head in his hands. "I can't believe you walked out. Do you have any idea how much I put on the line to make this happen?"

"Do you have any what it felt like when I saw her sitting there?" Hunter dropped his head back against the wall and closed his eyes. "You didn't even warn me, give me time to prepare." Hunter met his cousin's gaze. "All those times I asked where she was, if you'd heard from her. You lied to me. I mean, did you know when she left the rehearsal dinner she wasn't coming back?"

"No. I knew something was up, but she only said that she needed space to think, to clear her head." Brody let out a breath, then picked his beer up off the floor and cracked it open. After he took a long swig he added, I didn't expect her to disappear."

Hunter should have known better. The months leading up to his wedding she'd been acting strange. Distant and withdrawn. He knew she'd been struggling with migraines, or so she'd told him, and he'd chalked it up to stress over the upcoming album.

But he'd hoped that she'd trust him enough to come to him if there was a problem. Now he was starting to realize the problem went far deeper than trust.

"How long before the wedding did she know?"

"Remember when she had her eyes checked after she ran that red light?" Brody asked, and Hunter sighed.

He remembered all right. She'd nearly T-boned a delivery truck in the middle of the night. She'd called him from the side of the road crying. "She promised to go see her doctor."

"She did. The diagnosis was the same as her mom's."

A statement that hurt worse than Brody's titanium fists. Mackenzie had been given a diagnosis that to her must have felt like a death sentence. Leber's hereditary optic neuropathy wasn't some disease she'd have to look up. Mackenzie had already experienced it firsthand.

Had watched her world be torn apart by her mom's disease, watched as Susan's career as a photographer came to an end. Watched her own dreams of music school die when she sacrificed a full ride to the Berklee College of Music in Boston to take care of her mom.

With one diagnosis, Mackenzie's life had gone from *the world's your oyster* to serving oysters at a pub and caring for her mom.

It was just like Mackenzie to face her own diagnosis alone.

"How is she?" Hunter asked, hating himself for not following up with Mackenzie to see how her appointment had gone.

"According to my dad, the first year was hard."

45

"Your dad knew?"

Brody nodded. "A year before I did. Helped her through the worst of it. Took her to appointments, got her seen by the right doctors and into the best rehabilitation facility in Nashville."

Hunter gripped the back of his neck with his hand. "He never said a word."

"Dad wasn't one for gossip," Brody said, and Hunter nodded. "He was a man of his word too. And trust me, the only way Mackenzie would have told him anything was if he'd promised her complete silence."

Hunter cracked open his beer and thought about what all this meant. To him. To Mackenzie. To the rest of his family. Her need for distance had caused her to miss the funeral of a man she'd loved.

What else was she missing out on?

"She's doing better now," Brody said quietly. "She's got a Seeing Eye dog who helps her to get around more on her own, but the adjustment has been rough."

Hunter took a long pull, letting Brody's words settle. Trying to imagine how terrified Mackenzie must have been. "How fast did her sight go?"

It had taken Mackenzie's mom less than three months to go from normal to completely blind.

"I don't know," Brody said, and it was good, because Hunter wasn't sure he wanted to know. "She doesn't talk about it, not even to Savannah. She came to me about a year after your wedding, right when you were recording your third album."

Brody paused, as if waiting for Hunter to finally look him in the eye so he could see he was telling the truth. "I hadn't heard from her before then. I swear. She contacted me about some songs she wrote, asked if I would be willing to represent her independent work."

"You already represented her."

"She explained that was up for negotiation too."

"Sounds like her." Hunter let out a strangled laugh. Mackenzie had come a long way. She had emerged from her caretaker role focused, driven, and stubborn as hell. A potent combination.

"I asked her what happened, how I could help. She came unglued, told me in no uncertain terms that she was interested in representation, not a handout. Then she sat down at the piano and started playing." Brody smiled. "The shit of it was she'd gotten even better. I don't know how she did it, but before she hit the climb, I knew it was a hit. I told her I could pull some strings if she wanted to play at Big Daddy's. She said if she wanted strings pulled she'd ask Big Daddy herself, because she wasn't trying to be the next Carrie Underwood: she'd written the song for you."

Brody took another long swallow, fiddled with the tab of his can, and added, "Told me it would make your career."

"'Unrequited,'" Hunter said, more a realization than a question.

Eighteen months ago, the Hunter Kane Band had been about to propose a new deal with their recording label when Brody had come to him with a song written by a new writing duo he'd just signed. Hunter had listened to the song and asked to look at everything Mack and Muttley had in their library. There were only three songs, but he'd recorded all three.

A few months later, the first single off their album had released, and when "Unrequited" hit the airways, it became the smash hit of the summer. Then went on to earn the band their first GRAMMY, AMA, and Billboard awards.

"She pretty much took you from cult following to a household name, and she's been writing songs for you ever since." Brody polished off his beer and tossed it in the garbage. "Her only stipulation, besides complete anonymity, was that you get her songs first. That way you'd write or pick other ones with the same vibe for the album. She's always complaining you're the John Travolta of music."

"What's that supposed to mean?" It was clear from the smirk on his cousin's face it wasn't a compliment.

In fact, the accompanying shit-eating grin told Hunter that his question had not only made Brody's day, it had made his whole week.

"That you're talented as hell but couldn't pick career-making material if it came up and bit you in the ass."

Hunter nearly choked on his beer. "She always said I picked my songs like my women: flashy and too trendy to last." Images of her standing with wide, vulnerable eyes, stroking her guide dog, sobered him instantly. "I need to see her."

"Tried that. Less than twenty minutes ago. Yet you're here, determined to further screw with my night, which tells me she kicked you out or you ran from the room like a scared little girl."

"I needed time to absorb everything," Hunter defended.

Brody's eyes went wide with understanding. "Jesus, after all that pissing and whining, you ran? At least tell me you didn't say something to upset her." He held up a silencing hand. "Never mind, I don't want to know. As of this moment you are on your own. You may make me bank, but she's her own printing press."

"I'm family," Hunter argued.

"So is she," Brody said quietly. "I've been in the middle for two years, and I won't go there again."

◆ ◆ ◆

Heaven.

Mackenzie wiggled her toes, enjoying the unbound luxury as the sunbaked tiles warmed her bare feet.

The sunroom was Mackenzie's favorite spot at Brody and Savannah's house. It was open enough to allow her freedom to move around, yet cozy enough to eliminate disorienting echoes. It had become such a peaceful place for her that Mackenzie had added a similar one to the back of her own house.

She knew that three steps to the right rested a chaise longue covered in silk so temptingly plush it was the perfect place for a catnap. A step forward was a square coffee table, and four steps to her left sat a miniature table covered in nubby lace, which was the centerpiece for all of Caroline's tea parties, including the one currently in session.

Mackenzie sat with her knees nearly to her chest, squeezed into a square throne made to hold someone half her size. According to Caroline, it was painted princess pink with lavender stars.

Paper rustled and the distinct scent of vanilla, crayon, and everything little girl wafted over her as the princess in question snuggled deeper into Mackenzie's chest.

"Dat's your dress. See how floofy it is?" Caroline said. Her angelic voice and slight lisp were escorted by a pleasant smell of bittersweet chocolate that could only have come from sneaking one of her birthday cupcakes before the party started.

"Caroline, do I smell frosting?"

At Muttley's favorite word, the dog buried his nose in Mackenzie's thigh and let out a guilty whimper. Clearly he'd had a bite too.

Caroline shushed her and, as if that wasn't an admission of guilt, quickly guided the tip of Mackenzie's finger over the drawing in her lap. "And dat's me. I'm wearing a pink gown wif ruffles and bows and a big veil wif lots of sparkles."

"It sounds beautiful. What's over here?" Mackenzie asked as her hand drifted to the center of the paper, where she felt a buildup of waxy residue from the crayon.

"That's Muttley." Caroline outlined the dog's portrait, and Muttley barked in appreciation. "He's in da middle and has a sparkly collar wif a pink bow on his neck to match my dress. He broughted his own sleeping bag and everything for our party."

"Oh, a party. Is it a ball?" Mackenzie asked, playing along with Caroline's ever-growing imagination. "Will Prince Charming be in attendance?"

A noise erupted from Caroline's mouth, similar to a soda bottle exploding, and sent a light mist of spray onto Mackenzie's cheek. "No. I asked Uncle Cash to come and play da prince, but he's drawing a rose on a lady's back." Caroline leaned over and patted Muttley on the head. "I asked Mommy for a dog for my birfday but she said I'm not old enough, so den I asked for a sleepover wif Muttley instead."

Muttley started a low whining in his throat and pressed closer to Mackenzie's thigh, sneaking one paw onto the chair. Knowing it would take only a second to get all four on her lap, she said, "Down."

"See. He *wants* to come!" Caroline shifted to the side and rested her warm cheek against Mackenzie's chest. "I'm almost this many." Four little fingers danced across Mackenzie's palm. "Enough for a sleepover. I have all our favorite doggy movies picked out. Plus, Mommy gots us our own doggy-friendly cake, just for tonight."

Muttley's second favorite word had him sitting at attention, as if promising he'd be a good boy.

Mackenzie's heart sank at the simple request that was, for her, anything but simple. She depended on Muttley for her freedom, and there was no way she could function at home without him, even for just a night. Caroline loved Muttley almost as much as Mackenzie did. And even though she'd explained it several times, the concept of a guide dog was hard for Caroline to grasp.

Especially since Muttley looked like a giant polar bear.

Hoping to soften the blow, Mackenzie brushed a soothing hand over Caroline's hair and down her arm, feeling the short ringlets recoil as her touch passed. "Muttley has to sleep with me, sweet pea."

"I know. But I gots an idea. I could sleep at you and Muttley's house and den he can be wif me *and* you. Dat way you don't get scared at night."

Caroline's innocent remark hit so close to home Mackenzie had a hard time speaking. "I would love that and so would Muttley, but a sleepover at my place won't work until you're a bit older."

"I'll be on my gold-star behavior."

The sincerely whispered plea sounded close to cracking. Mackenzie cradled Caroline's little body closer to protect her from the disappointment. "It's not you, sweet pea, it's just . . . I can't be sure I can keep you safe."

"I can keep us all safe and sound." The promise was said with so much conviction Mackenzie's heart cracked a little.

They'd tried that once before, and Caroline had accidentally left one of her shoes in the hallway, causing Mackenzie to fall and wrench her ankle. With no other adults around and Caroline inconsolable, Mackenzie had been rendered completely helpless. All the possibilities of how much worse it could have been confirmed that she had no business taking care of small children alone.

"I know you can, but I'm just not ready yet."

The first sniffle came fast, followed by a little quiver and the slumping of shoulders. Caroline buried her face in Mackenzie's chest and mumbled, "'Cause on account of your eyes?"

Mackenzie opened her mouth to answer, to reassure Caroline that everything would be okay, but the words got stuck in her throat.

Mackenzie's stubborn determination and ability to focus on the positives were how she'd made it this far. But some times were harder than others to keep the doubt from creeping in. Like now, when even the positives couldn't distract her from the incredible losses she'd had to endure. The future losses she was destined to face.

She'd never let anything hold her back from what she wanted. Even growing up with a single-family income hadn't stopped Mackenzie from attending one of the top music schools in the country. But when her mother's condition worsened, Mackenzie had decided to cut her education short and come home to care for her.

Not that Mackenzie regretted a second of it. She loved the time she'd spent with her mother, playing music, looking through her mother's pictures, reminiscing about the beautiful places her mom had traveled to for her art. Had Mackenzie known that there was an expiration date on their time together, she would have made a bigger effort.

When Susan lost her sight, she lost her career but not her love of exotic landscapes. So when she hung up her camera, she took a job as a freelance travel writer. Susan revisited the places she'd been, and Mackenzie became her editor, her eyes, and her tour guide to the seeing world.

So much so that after her mother's death, Mackenzie had a hard time adjusting. She'd found herself at twenty-three, with a spotty education and an even spottier social circle, feeling very much alone.

Mackenzie had spent so much time chronicling her mother's journey she'd never given much thought to her own. She had no idea who she was or, more important, what kind of life she wanted. So she turned to her music, which was how she met Hunter, and he filled her world with some of the lightness she'd been craving.

The more time she spent with her music and Hunter, the closer she came to discovering her own happiness and how wonderful freedom could be. Then the Hunter Kane Band landed their first record deal, and one of the songs she'd cowritten with Hunter hit the Billboard list, and she had her first taste of success. Only it was so intertwined with Hunter's rise to fame she wasn't sure where his dream began and hers ended. She also realized that she didn't care, because as long as he was happy, she was happy.

Wasn't that a terrifying place to be?

She'd finally found someone who spoke her language, someone who was caring and nurturing, yet she'd still managed to tie her own happiness to his.

And if the three-carat princess cut wasn't proof enough that she needed to rethink her life, then the diagnosis that shortly followed was a clear sign from the universe that she was meant to be on her own for once.

Most days Mackenzie was at peace with that. But sitting there, holding Caroline, she was once again struck with the realization of just how much she'd lost. Travel, music, a family of her own—all the adventures she could ever hope for had been right here within reach.

One mutated gene had changed it all.

So yes, this was the closest Mackenzie would ever come to having a family. To deny Caroline something as commonplace as a sleepover killed her, but the reality was Mackenzie couldn't guarantee any child's safety.

Until Caroline was older, there would be no sleepovers. At least not at Mackenzie's house.

She cupped Caroline's face. "Yes, sweet pea, on account of my eyes."

"Maybe I can ask Mommy if we can do da sleepover at . . ." Caroline's face turned to the side, and her cheeks swelled with happiness beneath Mackenzie's hands. Muttley let out a growl from deep in his throat.

"You're here!" Caroline squealed.

"Hey there, kiddo."

CHAPTER 5

It was as if time shifted, moving slower and slower until it froze for a full heartbeat as recognition crashed into Mackenzie's chest. The familiar voice, smooth and husky, filled the room.

Mackenzie felt her balance falter, tasted the panic as it wrapped around her throat, suffocating her. The fear was even worse. It felt like leaded bullets lodged in her chest, and each pump of her heart shot a fresh dose of panic throughout her body.

"Is dat for me, Uncle Hunter?" Caroline asked, and every single one of Mackenzie's fears was muted, shoved to the furthest corner of her brain, until she had only a single focus.

Escape.

"Maybe you should open the lid and tell me," he said with that easygoing amusement in his voice that charmed women into doing stupid things. Thankfully, Mackenzie was too busy searching for her shoes to be charmed. Because she knew the power of that voice—and was convinced it should be outlawed.

She patted the floor with her palm, her heart doing some serious patting of its own, the thumps so loud it was impossible to decipher where Caroline had run to. But from the sound of the rustling taffeta and wet kisses, wherever she'd gone had landed her right in Hunter's arms.

Mackenzie slipped one shoe on, but with the other nowhere to be found, her panic began to rebuild. Then a wet nose nudged her hand toward the coffee table and—

Thank God—her shoe.

"You're getting a steak for supper," Mackenzie whispered to Muttley, who licked her hand.

An ear-piercing squeal lit through the room, so loud Mackenzie could feel the vibrations in her sternum. It was followed by a sound even sweeter.

A tiny little *yip*.

"It's a puppy! You gots me a puppy!" Caroline was jumping up and down, her feet and dress slapping with each movement.

Muttley, on the other hand, chose now to act like a working dog. He sat completely still, his ears perked but his body relaxed, almost bored. As if he couldn't be bothered by the addition of another dog.

"She's a pomapoo, so she'll look like a fluffy slipper with a wagging tail. And she'll never lose that cute little yip," Hunter said proudly.

"Ever?" Caroline asked in wonder.

Yipyipyip!

"See, isn't that cute? A powder puff that prances. Brody is going to love walking her downtown." Hunter sounded way too pleased with himself, which meant he was up to no good. Not that Mackenzie cared—she was too busy grabbing her own dog.

"Can I keep her?"

Hunter chuckled. "It wouldn't be a present if you had to give her back."

The commotion stopped, and the energy in the room shifted, became uncertain. Mackenzie strained to hear Caroline's voice. "But Mommy and Daddy said I has to wait until I this many."

"Good thing it's your birthday tomorrow, because you'll officially be older."

"I will!" Caroline swished back and forth, and then she was on the move again. The rustling of taffeta and *yips* became louder and louder until she squealed, "Snuggles, Miss Mack! We wants snuggles."

The air shifted as Caroline leaped up into Mackenzie's lap, securing her to the chair and eliminating any hope of a stealthy exit. A wet nose and hot doggy breath greeted Mackenzie's hand, then her arm, until she felt the puppy stretch to reach her face.

"Miss Mack, I gots a pomapoo," Caroline repeated.

"I can feel." Mackenzie made a conscious effort to bury her fear, push it down until she was alone. A talent she'd spent a lifetime mastering.

"It's just like the one I wanted. See." Caroline took Mackenzie's hand in her much smaller one and ran it over the puppy's body, showing Mackenzie what her new puppy looked like. The little thing's entire body trembled with nervous excitement. Not all that far off from what Mackenzie's heart was doing. "She's cream wif a brown spot around her nose, and her eyes are black. And she gots a glittery collar and little booties on her feet. And feel right here, her tail's curly."

Mackenzie loved the way Caroline always included her. If she wasn't describing the colors blooming in the garden, she was guiding Mackenzie's hands over some object, making sure Mackenzie saw what everyone else did.

Mackenzie squeezed the toddler a little tighter. "What are you going to name her?"

Mackenzie could almost hear Caroline considering all the options. With an excited gasp, she said, "Duchess."

"That's a perfect name," Hunter said with a smile. "I can already see her in a cute tiara and tutu prancing down the hallway of your daddy's office."

"Duchess!" Caroline bounced up and down on Mackenzie's lap. "Can I show her to Muttley?"

Muttley yawned, unimpressed with Duchess.

"Maybe later. He's working right now." Working on getting Mackenzie out of there.

"Dat's Muttley," Caroline informed the room. "I know you want to pet him, but you can't. See, his harness is on 'cause he's working."

And wouldn't you know it, Muttley was suddenly sitting obediently at Mackenzie's feet, alert and awaiting his command.

"You don't say," Hunter said, all that easygoing charm suddenly gone.

"He looks all sleepy, but he's working. Right, Miss Mack?"

"Yup." Mackenzie stroked Muttley's head, seeking connection and comfort.

"Miss Mack is his boss," Caroline whispered.

"Lucky dog," he said, and Mackenzie's nipples went on the alert.

Yup, time to go.

Mackenzie lifted the little girl off her lap. "Why don't you go show Duchess to your mom?"

"Mommy! Mommy!" And just like that, Caroline was off, racing down the hallway, Duchess's little claws sliding across the hardwood floors in her wake.

The invisible buffer, the only thing allowing Mackenzie to hold it together, left with Caroline. Even worse, the approaching clicks of boots on the slate floor sent a wave of pure terror racing through her body as a masculine and earthy scent caressed her cheek and confirmed her suspicions.

She hadn't been alone in Brody's office—Hunter had been with her. Which meant that Brody had sandbagged her. Supper hadn't been a sweet gesture. It had been a setup. Plain and simple.

And Hunter? He'd taken one look at her . . . and walked out.

Something she wanted to do right then, except she didn't know where to go.

The silence between them grew unbearable. Her stomach pinched from the intense anxiety pumping through her veins. Unable to keep still, she stroked Muttley.

"Is this another *coincidence*?" She threw air quotes around the word. "Or did Brody tell you I was going to be here?"

"It's good to see you too, Trouble." His tone said quite the opposite.

Refusing to let that affect her, she zeroed in on the sound of his voice and lifted her gaze. She knew she'd found his eyes when she heard his breathing shift. "Why are you here, Hunter?"

"To drop off a yap dog for my niece, a nice little payback for Brody *not* telling me about you sooner." The coffee table groaned under Hunter's weight as he sat. "And because we need to talk."

"You had your chance the other week in Brody's office," she said.

"Brody told you that was me?" He had the nerve to sound irritated.

"No, I recognized your cologne." She didn't know if he was impressed or just choosing to remain silent, so she said, "It must have taken a lot to get Brody to go against his promise and set up that meeting. Yet you didn't say a word." Not a single one. "Why?"

"I didn't know what to say."

It was strange how a simple statement had the power to cut so deep it actually ached to smile. But Mackenzie forced a grin, big and bold, because it would hurt less than his pity.

Since leaving rehab, Mackenzie had experienced her share of awkward conversations and even more awkward silences when running into people from her past. It was as if her disability had become her new identity, erasing the woman behind the illness, making her somehow a stranger to them.

What really got to her, though, were the people who would pretend nothing had changed. That this was just another bump in the road for her to overcome. As if all she needed to do was fight harder, really commit herself, and everything would go back to normal.

What people didn't understand was Mackenzie's life *was* normal. It was just a different kind of comfort and balance she sought. She was proud of the leaps she'd made in getting there.

Her doctors praised her for how fast she'd progressed, how she'd embraced her rehabilitation. The only thing she had yet to master was reentry. How to make her new normal work with everyone else's normal. So when those awkward moments happened, they wouldn't be so isolating—or devastating.

"Don't worry." She grabbed the harness and stood, Muttley steadily at her side. "I get that a lot."

"I wasn't talking about your sight," Hunter said, coming to stand in front of her. "I was talking about you, your music, everything else I've missed out on. You disappeared on me. I had no idea what happened."

His anguish was raw and real and made Mackenzie's stomach cave in on itself—and her feet shift to find a clear path.

"What was I supposed to do? Walk into your dressing room, a few minutes before you were supposed to walk down the aisle, and tell you I was going blind?" She took a step to the right and bumped into something large with rounded corners. "That all of the plans we had for touring and the band were over for me?"

"If that's what it took, then yeah."

She moved forward and felt the space tighten. Her emotions were out of control, so disorienting she couldn't remember the exact layout of the room. And she couldn't slow down enough to let Muttley do his job.

"It was your *wedding*. You had a honeymoon to go on and a tour starting right after. I didn't want to hold you back." Didn't want him to witness her independence wilting away. "I knew I could handle it on my own."

"This isn't about what you can or can't handle," he said, his voice right behind her. No matter how many steps she moved, he was right there.

A total Hunter move. Get close, get personal, then get sweet-talking.

Problem was, it had been a long while since someone had sweet-talked Mackenzie, a language in which Hunter was fluent. Although his tone was far from sweet. In fact, he sounded angry—an emotion she'd never felt from him before with regard to her.

"This is about our friendship. About you deciding how much I was allowed to care for you. *Jesus,* you were a no-show at my wedding, then disappeared without a word." No, not anger . . . fury.

"Big Daddy knew where I was," she said.

"And he was guilted into silence, I bet. *Jesus,* all I knew was that you'd quit the band and were going in a different direction. He never said much more, leaving me to replay the last six months before the wedding, what I could have said, what I could have done so wrong that you'd cut me out of your life."

A wave of guilt washed over her, moving around her stomach before settling like hot lead in her chest. She knew better than anyone how crushing the weight of uncertainty could be, how tiring it was to obsess over where things had gone wrong. Figure out exactly where she came up lacking.

Her mother's death had paralyzed her, but it was the all-encompassing guilt that had finally pulled her under.

"I was trying to do the right thing. My life was going to change, but that didn't mean yours had to," she said, finally letting Muttley lead her through the maze of furniture. "I knew if I told you about my disease, you'd want to help, postpone the tour to take care of me. But you deserved to enjoy your success, live a happy life with Hadley."

"You were a part of that happy life. And what went down between us had nothing to do with the band or Hadley." Suddenly he was directly in front of her, blocking her path, and it felt as if the walls were closing in. And that distress, the one she'd felt the first time she'd awoken to find everything had faded into the shadows, came rushing back.

Sometimes, being blind was similar to being bound: no matter how hard she fought, she'd never break free. Some days it was a lonely existence, and other days the darkness went far deeper than missing the spectrum of colors that made life warm.

"It had to do with you not trusting me," he said.

"It had to do with trusting myself," she clarified. "All I wanted was for you to be happy, but the engagement flew by, and working with you became harder and harder. I knew I would eventually lose my sight, next would come my home, and then my freedom." She pushed through the emotion. "I couldn't survive standing by and watching the last thing I loved slip away."

Hunter stopped breathing. She felt it. Felt the energy thicken and the reality of what she'd admitted push down on the both of them.

She couldn't see his face, didn't know what expression he was wearing, but knew she'd dropped a bomb so destructive it had splintered Hunter's foundation. Shredded the conversation until all that remained was her admission of love.

Mackenzie didn't know what was worse: unrequited love or her being so far under his radar that her admission came as a shock.

"You should have told me." His voice was so low she had a hard time picking up on the cues she needed to decipher his expression.

"Would it have made a difference?" A question she'd carried with her every day. A question that had expanded since news of the divorce hit, until sometimes it was all she could think about.

"Honestly, I don't know, but we would have worked it out. We've always worked it out. It's what made us such a strong team. Or at least I thought it had, but I must have been missing something if you thought your only option was to run."

"What other options would there be?" she whispered. "Sit on the porch and wait. For the band to leave on tour, for you to start living your new life, for everything and everyone I knew to keep moving in the same direction while I walked up and down those front steps of my house over and over until my doctors thought I could handle stepping onto the sidewalk?"

"Mackenzie," he said quietly.

"Y'all were in a different hotel room every night, while I was trying to memorize how many steps it was to the bathroom. How many tiles back my toothbrush sat on the counter."

Embarrassed by her admission and afraid she was about to cry, Mackenzie turned around to leave—and almost walked straight into a wall.

Muttley tugged her back before she could make contact, but she felt the cold air through the plaster close enough to know it was a near miss.

Humiliation warmed her face and stung her eyes. It had been almost a year since she'd walked into something, so why had her last four senses chosen now to abandon her? All she wanted to do was disappear into the darkness until the world didn't feel so big and ever-changing.

"Can we do this another time?" Her voice was hoarse.

Hunter came up behind her, his body heat seeping through her skin and his voice a soft husk. "We've been so busy moving forward we've lost too much time, Trouble," he whispered, her nickname falling from his lips as if nothing had changed, his hands resting on her hips as if they belonged there.

Slowly, *God, so slowly*, he turned her around and right into those big strong arms of his, then wrapped her up in a hug that was as gentle as it was devastating. Desire, and something much more vulnerable, rushed through her and settled in parts she'd thought long forgotten. But he didn't stop there.

Oh no, Hunter pulled her even closer, tucked a strand of hair behind her ear, and whispered, "And I don't plan to stand by and lose more."

CHAPTER 6

"Are you shitting me?" Mackenzie said and stepped back, right out of Hunter's embrace and—*whoa*, what was up with the you're-such-an-asshole glare she shot his way? "You just used a line from my own song to butter me up."

"I did not." Hunter quickly ran through every song of his and . . . "Nope. I didn't."

"Yes. You did. The line is from 'Wasting Time.' Which I wrote." She rattled off the singer's name, a nine-time GRAMMY winner, as if talking about the lady who did her hair.

"You wrote that song? Never mind, of course you did." He felt like an idiot for not recognizing her sound before. Mackenzie had a way with words that was exquisitely unique and undeniably hers.

"And the move you did there? I've got a song for that too. It's titled 'Good Luck with That.'"

He laughed. "What move?"

"That one." She waved an unimpressed hand at his chest. "It was straight from your playbook, used to charm the ladies. I've seen you do it a thousand times."

"There was no move and no ulterior motive. It was a hug."

"It was a move. Not to get laid or for a kiss on the southern region of your body," she said and didn't even crack a smile. "But to get me to agree to cowrite your album."

Okay, so maybe that was in the back of his mind. And sure, putting his hands on Mackenzie had been a serious lack of judgment. But he'd hugged her because she looked vulnerable, and lost, and like she could really use a friend right then.

Too bad none of his other friends were as soft and silky as she was. And he sure as hell didn't hug them until he could feel what kind of underwear they had on. Hell, his fingers had been inches from her ass. And her breasts, the ones he'd stopped paying attention to the second she became a band member, had been crushed up against him and—

Holy shit, he'd put the moves on her.

On Mackenzie, his artistic other half, who he'd spent a good five years putting in the friend zone because he never mixed business with pleasure—especially when that bandmate was also like family.

Mackenzie Hart, the sassy Georgia peach with the saddest fucking eyes on the planet, deserved more than a cheap line from a guy who could only go the distance if it was in a tour bus. "Move unintentional. And I'm not interested in talking about my album right now."

She skewered him with a look that—*damn*—if he hadn't seen her stumble earlier, he would never have known she was blind.

"I'm serious, I came here to see Caroline. And yes, I came to see you." He lowered his voice. "You look good, Trouble. I've missed you."

He'd missed her so much that the first few months after his honeymoon he'd found it impossible to breathe. He'd missed making music with her, missed that she got him—totally and completely. Most of all, he'd missed her laugh.

It took a lot to get her to let loose, a lasting effect from losing everyone she loved so young. Which was why when she did and that laugh of hers came out, sweet and care-free, it was like music for his soul.

Too bad she looked as if she hadn't laughed much as of late. Something he found himself desperately wanting to fix.

"The person you miss doesn't exist anymore," she said quietly, those mossy-green eyes locking on his, and a squirrelly feeling settled in his gut. "I'm not that girl anymore. And I won't ever be her again."

And wasn't that a damn shame, because the girl he'd known was remarkable. A survivor who had finally started to find her own strength, to discover all the things that made her so damn special. He'd hate to think that she'd come so far in the years following her mama's death only to retreat back inside herself.

"I'm not asking you to be anything more than who you are. I just want the chance to get to know you again." He wanted to see her thriving and living a full life, out from beneath the anger and the shadows. According to Brody, she barely even ventured out of her house.

"And what if you don't like the new me?" she asked, and *man oh man*, this lady knew how to break a guy's heart.

"Liking you is the easiest thing I've ever done," he said, and her gaze dropped to his chest. "I'm more afraid that *I* won't live up to the hype."

Hadley had told him he had problems opening up to anyone other than his guitar, and the only distance he'd covered during their brief marriage had been from the bunk of a tour bus. When it came to personal relationships with women, he was a one-hit wonder. But Mackenzie was back, right next to him, and he wasn't about to let her slip away.

Not this time.

He'd never really known his mother, and he didn't know how to do long-term with the female population. Just look at his disaster of a marriage.

Nope, Mackenzie had been the only constant woman in his life, and he'd naively believed she'd be that constant for him forever. Because whatever this thing was between them, it went beyond the surface, beyond the physical, and beyond all the BS that typically complicated relationships. Mackenzie was like family to him.

Sad thing was, just like his dad, she'd walked away too.

"Hunter—" she began, only Brody cut her off.

"I wouldn't worry about the hype, since you might not live to see tomorrow," Brody said, leaning against the wall, a prissy little dog tucked under his arm like a football. "First you crash a three-year-old's tea party. Then you bring her a dog?"

"I believe the dog has a name. It's Duchess," Hunter said, forcing a light smile to his face. "And if you're going to crash a party, you'd better bring a six-pack or a dog."

"You chose wrong," Brody said.

"The look on my niece's face said the opposite." Hunter rocked back on his heels. "By the way, Duchess is a pomapoo, a breed that is said to be the perfect bed buddy for idiot agents everywhere. I hear they like to sleep on your pillow, but they are known to be excited tinklers. So I'd stock up on some of those tinkle pads A-sap."

"I'll take the tinkle pads and a pair of handcuffs out of your commission. Because I will not have you two ruin Caroline's birthday dinner. So if it takes cuffing you together and shoving you in a room until you work this out, then that's what needs to happen."

The thought of handcuffs and a locked room with Mackenzie had all sorts of new and interesting ideas spinning through his head. Mackenzie's head must have taken the same track, because her face went an adorable shade of pink and she kept licking her lips.

Interesting.

"And you call me a diva?" he asked Brody. "I just came here to drop off Duchess and then head home. Your tea party is going to be just fine."

"You can't leave," a tiny voice said from behind Brody. "You promised we'd twirl."

Hunter crouched down to look at his niece, who was dressed as if she were going to high tea with the queen herself. "I'm coming back for your big party this weekend."

"But I wants you to stay tonight with me and Duchess. You're the only one she knows, and she might gets lonely if you leave."

"Caroline's got a point," Brody said with a smile. "You might want to stick around, make sure Duchess doesn't get lonely. Maybe even sleep with her on the couch. I'm short on wee-wee pads, but you can always use your jacket."

Hunter ignored his cousin to focus on Mackenzie. The nervous way she clung to the dog's harness, her body angled for the front door. He'd come here for answers, and yeah, he'd been pissed. He still was. But his goal was never to make Mackenzie feel unwelcome. Not when he was pretty sure she was about to spend her night alone. "I think you already have a full tea party."

"We can make room," Savannah said from the kitchen doorway. Her tone was honeyed, but her glare was glacial. "Can't we?"

Hunter hadn't a clue as to whom the question was addressed, but Mackenzie was the one to answer.

"You bet," she said with enough false bravado to have him squirming.

"Are you sure?" he asked, because the last thing they needed was one more thing between them. "I can always come back."

"No one should have to miss out on one of Caroline's famous tea parties," Mackenzie said, her smile strained.

"Not even overbearing, dumb fuc—" Brody looked down at Caroline, who was staring up at him with wide eyes, waiting for the bad word. "Funkles who show up uninvited."

"Even them," Mackenzie said and placed her hand on Hunter's arm.

Mackenzie was in desperate need of some girl talk.

So when Duchess, excited by the new people, started tinkling all over the floor, Mackenzie made a beeline for the kitchen.

"Fucking puppies" followed her down the hallway. "Jesus, Hunter, get some paper towels."

Mackenzie smothered a laugh. Muttley snorted, as if saying *puppies*. The two cousins were arguing when Mackenzie walked into the kitchen. She was greeted with the homey aroma of lime zest and warm cupcakes.

"Oh good, I was just about to bring you a mint julep," Savannah said as the cabinet doors rattled open and closed. "It's my great-grand-ma's special recipe, and I took a few liberties with the bourbon. Now I'm glad I did."

"Last time I had your great-grandma's mint julep, I woke up on your couch with Caroline braiding my hair and Muttley licking my face," Mackenzie said. "Plus, I'm not talking to you."

"You were a minute ago."

"That's because I didn't want to upset Caroline on her special night." Mackenzie narrowed a gaze in on Savannah's general direction. "A little warning would have been nice."

"For you and me both." Savannah popped the top off the cocktail shaker and poured two glasses, setting one in front of Mackenzie.

"I'll stick with some sweet tea."

"Okay," Savannah said, but she never moved to the fridge. "And maybe it happened this way for a reason. All that stress about the *when* it would happen had almost paralyzed you, but now it's gone."

Only to be replaced by the *how*. And as far as Mackenzie was con-cerned, how this was going to play out moving forward was a heck of a lot more terrifying.

"Don't misunderstand, I will forever be grateful for your patience and support, and I understand that Hunter has every right to be here. Caroline is his niece, and I would never expect y'all to leave him out."

After all, he was family, and Mackenzie was somewhere on the periphery.

"And of course I imagined, if I ran into him again, what I'd say." After she'd pulled her life back together. "But not like this. This was so . . ." *Shocking? Confusing? Fucked-up?* "Unexpected."

Meeting Hunter again without any warning had rocked the carefully laid foundation she'd constructed in the aftermath of her illness. Her ability to know what was coming had been the key to her rehabilitation and continued independence. In the beginning, she'd let go of everything and everyone she loved so she could build a new life, create a new existence, and grow into the person she needed to become in order to thrive.

But after that hug, she wanted to go back and be the person she'd been before. The person she'd been with Hunter.

"Expectedly unexpected," Savannah said, apology thick. "If I had known Hunter and Brody were going to ambush you, I would have stopped it. Or at least warned you."

"So you didn't know?"

"Of course not," Savannah said firmly, and Mackenzie felt some of the tension dissipate. "Have you ever known me to betray a friend's trust?"

"Never," Mackenzie acquiesced.

Although Mackenzie had known Savannah for years, it was only after Mackenzie lost her sight that the two women had really become close. Savannah was such a loyal and generous friend that Mackenzie was relieved to know she hadn't been a part of the con—and embarrassed that she'd wrongly accused Savannah.

"I'm sorry I even considered it."

"Don't apologize," Savannah said gently, resting her hand on Mackenzie's. "I know from experience just how unsettling a Kane's surprise appearance can be on a girl. Just like I know from experience that being surprised by a Kane doesn't always have to be a bad thing. In fact, if you let it, it can be pretty amazing."

Savannah and Brody had been high school sweethearts who'd gone separate ways after graduation. Savannah had big dreams, and Brody was content to work at his dad's bar. Two degrees later, Savannah had come home to Nashville with a degree in law and six carats on her finger. Brody had taken one look at that ring and known he had to grow up, and fast, or risk losing the love of his life.

It had taken him a year to convince Savannah he'd changed, and another to make her his wife. There wasn't a day that went by when Brody didn't show Savannah just how much she was loved.

Their love was the kind that went soul deep and grew with each passing moment. The kind of love Mackenzie dreamed about but feared she'd never experience.

Mackenzie rubbed the familiar ache in her chest. It had been a long time since a surprise had been in her favor. "I knew that running into him had to happen sometime. I couldn't expect you and Brody to keep my secret forever. I just wish I had been more prepared."

"That's the thing about secrets," Savannah said gently. "They wait until the worst possible moment to unravel. It's like some sick joke the universe plays. He waits until you think you're in the clear, and then, *boom*, he goes all Ghost of Christmas Past on you."

"He?"

Savannah laughed. "Honey, no woman would wait two years to tell you what your problem is, then drop it on you at a kid's tea party. Oh no, women are more sensitive than that. We come to your house with a tub of ice cream, a jug of moonshine, then let you cry it out in private."

A warm hand tightened around Mackenzie's, then slid a cold mason jar into her palm.

"This doesn't feel like sweet tea," Mackenzie said.

"Bless your heart," Savannah said as if Mackenzie were dim-witted. "At this point you need something a lot stronger than tea."

Wasn't that the truth.

Mackenzie rarely drank. She didn't need to add the world spinning to her already complicated situation to realize it was a bad decision. But one glass couldn't hurt.

"Does it come with ice cream?"

Savannah sat next to her at the counter. "I'm more of a cake girl, but after your day, I wouldn't judge if you wanted to go straight for a gallon of double chocolate chunk."

"Double chocolate chunk is reserved for pity parties of one. This situation calls for something a little more hopeful."

"Are you saying you're hopeful about all of this?"

Mackenzie shrugged. "I understand my reality." *But I want to believe in the dream.* Because by *this* Mackenzie knew her friend was referring to more than just working with Hunter again.

It was her inability to let go of the hope of more that made Mackenzie such a great writer. It also made her a heartbreak waiting to happen. And Mackenzie's heart had been broken enough for a lifetime.

"And what reality would that be?" Savannah asked.

Mackenzie laughed, but it was heavy and raw, and *well, shoot*, she was going to cry. Something she rarely did, and never in public.

She wasn't sure if she was angry or hurt or relieved. Maybe it was a mixture of all three that had her eyes burning. Or maybe the part of her that refused to let go of Hunter was pushing through common sense, because she knew letting go would eventually help ease the pain. She should be jumping into survival mode, but all she could think about was this second chance she'd been presented.

Not at love or forever—those weren't in the cards for her. But maybe she could find closure. Repair the damage she'd caused by leaving and find whatever it was she needed to finally let go.

"What are you going to do?"

"I don't know, I guess let him get off his chest whatever he needs to," Mackenzie admitted. "He has the right to have his questions answered."

"And what if he asks you about how you feel now?" Savannah asked, and Mackenzie shrugged. "Do you *know* how you feel? About him?"

Sadly, yes. She felt the same way she always had when it came to Hunter. She was hopelessly in love with a man she couldn't be with. Time may have passed, her life had been flipped on its head, but her feelings for him hadn't changed in the slightest.

"I am such a loser." Mackenzie dropped her head to the countertop. "It has been three years, and I still can't move on."

"Love doesn't work like that. It's forever."

"Even when you wish it wasn't?"

"Especially then. You can either hide from it or face it, but it isn't going away."

Mackenzie had hidden from it before, and look where that had gotten her—relying on Savannah's home-crafted courage in a mason jar to get her through the night. She wasn't sure that confronting it would end any differently, but at least there wouldn't be those annoying *coulda-shoulda-wouldas* haunting her.

Savannah gave Mackenzie's hand a gentle squeeze. "You okay?"

"I will be," she said, lifting her head. "But ice cream might help."

CHAPTER 7

Hunter owed his cousin. Big-time.

Not only had Mackenzie stayed through dinner *and* dessert, she didn't seem in any rush to cut and run. Even though Savannah and Brody were taking their sweet-ass time putting the munchkin to bed—something about covering the floor with wee-wee pads—Mackenzie hadn't reached for her purse once.

Bedtime would have been the perfect excuse for her to make her exit, no questions asked. Instead, she'd sauntered out to the front porch, asking if he was coming, since, apparently, *she* was ready to talk. Although they hadn't done much talking.

Nope, it was forty degrees, a light drizzle coating everything in sight, and Mackenzie sat on the porch swing, sipping her julep as if it were summer in the Caribbean instead of March in Tennessee.

From Brody and Savannah's place in Oak Hills, Hunter could make out the bright lights of Broadway flickering in the distance and the blue bulbs of the bridge reflecting in the smooth waters of the Cumberland River below.

It was so tranquil and stunning he'd often considered giving up his loft downtown to move up here. Be near Brody and his niece—and away from the chaos and noise that filled the city.

His gaze landed on Mackenzie.

Talk about stunning.

Her hair was pulled back into a messy bun, and a few curls had escaped and were dancing in the wind. She had her feet tucked beneath her, those elegant fingers wrapped around her empty glass, as her eyes stared out on the horizon. She looked relaxed, completely at ease, and so damn beautiful it was hard to look away.

So he didn't. He took the time to study her, noticing the subtle changes in her face. Her cheekbones were more pronounced and her lips still full and lush, but the laugh lines didn't seem as defined as they'd once been. The elegant slope of her neck drew him in, feminine and silky, her pulse pounding at its base.

"What are you looking at?" she asked, her gaze never leaving the horizon.

"You," he admitted quietly. "How did you know? Can you see shapes and shadows?"

Hunter knew from Susan's situation that there was a wide spectrum for those deemed legally blind: everything from the ability to see up to twenty feet away, to light perception, to complete darkness. Susan had lost her central vision, leaving her with some peripheral awareness.

"No shapes or shadows, just blackness. But I can feel your breath on my cheek, sense that you're watching me."

A nauseous feeling churned in his gut at the reality of her life. And how challenging it would be for a woman who'd spent her early twenties confined by her family situation to finally gain her freedom only to be thrown into complete darkness, with no hope of escape.

It was Mackenzie's worst nightmare. Yet she'd managed to come out the other side stronger than before. More in tune than ever.

"During supper, it felt like you could track me. Track everyone in the room."

"I didn't want to ever be caught off guard, so I practiced following sounds and voices until I was good enough that nothing could surprise me." She turned her head his way, and proving her point, those bright green eyes locked on his. "Which is why what you and Brody pulled was mean."

The hit was a lot like the woman. Honest and direct. "I wouldn't call it mean, more of a step in the right direction."

She snorted. "I haven't seen an ambush like that since you and your cousins cornered Ben Backster in the alley behind the bar for trying to look up my skirt."

They'd done a lot more than corner the prick, but she didn't need to know that.

"Every time you leaned over to serve a tray of drinks, he'd decide to rest his head on the table, sideways, to get a better view of what color panties you had on. You were the reason Big Daddy changed the dress code for waitresses: 'Skirts must cover more than butt cheeks.'"

Hunter had written the rule, then forced Big Daddy to implement it. His cousins had given him shit for months.

"My skirts were not that short," she said, and speaking of skirts, the breeze picked up, causing her current skirt to flirt higher up her thighs. "I think you're being dramatic."

Hunter averted his gaze. "I think you're drunk."

"I don't get drunk," she explained, her tone so serious Hunter found himself laughing. "But can you stop moving the swing? I don't do so well with motion anymore."

"The swing isn't moving, Trouble. That would be the first sign that maybe you should hand over the booze and slow down a little." When she didn't, he snatched her glass and set it on the patio table.

"I'm tired of slowing down. Last week, Muttley got so impatient he tried to drag me across the street." She crossed her arms, showing more than enough cleavage for Hunter to know she was drunk—and chilly.

"Well, if you were slurring your words then, like you are now, maybe he misunderstood your command."

"Maybe I am a little tipsy, but nothing I can't handle." She went to stand, and Hunter pulled her back down before she tumbled over and right out of her strappy sandals and onto her very fine ass.

"A little?" He wrapped an arm around the back of the swing and pulled her to his side. "It only took two glasses for you to stop scowling at me every time I opened my mouth, and this looks like your third."

"I wasn't scowling," she argued, but her smile said she was happy he'd noticed her displeasure. "I was concentrating on what you were saying." She dismissively waved her hand in his direction and nearly smacked him in the chest.

He caught it beneath his and trapped it there. "Trouble, your scowl packed enough ice to cryogenically freeze my nuts. Now it's just warm and bright, telling me you're well past drunk."

"That must have been some scowl." She patted the swing for the throw Savannah always kept outside, but since she was two sips from shit-faced, her aim was off in left field.

Hunter picked up the blanket and tucked it around her body, noticing more of those curves he'd been trying to forget.

"I've always said you had quite the mouth." He waited for her to get comfortable, then rested his hand on her thigh and transitioned seamlessly into implementing his plan. "Speaking of which, we need to talk about the album."

With a cute little sigh, Mackenzie rested her head in the cradle of his shoulder. "Yeah, we do."

"What, no argument?"

"Nope, you smell too good," she murmured into his neck. "And come tomorrow, when I'm not so . . . *drunk*"—she threw up air quotes—"I won't have this chance again."

And Hunter knew that, even though it was a shitty move, if he didn't push now, he'd never get this chance again. "There's still a lot for us to talk about, a lot of feelings to lay out in the open, but the bottom line is . . . I need your help, Trouble."

"You don't need anyone's help," she said with a yawn.

"Not true." He needed her more than he could admit. "I need yours."

"Can't happen. The thought of getting downtown every day, navigating a busy office building, learning a new floor plan . . ." She shivered. "That sounds about as inspiring as rehab."

Hunter had never considered how the little everyday things he didn't have to think about were just more obstacles for her to overcome. Thankfully, he was excellent at finding solutions.

"I can pick you up, and we can use a familiar place," he suggested. "Maybe the back room at Big Daddy's."

"I have a driver I use when I need to, but the bar is too loud and busy." She shook her head. "You'll do fine on your own."

"I don't want fine." He'd tried fine. Found it incredibly boring. But nothing about Mackenzie was boring. Hell, she could send his world spinning with one look.

Hunter placed a crooked finger under her chin and looked down into her face. Holy hell, he'd forgotten how potent those mossy pools could be.

"Not when it could be incredible with you," he finished.

"It would be incredible for a while, but"—she shook her head—"eventually it will end, and nothing would ever be incredible again."

Will end, as in a definitive expiration date. Not what he wanted to hear.

"It doesn't have to. This can be whatever we want it to be, last as long as we choose." And he hoped she'd choose the long-term. Because even though he was still working through his anger, he'd take her at his side any day over the alternative.

He'd lived through losing her once, wasn't interested in a repeat.

"What if I choose wrong?" she said, and to his horror, her eyes went misty. "What if I choose wrong and ruin everything?"

He wanted to tell her that as long as they were honest with each other, there wasn't anything that could go wrong. But then the misty turned to more of a glisten, and he was pretty sure she was one sniffle away from real tears. And suddenly he wasn't sure how to handle the turn of events.

Tears didn't scare Hunter. He'd learned the power of embracing waterworks in the sixth grade when he'd found Carrie "Full-C" Callahan crying over her English grade behind the schoolyard. Instead of walking past her, like his buddies had done, Hunter had asked her what was wrong.

Ten minutes of tears and a hug later, he'd become the first kid in his class to round second base. And junior year, when Carrie's boyfriend dumped her for a gymnast, Hunter made that home run. Not that there were going to be any home runs with Mackenzie, besides the chart-toppers they'd make.

No, tears weren't a problem. Tears led to talking, which led to hugging, which for Hunter usually led to a whole lot of lip action and hip traction and—*Sweet baby Jesus*, when did his mouth get so close to hers?

Had she moved, or had he? Not that it mattered, because one little dip of the head and he'd know exactly how much bourbon was in those juleps. And talk about the wrong way to start this partnership off.

Kissing his cowriter was a big no-no. Kissing Mackenzie Hart when she was feeling cornered was a fast track to never seeing her again, and—*fuck*, her hands somehow had slid down his chest to fist in his shirt.

And why was it when he needed one of his nosy family members to interrupt, there were none to be found? Even her dog had passed out on the edge of the deck, back to them, face buried beneath his big paws, leaving them virtually alone.

So they sat there on that porch swing, a breath apart, for a long-ass time. Nothing 'round them except the cool Tennessee breeze and the growing sexual tension.

It was as if the universe was saying, *Go for it, Hunter. Take a taste.*

His dick was saying something infinitely worse. But his head, the one he tried to use when it came to Mackenzie, was telling him that if he played this wrong—and by wrong he meant kissing her—he could blow whatever this was before it even began. And leave tonight wondering if he'd ever see her again.

"As long as we're honest with each other, everything's going to work out perfectly," he assured her.

"You promise?" she whispered, reminding him of that lost girl he'd first met in the bar all those years ago.

"Yeah, I promise." But if she pressed any closer, things were bound to get screwy. And wouldn't that just make everything a hell of a lot more complicated.

"Good," she said, tightening her fist and tugging him toward her. He'd like to say he put up a fight, but then he caught a hint of her scent and, *damn*, she smelled good. Like mint and tangled sheets. She tasted even better, he realized, as her lips ever so gently brushed his.

Once. Twice. Only to go back for another pass.

This one a little firmer.

"What are you doing?" he asked, holding himself stock-still, as opposed to Mackenzie, who was making moves he hadn't seen coming.

"Skipping the cake and going straight for the icing," she said against his mouth, and Lord help him, all he could picture was Mackenzie covered in icing.

And her lips. Her incredible lips. Full and soft and, *whoa now*, working his with a shy confidence that blew his mind. Mackenzie Hart was kissing him on his cousin's front porch swing, and Hunter would be a liar if he said he wasn't dying to kiss her back.

To take what she was offering, because he'd be the luckiest son of a bitch on the planet to be on the receiving end of a woman like her. Only what he wanted and what he *wanted* were at odds.

He'd come here to talk, to get back to the place they'd left off. Only now they'd taken a detour, a sexy-as-hell detour, which he was pretty sure would lead to a dead end. He was confident, even, that skipping straight to the chemistry would be like pulling the pin on a grenade: a few seconds of excitement before everything blew to hell.

The only way this would have a happy ending was to keep things as simple as possible. Sure, he'd come because he needed her help on the album, but things had changed.

And he had a feeling she was feeling the same shift. Which was why he had to take this slow. Start with the thing that had connected them originally. The one thing that made her feel safe and alive.

Music.

"Mackenzie," he said without all that much conviction, so he put his hands on her hips.

"Yeah." She opened her eyes, and they were warm and heavy-lidded.

"Maybe we should start with the cake, work our way up to the icing?" Or better yet, go back inside and talk about things that didn't include icing and kissing.

"I always took you for an icing kind of guy."

"Yeah, but there's something to say about savoring the cake."

She sat back, uncertainty flickering across her face. "Why? What's wrong with my icing?"

"Nothing's wrong with your icing." He laughed. "I don't know enough about your icing to have an opinion."

To prove his point, he did not look at her cleavage when she jerked back and crossed her arms. "Well, I can tell you that my icing is top rate. In fact, most guys would say my icing rocked their world."

"Well, I'm not most guys," he lied. "And you're not most girls. You're—"

"What?" she said, those eyes sparking with challenge. "I'm what, Hunter?"

"First off, you're drunk."

"Not that drunk."

"Drunk enough." And no way was he going to open himself up to being tonight's bold move and tomorrow's big regret. Been there, done that, wrote a song about it. "Second, your friendship is important to me, and I won't do anything to complicate that."

"That's the same speech you gave me when we first met, then when my mama passed," she said, and he could hear the embarrassment in her voice. See it in the way she wrapped her arms protectively around her. "Let's see. First I was too young, then I was too sad, and now I'm what?" She stood. "Too much of a complication?"

"That's not what I said." He reached for her hand. "The problem is, you're too special."

"I never knew being special could feel so humiliating." She pulled away, her chin high, her shoulders back, her eyes sad as fuck. "Now, if you'll excuse me, it seems I have a mint julep calling my name."

CHAPTER 8

A pounding woke Mackenzie from a dead sleep.

She opened her eyes and, for one terrifying second, couldn't figure out her surroundings. The sheets were knotted around her, holding her prisoner, and the world was completely black. She strained her eyes even further, trying to make sense of why she could feel the warmth from the morning sun radiate through the window when the room was dark enough for it to be the middle of the night.

Her head spun painfully, and panic gripped her by the throat as she reached for the light switch, but nothing happened. Then the sharp edges of frustration churned in her gut as she tried again. With the same results.

She squeezed her lids tight and breathed in deeply, only the churning worsened and the pounding settled behind her eyes. Then she wished like hell it was the middle of the night, because that would mean the sun hadn't risen, rather than she couldn't see it.

She also wished she'd stuck with tea and her usual MO of pretending everything was just fine. In her attempt to eliminate the *coulda-shoulda-woulda*s in her life, Mackenzie was left with a big *Oh no you didn't!*

But, oh yes, she had.

She'd gone big, then gone home, and she could still feel the bitter bite of humiliation. Had she not been intoxicated, she would have recognized the hesitation in Hunter's tone. Could have evaluated the pros and cons of kissing America's Sexiest Man, who happened to be the former love of her life.

Convincing herself that the nauseous feeling in her stomach was nothing more than a hangover, Mackenzie lay back down.

Big mistake. Being horizontal was like being adrift at sea in one of those tiny inflatable rafts in the middle of a hurricane.

"This is why I don't drink," she said, tossing the covers over her head. The motion offered nothing in the form of help, unless she counted the small comfort of familiarity. It was strange how habits stuck with a person, even when they no longer held a purpose.

Mackenzie had lots of habits—rituals, as her rehabilitation therapist called them. An order of doing things that gave her a sense of control, kept her safe.

Kept her moving forward.

Last night she'd been too thrown to think, let alone stick to the rules. As a result, she'd abandoned her nightly routine. And her common sense.

End result?

She hadn't a clue as to what time it was, where she'd left her purse and phone, or if Muttley had gone out for his morning tour of the backyard. And, as if the day couldn't get any worse, Hunter had driven her home last night. Which meant now he knew where she lived. And avoiding him would be that much more difficult.

What had she been thinking?

She hadn't been. That was the problem.

Hunter had this assuredness about him that said he could handle anything thrown his way and a charisma that pulled people along for the ride, making it easy to sit back and let him take over. He was the kind of guy who would get it done—and done right.

Hunter Kane was a sure bet.

That kind of magnetic confidence was rare. The industry term for it was *X factor*. Mackenzie called it swagger. And Hunter had enough swagger to convince Garth Brooks to sing backup.

Metal tags jangled down the hall and into her room, stopping inches from her bed. She was immediately met with warm dog breath wishing her a good morning, although there was nothing good about what that breath did to her stomach. When she didn't move, a wet nose nudged her foot, which was peeking out from the covers.

"Morning," she mumbled and dropped her hand to give Muttley a quick pat.

His tail tapped the hardwood floor in pure pleasure.

"Bet you want your breakfast, huh, big guy?" Muttley nudged her hand, then let out an impatient bark. "All right. All right. I get it."

Mackenzie needed another hour of sleep, followed by a hot shower. But Muttley was making it clear that neither of those was an option, so she settled on a cup of coffee and dragged herself out of bed.

Slipping on her house boots, she trudged down the hall and into the kitchen, to the familiar sound of her automatic coffee maker already percolating. The earthy hazelnut aroma wafted over as sunlight from the big windows that spanned the back of the house warmed her skin.

When her boots met the tile floor, she took five precise steps forward and three to the left, then ran her hand down the pitted texture of the refrigerator door and opened it. Second shelf, left-side front, she grabbed the carton of cream.

Five steps to the right and one forward was the cabinet with her mugs. She grabbed one and set it and the cream on the counter. In the lower cupboard was the sugar.

Mackenzie bent over and opened the cabinet door, and the pressure in her head swelled to the point of near explosion.

"I'm never drinking again," she grumbled to herself while pinching her fingers to her forehead in a lame attempt to hold her brain in place.

"That'd be a shame, since I like you better drunk," a masculine voice said from behind her. "You're friendlier."

Terror caught her off guard and she spun toward the voice, her eyes darting frantically around the room. A habit that did nothing to help the situation. She couldn't see a thing.

Her hand grabbed the mug off the counter, and she threw it in the direction of the voice.

"What the—"

Porcelain shattered against the wall, the sound exploding through the room as she reached for the carton of cream.

"Whoa there." A hand came up to stop her as she took aim. She jerked back and lost her balance, tripping over Muttley, who was barking as if he meant to tear off a limb. But instead of her falling backward, two strong arms circled around her, holding her steady. "It's me."

Hunter.

Relief washed through her, bringing with it a double shot of irritation. Hunter had let himself into her home.

"It's me?" she repeated in her best Hunter impression, trying to get her heart to slow back to a speed that wasn't bordering on stroke levels. "Unless you want me to give my dog the command to eat your nuts off, you need to be more specific."

When she'd lost her sight, Mackenzie had lost a part of her independence that had been hard-won. Situations where she couldn't anticipate the outcome fueled a heated panic that swept through her body, churning up her deepest fear: that something would happen while she was alone and utterly defenseless.

Not that she was going to admit that. Not to him, at least.

"Eat my nuts off?" he repeated, sounding way too amused, which ticked her off.

That easygoing confidence of Hunter's slid beneath her barrier. She told herself she was immune to his woman-whispering ways but knew it was a lie.

"Your charm doesn't work on me," she said as she reached for the sugar jar. "And since the only guy with a key to my door is Arthur, and you're clearly not him, I'd cover your boys."

"Arthur?"

"My neighbor," she said. "Now state your name."

"According to *People* Magazine, I'm the Sexiest Man Alive and have the best buns two years running," he said, taking the sugar jar from her and setting it down. "Want to feel?"

The familiar texture of his callused hands on her skin registered, and Mackenzie knew she wasn't out of danger. Not by a long shot. A stranger there to steal her valuables would have been less of a threat than Hunter, who had that swagger dialed to panty-melting levels.

He took her hands and drew them around his waist to—

Oh.

My.

God.

If she didn't do something, she was actually going to touch Hunter Kane's butt. And then what? He'd get all charming and funny and ask her if she agreed with the press, and what was she supposed to do, lie?

"No thanks." She jerked her hands back. "Buns aren't on my diet," she said, remembering just how magnificent his butt was. She'd often spent entire shifts watching it strut around the bar.

As far as she was concerned, he had the best buns *seven* years running.

"What? Are you gluten-free now?" he asked, and she could feel him smile.

After last night? "Man-free."

"Does *Arthur* know that?" he asked, and Mackenzie had to bite back a smile. If she didn't know better, she'd say Hunter was jealous of her sixty-nine-year-old neighbor. Not that he needed to know how old Arthur was.

"Arthur is very considerate of my need for privacy."

"Sounds boring." Hunter's voice dropped to a low rumble that rippled through her. "And lonely."

It *was* lonely, but it was also necessary for her growth and independence. And her pride. Hunter wasn't just charismatic—he was in charge of his world. And Mackenzie needed to make sure she didn't let him take charge of hers.

"Are you okay?" he asked, taking her hand.

"I think the wall got the worst of it," she joked, but he didn't laugh.

"I wasn't talking about today," he said, and she could feel him taking in every nuance of her face, tracking down her neck.

"Why are you here?"

"I was worried about you. Wanted to make sure you were all right."

"I'm feeling a little awkward after last night," she admitted. "But nothing so bad it won't pass."

"If it makes you feel any better, I'm feeling a little awkward myself," he said softly. "We're still feeling each other out, seeing how we fit."

"What if we don't fit anymore?" she whispered.

"What if we fit better than before?"

Always the optimist, she thought. She could even picture that crooked grin of his slowly lighting up as he said it.

Her hands ached to glide over his laugh lines, through his hair, feel if he still kept it a little shaggy. Would his smile make her heart two-step like it used to?

"Do you want me to show you what I look like?" he asked.

"How did you know?"

"You keep scanning back and forth like you're trying to figure out what's changed and what's the same."

"Old habit."

Hunter brought her hands to his lips and brushed a light kiss over the tips of her clasped fingers. "Let me show you."

Mackenzie almost said no. The reality that he'd be different, that he wouldn't look like the image she carried with her to bed each night, was terrifying. It wasn't the him-looking-different part that ate at her. It was finally having concrete proof that everything had changed that had her hesitating.

They were different people now, with different desires and needs. Once she touched his face, the last piece of the fantasy would finally shatter.

Maybe that's what she needed to move forward. To let go completely. Push past the *ignorance is bliss* and *what-ifs* so she could accept the here and now.

With a hard swallow, Mackenzie lifted her hands to his face, her fingers trembling as they lightly brushed his cheeks. She let him guide her at first, breathing in the scent of him as her thumbs slowly trailed over his wide jaw, hard and masculine, the scent of his skin rising from the heat of her touch.

He released her wrists, dropping his head slightly, encouraging her to explore. After a moment's hesitation, she moved her hands toward the high planes of his cheekbones, then smoothed them over the ridges of his eyebrows.

His long lashes fluttered shut and twitched lightly under her gentle inquiry. Willing her hands to stop shaking, she trailed her fingers down the bridge of his nose, detecting the slight bump earned in a bar fight in Denver. She smiled.

Hunter's hands slid down her arms to her shoulders, finally settling on her waist, sending a familiar zing through her body. And what a zing it was. Electric, exciting, and tempting.

He tugged her closer, their hips brushing, her breath hitching.

She continued her exploration, lingering at a puckered slice of skin over his right brow, brushing back and forth over the angry mark. "A cut? It's recent."

His hands splayed across her waist, urging her even closer, their bodies perfectly aligned. "Brody and I had a, uh . . . minor difference of opinion over his decision to keep you a secret."

"A minor difference, huh?" She laughed softly, because nothing was the same, yet nothing was all that different either.

Sure, his stubble was rougher, his hair thicker, shorter. He even seemed bigger, his arms and chest more muscular, defined. But that smile.

Mackenzie feathered a single fingertip over his lips and laughed. Oh, that smile was charming, sexy, and all Hunter. It was also playful and soft. So soft she ran a finger over his upper lip, then his lower, loving their velvety texture.

"Mackenzie." Hunter's mouth moved under her touch, and a feeling so simple and wholly erotic shot through her, from her fingertips all the way to her toes.

Startled by how strong the attraction still was, she pulled her hands back. "Thank you," she said. "Most people find it awkward, like their personal space is being invaded."

"I liked it."

So had she. Too much, in fact. "How did you get in?"

"I left the back door unlocked when I went out to go get coffee."

When he left? Mackenzie vaguely remembered him driving her home and walking her to her room. But she thought he'd gone to his place. Only Hunter wasn't the kind to leave the back door unlocked until morning.

"You stayed here?"

"On the couch with your dog glaring at me all night."

"He was probably trying to tell you that camping out on a drunk girl's couch is a huge invasion of privacy," she said, blaming the warm pit in her belly on irritation.

"I call it being resourceful," he said, completely unfazed. "My intentions weren't to scare you."

"Well, that clears things up." She angled her body toward the front entryway, because his tone implied that he had no intentions of leaving anytime soon. "You can apologize as you let yourself out. I have a long day ahead of me."

"Which is why I brought fresh-pressed coffee. I figured after last night you could use some caffeine. And maybe a doughnut. They were out of chocolate, so I got powdered sugar."

He was playing dirty.

"I can make my own coffee." Ignoring her kryptonite, she carefully walked to the cupboard and pulled out another mug.

"Yeah, but you get the prepackaged stuff. It tastes like shit."

"It does not." She set a second mug on the counter and made a mental note to call Arthur to help her clean up the floor. But first she had to get rid of Hunter before he asked her to touch something else.

"Only because you don't know any better." He took her hand to give her a paper cup, and there was that zing again. Warmer than before, sliding through her body like butter on a hot biscuit.

Her breath caught, and Hunter whistled—low and smug. "Impressive, right?"

"I haven't taken a sip yet." She tried to pull her hand away, but he held it.

"I wasn't talking about the coffee." With a squeeze, which took her good parts from hibernation to fully caffeinated, he let go.

Rolling her eyes, she took a sip and—*sweet baby Jesus*—her world felt right again. Her headache disappeared, the sun felt radiant, and she could have sworn she heard birds singing if she listened carefully.

This coffee wasn't just better. It was *magical*. Smooth and bold, with a surprising sweetness on the end. Kind of like the man who delivered it.

"It's a little too sweet and smooth for my taste," she said, handing it back. "Plus, I like drinking my coffee while reading the morning paper." She held his gaze, waiting for him to point out that she couldn't read anything.

"Great, where is it, and I'll go grab it."

"It's at the market around the corner. It's a special braille edition," she lied. "You have to ask one of the clerks behind the counter."

"You want to walk or take my car?"

She smoothed down her hair. "I have to shower and get ready. You go and catch me up later."

"I can wait." He pulled out a chair at the counter and, making himself at home, took a seat.

"Okay, let me be clearer. I need to shower, so I'd like you to leave."

"I know." He took a leisurely sip of his coffee. "And I'd like to finish that talk we started."

Mackenzie frowned. "I'm not in the talking mood."

"Again, I can wait."

Mackenzie threw her hands up in frustration. "God, you're such a pain in the ass!"

"You'll find that I grow on you."

That was the problem. "When did the guy who'd drink convenience-store drip decide to become a coffee snob?"

"I'll tell you, if you tell me when you decided to start investing in so much lace," he said. "I must say, teal really brings out the color in your cheeks."

"My cheeks are probably as pale as the rest of my face from too much bourbon."

"I wasn't talking about those cheeks, Trouble."

Mackenzie rolled her eyes. So she liked to sleep in nightshirts. So what? She was a single woman living alone. What she wore to bed, or didn't wear as the case was, wasn't any of his business. He was the guest who'd worn out his welcome.

Ignoring the cool breeze blowing past her lace-clad backside, Mackenzie crossed her arms over her chest. "Grow up, Hunter."

Hunter smiled, so big she actually felt it. "If Ben Backster could see you now."

Mackenzie yanked the bottom of the tank top down, stretching it to cover as much of her un–award-winning buns as possible.

Hunter gave a sound of male appreciation. "I'll be sure to tell good old Ben you like to match your lace."

She let go of the tank and it popped up. She heard a low whistle. "Stop looking at my panties."

"I'm too busy staring at your ass to have time to take in those panties of yours. But if you'd hold still, I can take in both."

"Oh, for God's sake, they're just panties."

"Have to disagree, Trouble. Panties are cotton with little flowers or the days of the week on them. Those there would fall under lingerie. Cheeky cut, I believe."

"I need a shower," she said, noting that Muttley had moved to her side and was forming a barrier between her and the broken mug. "Be sure to lock up when you leave."

"Let me know if you need help scrubbing your back. I've been told I'm very thorough."

◆ ◆ ◆

Hunter watched Mackenzie strut down the long hallway, hand lightly brushing the wall on one side to guide her, her ass swishing like she knew he was watching.

And he was.

Hunter hadn't stopped staring at her since she'd stumbled out of her bedroom dressed in nothing but a T-shirt, teal lace, and those fuzzy pink boots. Then there was the morning sunlight, shining on her sleep-tousled hair and making that lace more like cheesecloth than clothing.

Damn, she knew how to put the good in his morning.

Which was the only excuse Hunter had for how he'd handled things. Had the blood not been pumping south, he'd have known to gently announce his presence. Instead, he'd taken one look at that lace-covered backside, remembered how she'd felt pressed up against him last night, and immediately forgotten the plan—to keep things simple.

Then he'd scared the shit out of her.

He'd never really considered how vulnerable she was. A blind woman alone in a house with a strange man. The possibilities of what could happen if that man were an intruder instead of him made him rethink everything.

Hunter walked into the pantry and grabbed the broom and dustpan. He needed to make sure he got all the pieces of the broken mug cleaned up.

He'd just tossed the last of it in the trash and was using a wet towel to catch the tiny fragments when he was met with two big black eyes—and a growl.

"Hey, fella," he said, but those eyes only narrowed. Hunter reached out his hand, and Muttley decided it was time to show Hunter his teeth—and whose house this was.

Hunter had been around territorial males enough in his career to recognize one. And know how to deal with him.

"You hungry?" He went to the cupboard and pulled out a bag of kibble he'd seen earlier. Filling up the bowl, he said, "How about we eat some chow, get to know each other, maybe even play some ball?"

Muttley peeled back his lips and let out a loud *whoof*, and Hunter began to worry that the only balls Muttley looked interested in were between Hunter's legs.

"Right, well, that isn't going to happen, so why don't we get back to playing friends?"

Muttley's eyes darted around the room, landing on the shattered mug in the trash, then back to Hunter.

"I apologized for scaring her, and then I offered her breakfast, but she turned her nose up at the coffee and disappeared into the bathroom." With a dismissive snort, Muttley headed out of the kitchen and down the hallway. "You might be there awhile. She didn't seem in a rush to come back out."

Unconcerned, Muttley made three circles—his eyes never leaving Hunter—and laid his body against the bathroom door as if prepared to wait an eternity for his mistress to appear.

"Right there with you, pal," Hunter said, tossing the paper towel in the trash.

As luck would have it, the trash can was next to a stack of unopened mail and her phone. If Mackenzie didn't want to talk about what she'd been up to since he'd seen her last, then Hunter would do a little exploring on his own.

He swiped her phone screen to get a look at her playlist, wondering if his albums were in her favorites, except he became distracted by an unanswered text from last night. It was from some guy named Arthur.

Had it been from a Mary or Delores or Jenny, Hunter wouldn't have paid it a second glance. But it was from Arthur and began with the word *Darlin'*. So, yeah, he may have "accidentally" opened the text.

Only when he opened it, a computerized female voice came from the phone.

"Yesterday at seven-oh-nine p.m.," the phone began, and Hunter pressed his hand over the speaker to muffle the sound. "From Arthur. Darlin', it is time for supper. Chicken is on the grill and corn bread is in the oven. Table's set for two and door's open." There was a beep. "Would you like to reply?"

Hunter checked the bathroom. With the door still shut, he whispered into the phone, "Yes."

"Go ahead with reply."

"You are one confident prick," Hunter began. "Too bad for you, *Darlin'* was sipping bourbon with me on the porch swing last night."

He watched the text appear on the screen.

"Would you like to send message?"

Hunter looked at the ceiling and, after a long moment, said, "No," then set the phone on the table. With a final glare at the screen, he headed to the office, which sat off the main room and housed a baby grand.

Pushing the door all the way open, he walked into a home studio that was beyond impressive. A dozen or so instruments lined the wall, the piano sat in the middle of the room, and a big overstuffed chair rested next to a window, drenched in sunlight. There was her first guitar, a gift from her mama, leaning against the windowsill, and vases of bright flowers were scattered through the room. So many fresh-cut flowers it smelled like a rose garden.

Gone were the computers and digital production boards he'd gotten accustomed to. Instead there was sheet music, a mic, and an old-school soundboard. Mackenzie's studio had been designed by an artist for an artist.

What caught his eye, though, was one of the sheets of music. Not one on the piano, but some chords and lyrics scribbled in an open journal, which sat next to her chair. Handwritten and incomplete, but two beautiful pages of music, begging to be uncovered.

To be played.

Hunter sat in the chair and picked up her guitar, resting it on his knee. Then he looked at the journal and began playing. A grounding warmth washed over him as he strummed the opening chords. The melody was soft and soulful, a complex combination of familiar and unexpected that drew him in and held on long after the song had ended.

Just like its composer, he thought with a smile. Because while the scribbled notes on the sheet were too masculine to have come from Mackenzie's hand, the music absolutely had.

But it wasn't only the chords that had him convinced. No, that honor went to the words scrawled in the lines. His heart rolled over in his chest as he read the raw honesty in the lyrics. They spoke of a love without limits, without restrictions or prejudice. A love that went beyond circumstance, to a level that was as forgiving as it was understanding.

The notes were strong, deliberate, and purposefully unique, but the lyrics . . . *Christ*, the lyrics. There weren't a lot—it was a work in progress, and he could tell by the different colors on the page that the process had spanned months, maybe even years—but there was enough there for him to know it was Mackenzie. Right there on the page for him to see.

Her hopes. More important, her fears. He could feel them all as he gently strummed the strings, played the notes she'd kept to herself. He reached the end of what he knew in his heart was a hit and started over, understanding more and more about her with each note he played.

Mackenzie had always been a mystery. She never seemed to need anything or anyone. She was content to stand alone, take on whatever life threw her way with a brave smile. And it was that brave smile that had him so determined to stick around.

Hunter had never been good at sticking, but he wanted this more than he wanted another hit album. And that was saying something.

So before Mackenzie walked in and caught him peeking through her private journal, Hunter set down the guitar and removed any trace of his snooping.

He was just leaving the studio when he spotted a note resting against a vase of roses that were so big it was clear they weren't of the average flower-shop variety. Nope, these were special-order flowers with a single purpose: to charm.

It was a play from Hunter's own handbook. A rookie play but an effective one. As he well knew.

And the note? Made from high-quality card stock with silver edging and some fancy AC monogram branded into the front, it was bold, masculine, and enough to make his eye twitch.

He picked up the card and flipped it open. The sunlight pierced the hundreds of holes, which all had a place and purpose. Neighbor Arthur knew how to cook and write braille and had *Darlin's* personal number and a key to her place. So what? The dude was clearly long-winded and a pushover.

Mackenzie didn't like pushovers. Plus, she shared a history and connection with Hunter that couldn't be surpassed.

Unfortunately for Hunter, Neighbor Arthur also had a signature that was identical to the scribbles in Mackenzie's journal. Which meant she already had a writing partner in her life.

And it wasn't Hunter.

CHAPTER 9

When Mackenzie came out of the shower, she found Muttley sleeping on the couch and the rest of the house empty. *Back to normal,* she thought, grabbing the bag of doughnuts off the counter.

She stood next to the stove and sank her teeth into the first one, moaning as the powdery goodness melted in her mouth.

"Gawd. So good."

Taking another bite, she considered sitting at the table, then shrugged it off. It seemed silly to sit there all alone. Especially when she could have enjoyed her meal with Hunter. But he'd left, which was what she'd wanted. So then why did she feel this ping of disappointment?

Not wanting to think about what *that* could mean, Mackenzie decided she needed some chocolate with her breakfast. Which required a short walk to the Bark 'N' Bean, the local dog-friendly café a few blocks from Mackenzie's house, and perhaps conversing with other humans.

Her therapist would be so proud.

She grabbed Muttley's harness. "Time to go be social. I was thinking a walk to work off the cupcakes you had last night, then breakfast."

A loud snoring filled the room.

"You don't snore, buddy," she reminded him, then jingled his harness. "This is where you hop up off the couch and prove those teachers were wrong and that you are the best guide dog in Tennessee." Nothing. Not even a tail swishing against the cushions of the couch. "At least you can pretend to earn your keep."

It seemed Muttley was more interested in holding down the couch. Not that Mackenzie blamed him—pretending was exhausting.

"Your choice. But don't whimper to me when your butt gets big and the lady doggies don't come sniffing around anymore."

Mackenzie plopped down on the couch and slipped on her tennis shoes. Muttley didn't budge, except to stretch out his legs even farther, taking up the entire length of the settee.

"We have to stop by the Bark 'N' Bean and see Tia," she said, and Muttley hit the floor with enthusiasm.

He had his vest in his mouth and was standing at the front door before Mackenzie had her shoes tied. Nothing got Muttley moving quite like the mention of his first doggy-mommy. Well, except the promise of treats.

Tia Flynn managed the Bark 'N' Bean. She was also one of Muttley's favorite humans. Not only were her pockets filled with treats for her favorite canine customers, but she had a soft spot for difficult dogs. Which was how she had been hand selected to train Muttley.

Tia was also Mackenzie's health-care advocate, and part of Mackenzie's rehabilitation was to meet with her twice a week in a public place.

Mackenzie had become a pro at finding reasons to avoid their little get-togethers, but instead of the content feeling that usually came with a day spent in solitude, the prospect suddenly felt suffocating. The good news was she'd make her meeting today—and do it with a smile.

When she stepped into the crisp spring air and the sun hit her face, she didn't have to pretend. The morning chill seemed to make everything better, clearer. It was as if she could breathe again.

Leaves rustled in the canopy of black oaks above as Muttley led her through her quiet neighborhood on the outskirts of downtown. The streets were lined with Queen Anne–style homes and historical bungalows, and most of the residents were either retired or young families. The pace of life was slow, traffic was light, and a sense of community was as sweet as the blooms on the crape myrtle trees.

But it did nothing to quell the irritating unease that grew every time a car drove past or a rock got caught underfoot.

Mackenzie pushed through the door of the café and was met with a warm blast of sugar-sweetened air. She took in a deep breath and allowed her body to relax. Then she heard the hum of the customers, the clattering of silverware, and the uncertainty came back.

She'd been so focused on fresh air she'd forgotten that today was Saturday, and the place was packed. It was a seat-yourself kind of café, and Mackenzie was afraid she'd seat herself on someone else's lap. Or worse.

"Crap," she mumbled and turned to head right back out the door.

"Leaving so soon?" Tia called out from somewhere behind the counter.

Mackenzie closed her eyes, knowing she was stuck now. Muttley barked.

Tia walked over and made a shushing sound, and Muttley immediately dropped to his butt and hit his best-in-show pose.

"Now you behave," Mackenzie whispered to Muttley, who panted happily.

"Tables five and seven are open," her friend said, not giving a single direction to remind Mackenzie where tables five or seven were. Not that she needed it. Table five was in the corner, next to the window and out of the way of any major foot traffic.

"Table five sounds nice."

"Whoops, someone just snatched it."

"Story of my life," Mackenzie grumbled, picturing the table in the center of the café. "Table seven it is."

"It needs to be cleared. Just a coffee mug and a plate, but a fresh water bowl is already there for Muttley. I'll meet you in a sec."

"Thanks," Mackenzie said, grateful for that tip.

Tia wasn't blind, but she'd grown up with an autistic brother who benefited from an emotional support dog and dedicated her spare time to helping others in similar situations. Her superpower was to recognize dogs with the right temperament for service training and understand the obstacles the impaired faced every day.

She didn't pity Mackenzie. In fact, Tia rarely gave Mackenzie any special breaks—one of the reasons she made such a great sponsor. Tia was conscious of what Mackenzie was up against and was always willing to lend a helping hand—as long as it wasn't used as a crutch.

Feeling bold, Mackenzie walked to table seven and—would you look at that—carefully navigated around the table without knocking anything over. With a proud snort, Muttley settled at her feet.

He was on his best behavior. In hopes of snagging a treat, he kept all four paws on the ground, choosing to rest only his head on Mackenzie's lap.

Mackenzie gave him a nice cuddly ear rub when Tia came over. "What can I get you?"

"A double chocolate chunk muffin," she said. "Heavy on the chocolate."

"That sounds ominous." Tia pulled out the chair and sat down, purposefully ignoring Muttley, who was vibrating with excitement over the impending treat. "Does this have anything to do with the shiny truck with the mud tires and lift kit parked in front of your house last night? *And* this morning?"

Mackenzie's face heated. "You saw his car?"

"I think everyone who drove past your house saw the car. But I didn't know your houseguest was a *him*." Tia leaned forward. "Spill."

"Not much to spill. It was a guy I used to work with. More of an old friend. He gave me a ride home, then stayed the night to make sure I was okay because I'd had a drink or two."

"That's a long explanation for some guy. Unless?" There was a long beat of silence. "Oh. My. God. I know that look." Tia snapped her fingers. "It wasn't just *a* guy, it was *the* guy."

Tia had spent a lot of hours over the past year working with Mackenzie and Muttley. In that time, they'd both opened up about their pasts, shared their secrets. Some dark, some hilarious, but all of them told in confidence.

The quiet life Tia had left behind in northern California hadn't been one of her choosing. So one night, she'd packed up her car and made her way to Nashville, searching for a radical life makeover. One that included living loud and following her dreams of starting a training school for guide dogs.

Mackenzie had been fleeing the heartache that came from losing everything she held dear. She had known she'd needed to change things up as soon as Hunter proposed to Hadley. Being secretly in love with your best friend was one thing. Being secretly in love with your married best friend? Talk about tempting karma.

Neither one had ever revealed what they were running from, just why they were running. But that too was about to change.

"He ambushed me at a friend's party," she said, silently flipping karma the bird.

"You, at a party? Socializing with people other than your agent? Wow, talk about a gold-star week." Mackenzie would take that gold star and leave out the part where it was Brody's party. "But being ambushed?" Tia grimaced in sympathy. "How did that go?"

"I kissed him."

Tia choked on her own air. "I'm sorry. That is so not what I thought you were going to say."

"Trust me. The shock is mutual," Mackenzie whispered through the embarrassment. Although embarrassment wasn't enough to dull the residual tingling. "I told him I liked him and then I kissed him." Mackenzie held up a hand. "And before you get all girlie on me, he didn't kiss me back."

There was a complete beat of silence. "You made it clear that you were kissing him?"

"The only other clue I could have given was sticking my tongue down his throat."

"But he spent the night? Doesn't sound like a total disaster."

"He slept on the couch and only hung around because he wanted to talk about collaborating with me on a project." Mackenzie took in a big, humbling breath. "As for kissing me back, he said I was too complicated." Or had he said he didn't want to complicate things? Bourbon-brain made remembering all the details difficult, but either way it stung. "We finished the night with him stating he wanted to be friends."

"That long silence is me rolling my eyes, because what a jerk," Tia said. "He's missing out." She paused to instruct Muttley through a series of commands, ending with ordering him to give her a high five and then lie on the ground. All of which he did without question.

Show-off.

"I mean, what kind of guy takes a drunk girl home, a drunk girl who'd just kissed him, and then sleeps on the couch?" Tia asked.

"I can't be certain, but I think they call them nice guys," Mackenzie joked, knowing that Hunter was as good and as nice as they came.

"Nice guys are like unicorns. I hear about them, people swear of their existence, but I've lived in the birthplace of the southern gentleman for three years now, and I have still never seen one with my own eyes."

Tia rested her hand over Mackenzie's but didn't say a word. The longer the silence, the more self-conscious Mackenzie felt.

"There must be something magical about him, because you're here and I didn't have to threaten you." Tia laughed. "I was beginning to wonder if I'd have to come over and bribe you with the new Nicholas Sparks movie in order to see you again."

"No bribe necessary." All she needed was an empty house that smelled like a big, sexy good old boy with an interest in lace to get her moving.

"How is Muttley doing?" Tia asked, still ignoring the dog in question, who was displaying model behavior.

"He got into the dishwasher again last week to clean the dishes, and he still hides under the covers whenever the garbage truck comes. But last night he rode on the floor of the truck the entire way home," Mackenzie said with pride, but from the sounds of Muttley's panting, Tia still hadn't given up the treats. She was a tough-love kind of person.

"Is he still growling at Arthur's shoes when he visits?"

"No." Which was not a lie. He wasn't *growling* at anyone's shoes anymore.

"Did anyone ever tell you you should never play poker?"

Mackenzie let out a frustrated sigh. "No more growling, but he has started stealing any shoes left around the house and hiding them in his bed." A habit he'd started after the ill-fated playdate with Caroline.

"I trained a search and rescue dog who used to steal stuffed animals from kids and hide them in his bed. What started out as a reward system for the dog led to a really bad habit," Tia said. "So learn from my friend's mistakes and don't be a pushover. What's cute now will become a pain in your backside later. Trust me. You need to nix this before it becomes cemented and Muttley uses his protectiveness of you to justify a shoe problem."

"Stop being a pushover, got it."

"I worry about you," Tia said softly.

"I know." Mackenzie worried about herself sometimes. "On a brighter note, Muttley led me through the park on the way here and didn't give out a single doggy high five," she said, referring to Muttley's bad greeting habit of sticking his nose in places it didn't belong. "There was even a Mommy-and-me playdate going on in the playground."

"That's progress," Tia said, and from the excited smacking sounds, Muttley had finally received his good-boy treat from his teacher. "And how about you?"

Mackenzie plastered on a big fake smile, knowing there was no treat in store for her. "I'm here today."

"Which is great, seeing as you skipped out on our last three sessions."

Mackenzie cringed. "Yeah, sorry about that. I've been in the writing cave."

"Yay you, for gracefully falling back into your writing," Tia said, the sarcasm thick. "Music is therapeutic for you, makes you feel closer to the life you used have. But it's also a vice." Tia lowered her voice. "There's more to reintegration than going from one cave into another. Which is why I keep stressing the importance of gaining your freedom back, finding a peer group, making new friends."

"I have Arthur."

"Who is as dependent on you as you are on him," Tia pointed out. "I want to see you challenge yourself. Really put yourself out there and practice some of the new skills we've been talking about."

"Muttley and I went to a business meeting the other day," she said with a big grin. "And we didn't get lost."

"Did Arthur take you?"

Mackenzie's smile tightened. "Maybe."

What she wanted to say was, so what if her friend had driven her and walked her into and out of the building? She'd gone downtown and lived to tell the story. As far as she was concerned, that deserved a good-girl treat.

Tia clearly disagreed. "Arthur isn't going to be around forever, and it isn't fair to place that kind of responsibility on him, especially after he spent so much time caring for his wife."

"Which is why he's going on a fishing trip next week with his old army buddies." A trip Mackenzie had given him as a thank-you for helping her get settled in her new house. "It's two weeks in Alaska, so I'll be managing all on my own," she said, and the reality of exactly what that meant finally settled.

It was not a good feeling. At all.

"That's great," Tia said proudly, and Mackenzie felt her spine straighten, her shoulders go back, and her chest relax a little. "I was afraid Arthur would stock your fridge with premade meals or hire one of those driving services so you wouldn't have to take the bus."

"Nope." He'd done both.

"Good, because you need to learn how to be more self-sufficient in navigating downtown."

"Who needs downtown when I have everything I need right here?"

"The hospital isn't here, your doctors aren't here, and the support groups you're supposed to be attending but haven't shown up to since week two isn't here either." Tia closed the distance and spoke slowly. "The more you cut yourself off from the outside world, the harder it will be to find peace."

Mackenzie wanted to argue that she had all the peace she could handle, then remembered how unsettling her morning had been.

"Keeping cooped up in the house isn't good for you."

"I get out."

"Hiring a car to take you from one building to another isn't getting out in the world. You need to get comfortable in all kinds of situations, step out of your safe bubble. And if that isn't enough to get your butt moving, it isn't good for Muttley."

"I know," Mackenzie admitted. "I'm working on it."

"I'm only saying this because I care about you, and I think you and Muttley are the perfect pair or I never would have agreed to the placement." Tia's voice went serious. "But you need to work faster, because if we can't prove progress, we might have to find another placement for Muttley."

Mackenzie's heart dropped, and her hands instinctively went for Muttley's harness. He was the one stable thing in her tiny world. She couldn't lose him. "You'd do that?"

"If it meant Muttley would get the kind of exercise and challenges he needs to be good at his job, then yes." As if that wasn't scary enough, Tia's voice went even softer. "But it's the foundation you need to worry about, not me."

Oh boy. Guide Dogs of Tennessee had never been 100 percent behind Muttley's placement. It had taken a lot of convincing on Tia's part for them to agree to the match, but in the end GDT had approved the placement on only a trial basis. Their concern had stemmed from how hard rehabilitation had been for Mackenzie and how desperately she'd needed a companion. They'd made it clear that, while Muttley would be by her side always, he was not a companion pet. He was a working dog, who needed structure and to be challenged.

"Have they said something?"

"Yes. GDT is concerned that keeping a ninety-five-pound animal locked with you in your house for days on end isn't fair to him." Mackenzie's panic must have been all over her face, because Tia added, "I'm not saying you have to start doing marathons. You just have to be consistent with your progress and Muttley's routine. To be safe, I think both of you need to gain and display new skills as a team every time we meet. Muttley is a special guide dog with special needs, the main one being consistent discipline."

"I love that he's a snuggler." Doggy hugs were the only regular contact she had.

"Then snuggle away at night. But during the day you need to get out with him, let him practice his skills, be confident in what he's been trained to do. That was our deal," Tia reminded her. "A guide dog is only as good as his owner allows him to be. And right now, you're holding both of you back when the foundation needs to see forward movement. Even if it's one step at a time."

"I can do that," Mackenzie vowed, knowing she would do anything if it meant keeping her little family together.

◆ ◆ ◆

After three straight days locked in a recording studio, Hunter was desperate for a cold beer, a hot shower, and a solid twelve hours in bed. Preferably with a woman. None of which should have been a problem.

Tonight was ladies' night at Big Daddy's. With two-for-one drafts on the menu, ladies outnumbered the gents two to one, making the bar a sea of midriffs, miniskirts, and mile-long legs—many of them aimed in Hunter's direction.

His problem wasn't getting laid. It was mustering up enough interest in someone.

His mind kept winding back to Mackenzie in the fuzzy boots and sleep-tousled hair. The teal panties had been a showstopper. She was a pint-size bombshell with the face of an angel and the curves of a pinup. Every guy's fantasy.

And *this* guy's biggest problem, since she'd been avoiding him since Saturday. Okay, she'd been avoiding him since his wedding, but now that he knew where she lived, he couldn't focus on anything else.

The band had spent the past few days trying to finalize their song list for the label. They'd listened to more than a hundred demos and found two hits. Both written by Mack and Muttley. Leaving Hunter with the few songs he'd been trying to write himself.

"At least consider using one or two of them," Brody said, trying again to get Cash's attention—which was securely affixed to a stacked blonde at the end of the bar.

"Did you even listen to the songs *I* sent you?" Hunter asked, but he could tell from his cousin's expression he had—and they were as bad as Hunter feared. "Was any of it good?"

"The bones were there, but it was missing . . . I don't know. Something."

Yeah, Hunter knew what Brody meant. His songs were lacking the same thing his life was: something authentic enough to hold on to.

"What did the label say?"

"They loved the sampling you submitted and are optimistically hopeful," Brody said, and Hunter relaxed with relief.

He took his first deep breath since he'd signed on the dotted line for this upcoming album. The expectation he'd been drowning in lifted enough for his chest to ease up. "Not what I thought you were going to say, but Christ, this is great news." He paused. "You're not screwing with me, right?"

Hunter knew he was far from a solid album, but now he had the freedom he needed to make it happen.

"I never screw around when it comes to business. Ever." Brody grinned at him. "Which is why I replaced all your songs with the two from Mackenzie, then explained to the label that it was only a small sampling of what was to come."

And just like that, Hunter's lungs stopped working. "I haven't fully convinced Mackenzie to get on board." It was only a matter of time before she caved. "If she finds out we are using her songs, I lose all my leverage with her. You have to call the label back, tell them those songs aren't locked in."

"No can do, cuz. They already started the paperwork to secure them. And before you go all menstrual on me, those songs are the only reason I didn't show up with another Cody Kelly in tow," Brody explained. "We take Mackenzie off the table and peach fuzz will just be the start of your problems."

"I don't want to take her off the table. I want to bring her back into the fold."

"Until I hear from her that she wants to change the terms of your working relationship, we move forward with those songs."

"We don't have a working relationship. That's the problem!" *Jesus,* was he the only one who was looking at the big picture? "And I need time to fix it."

"Did you ever stop to wonder whether maybe by fixing your problem, you're creating a truck full of ones for her?" Brody asked.

"The only way this can become a problem is if I let her walk away again," Hunter explained. "And that's not an option."

"Right, I forgot—your big plan. The one where, when this is all said and done, she'll go back to sitting in that same house while you're off living the dream."

"Maybe it's time she was reminded of her own dream," Hunter pointed out, still trying to reconcile the headstrong and vibrant Mackenzie he knew with the hesitant and scared woman from the other day.

"Dreams change," Brody pointed out. "Sometimes they die."

"Yours didn't," Hunter said. "Even when Savannah was one step from saying 'I do' to that suit, you didn't stop dreaming about her."

"My situation was different."

"The woman you loved was marrying another man, making the likelihood of living out *that* dream impossible. Yet here you are, married to her and raising a family with her," Hunter said, because if there was ever a time to give up hope on a dream, that was it. But Brody had never let go, and even though his life hadn't panned out exactly how he'd imagined it, he'd found his way back to Savannah, finding his own happiness in the process.

Brody thought about that for a moment, his face going soft. "Mackenzie's still healing, Hunter. Tread lightly."

"What better way to do that than with music?"

"This could be a good thing for her," Brody said, his focus lasered in on Hunter. "But you need to ask yourself if you are the right guy for the job."

Well, that pissed him off more than it should. "I'd never do anything to hurt Mackenzie."

"I believe that *you* believe you won't. But your drive is infectious." Brody shook his head. "You're like a tornado when you get focused on something—you kick the door down and sweep up everyone along the way and carry them with you."

"Maybe Mackenzie *needs* to be carried for a little while, so she can remember what it feels like to fly," Hunter said.

"This is all about Mackenzie, then?" Brody asked, studying Hunter as if he wasn't buying what Hunter was selling.

Hunter ignored the warning bells going off in his head that suggested his cousin was onto something and nodded. Confident and firm. "Yeah, and if a hit album comes from it, it's a win-win in my book."

Brody skewered him with a look. "*Your* book being key in that statement. What about Mackenzie's book? Maybe working with you won't be a win-win for her."

"I'll make sure it is," Hunter vowed. "Why are you so against this? I thought you'd be on my side," he asked, wondering how Brody wasn't grasping the situation. "Ninety percent of our sales from the last album came from single downloads. Two songs, to be exact. The rest of the album tanked. With the right writing partner, that won't happen again."

"Which is why I'll be sending over some tracks for you to listen to tonight." Brody pulled out his phone and scrolled through a small list of names. "Before you ask, no, Mackenzie won't be there to throw more of her time into the hat. I asked. She declined. End of story."

She'd also stayed in the shower for more than an hour to avoid seeing him out.

"She told me she was going to think about it," he said, and Brody leveled him with a *bullshit* look.

"Really? Because she told *me* she wasn't sure if she could trust me enough to keep me on as her agent just because I told you where she was. So somehow I can't picture her agreeing to work with you."

"It will happen, and she won't fire you," Hunter said with confidence. Mackenzie might be pissed about the other night, but she'd never fire Brody. "The idea of someone other than your family getting a cut of her success? Never going to happen."

Mackenzie would never do anything to harm a friend's career. It wasn't in her nature.

"Only because hiring a new agent would mean interacting with strangers." Brody leaned back in his chair. "And she can't work with you because she's working on another project."

"With Arthur?" Hunter said, and man, he sounded like a pussy.

Brody hiked a brow. "You met Arthur?"

"Nope, but his flowers were stinking up the house."

"The roses," Brody said with a smug-as-shit smile. "He brings Mackenzie a vase every few days from his garden to brighten up her studio. You should see her place after she sells a song."

Hunter snorted. "What kind of guy gardens?"

"The kind Mackenzie trusts to help her with her music," Brody said, then pointed to the list again. "These writers here, they don't have a Mack or Muttley. But they do have talent. They are top-shelf writers, in high demand, *and* willing to work with you on the album. Something Mackenzie is not. Plus, they were all vetted by me. Not the label."

Hunter looked at the list of names. Every single one of them was an award-winning writer he'd dreamed of collaborating with when he'd been coming up in the industry. Now they were willing to work with him. Talk about surreal.

He slid Brody a look. "Most of these guys are booked years in advance."

"They were interested enough in working with you to free up their schedule for the next few weeks."

An honor that should have left Hunter feeling hopeful and inspired. And for a moment, he bought into it, enjoyed the surge of pride and excitement that surfaced, and gave himself over to the idea that this was the solution.

Except with all the emotions rushing through his body, he couldn't find the one thing he'd been desperate for.

Direction.

"I know you had to pull a lot of favors to make this happen, and I am going to listen to the tracks when I get home . . ."

"Ah, Jesus." Brody reached over the bar to grab a frosty mug and poured himself a beer from the nearest tap. "I am practically handing you a GRAMMY and you've already come up with a dozen reasons to say no because you aren't getting your way."

"I'm not saying no, but I'm not sure bringing in someone new at this point in the game is the right move for the band. We're still trying to figure out what we want this album to say, and a new voice, who shares the label's direction, might lead us down the same path as last time."

Because, in truth, the last set of writers hadn't been the problem. They'd just been brought in too early. The Hunter Kane Band had still been figuring out the feel and sound of the album when the writers had come in with a vision that didn't match the band's. Hunter had been too distracted by his personal life to come up with a better idea and deferred to the writers.

Huge mistake.

"Some of the band members might disagree."

Hunter froze. "You've talked to them?"

"Not yet," Brody said. "I was going to see if you wanted to talk with them first, because when Mackenzie says no, and she will, you'll need a backup plan. And this decision doesn't just affect you, Hunter. It affects everyone involved."

"You don't think I get that?" he said, a little harsher than he'd intended.

His Superman complex, as Hadley called it, was one of the biggest factors in why his marriage fell apart. Hadley wanted him to go solo, and so did the label. The band shared equal ownership in the Hunter Kane Band, but as the front man, Hunter was the one who did the majority of the press junkets, radio tours, and interviews.

His face was splattered all over the magazines, his personal life talked about in the gossip rags. And in between touring and recording albums, while the rest of the band went home to their families, Hunter was tasked with the responsibility of promoting the band. A responsibility that, most days, didn't bother him. But lately, the weight had become suffocating.

"I think you've had a hard couple of years, and I agree that you need some help with the heavy lifting. A writing partner could ease that pressure, help you get back in the right mind space."

His mind already knew exactly which writer's space he wanted to be in. Only she wasn't returning his calls. "I need more time."

"You've got three weeks," Brody said, reaching for another mug and handing it to Hunter. "That's when the studio time is booked, and the label won't give you another extension."

Hunter took the beer and laughed. "What will they do? Fine me the studio time?"

"No," Brody said with a seriousness that had Hunter swallowing hard. "They'll drop the band."

"What?" Hunter choked on his beer. "They said that?"

"Right before they explained that you'd have to pay back the advance or they'd sue for breach of contract."

Which meant his band would have to return the multimillion-dollar advance they'd received, most of which his bandmates had already spent. Hunter could come up with his part of the money, easy. The rest of the band had dependents, mortgages to pay, and kids to send to college someday.

"Can they do that?" Hunter asked.

"Yes, and before you go all gladiator on me, you'll lose," Brody said. "Which is why I expect the name of the writer you choose in my inbox tomorrow morning. Use the list, don't use the list, I don't care. But, Hunter, if you don't pick someone, the label will."

CHAPTER 10

The late-afternoon sun was starting to set, radiating a soothing heat through Mackenzie's body. She reclined on the settee, stifled a yawn, and stretched languidly, basking in the feeling of her skin gliding over the sunbaked slipcover. Picking up her guitar, she ran her fingers down its neck before cradling the instrument.

Outside, a strong wind whistled through her back courtyard, the branches of the great oak creaking under the pressure. Mackenzie loved springtime in Nashville. With its rain-washed freshness and lack of major holidays, it was her favorite season.

It was as if Mother Nature was wiping the slate clean. Something Mackenzie could get firmly behind.

She'd been trying to work on this song for the past week. Which would have been a lot easier to do if she weren't still thinking about Hunter. Or the dozen or so times he'd called her. Or how her house still smelled like him. That's how potent he was.

She'd opened all the windows, hoping to erase his visit completely, then pulled out her lucky sweatshirt. It was ratty and old, two sizes too big, and had the Berklee College of Music logo on the back, but it felt like simpler times.

Guitar cradled in her lap, hand lightly resting on the strings, Mackenzie settled her head back against the settee. She didn't strum but silently listened to the branches tapping against the glass roof of her sunroom.

Only, instead of channeling independence and female-inspired rebellion—the two themes her client had requested for their album—all she could picture was strong, firm, masculine hands sliding down her body to her teal panties . . .

Gaah.

Mackenzie grabbed the remote and punched in her "Get Focused" playlist to distract herself. The theme song from *Schindler's List* filled the room, bouncing off the walls in such a rich, heartbreaking way she held her breath and listened.

She braced herself for John Williams's notes to flow through her, the first verse of the song leaving chills rising in their wake. At the chorus, her heart slowed to a stop as the sorrow of the violin wove around the hopefulness of the harp, creating a gentle melody that pulled her into another world. Made her forget reality and exist only in the notes.

The song came to the final chorus and her fingers began to glide across the strings, finding their way to the right notes, one by one. Not quite a melody, but she was headed in the right direction, building toward something that resonated. She could feel it.

And then she heard it.

Another guitar lightly strumming in the background, adding a little flash to her folk.

Hunter!

She could recognize his riffs anywhere. And the melody was as inspiring as it was irritating. Inspiring because, for the first time in weeks, she didn't feel lost in the song. The irritation came when she realized that all it took was a few keys from Hunter and she completely gave in to his lead.

With a frustrated strum across the strings, she came to a hard stop. "You're trespassing," she said loudly.

"You're right. You should call the cops," Hunter said from the other side of the open window. He was on her porch—she could tell from the proximity of his voice—and he'd been listening to her play. "Oh wait, that would mean picking up the phone."

He sounded annoyed. *The feeling's mutual, buddy.*

"What are you doing here?" she asked.

"Getting ready to write my new album."

"The studio is that way." She pointed her finger to the north. "About twenty minutes in the opposite direction."

"Twenty minutes, huh?" The porch swing creaked under his weight. He was making himself at home. "You want to go back to the top or pick up where we left off?"

"I want you to go back to your studio so I can get back to work."

"Can't," he said simply, then started strumming a catchy hook that sounded like a Hunter original.

"Why not?"

"By now I'm sure my studio is filled with a bunch of record executives waiting for me to tell them what writer I chose." He rattled off a few names that collectively held more awards than the Beatles.

"Impressive list," she said, telling herself that it was a good thing. In fact, it was exactly what she wanted and exactly what Hunter needed.

"Turns out, even after a few flops, I'm an impressive guy to work with."

He was more than impressive. And that was the problem. "Who did you choose?"

"That's a secret," he said, and the lighthearted flirt in his tone was as tangible as a touch. "Which I'm willing to share, if you are. A secret for a secret."

So annoying! Hunter could make her feel safe and defensive all at the same time. Once upon a time she'd shared all of herself with him— and he'd given his heart to a social media socialite. "I'll pass."

"Later, then," he said as if it were the start of a conversation instead of the send-off. "Probably for the best, since the label wants to get started on the rest of the album right away."

"The rest of the album? So you're keeping the songs I sent over?" she asked casually, as if her future happiness didn't rely on his answer.

"Seems so," Hunter said, his fingers stopping for only a moment before going back to work.

"You told Brody you wouldn't record an album created by a mish-mash of writers ever again," she said. "That you 'being a creative part behind every song on the album' was important."

"*Nonnegotiable* was the term I used," he said. "And it still stands, so when Brody sent your songs to my label and they fell in love, our fate was sealed, Trouble." He lowered his voice and whispered through the screen, "Whoops, I blew the secret. I choose you. Think of how fun it will be. Just like old times."

Yeah, she'd barely made it through those old times. It wasn't a road she wanted to head back down.

"We will not have old times or new times." She set the guitar on the ground and walked over to the window. Even though he wasn't in his work harness, Muttley stood and came to her side. "I'm not writing this album with you."

"Write it with me or don't. But for the next three weeks, I will be right here, making music, the way we used to."

"Oh no you won't." She closed one window and locked it, then moved to the other, Muttley growling at the back door. "You are not going to camp out on my porch. I have work to do."

"Sounded like you were a little stuck on that last riff. Need help?"

Did she ever. Not that she would admit that. "I'm fine, thank you."

"Your lucky sweatshirt says differently," he mused. "We can add that song to the agenda. Unless it was already for me."

"It is not. And there is no 'we,'" she argued, closing another window. "There is *me*, going into my studio to work, and *you* heading to the studio to meet with your new team."

She was struggling with the last window when Hunter spoke. And Mackenzie knew he was right on the other side of the screen. "See, that's the problem, Trouble. If I walk in there to meet with them, the label will look at it as a done deal and we'll be stuck with a writer who, yeah, is talented but doesn't know what direction to go in or avoid. It will be like the last album all over again, and I can't do that to the guys."

But he could do this to her.

Mackenzie's throat tightened. "How is everyone?"

"They miss you," he said quietly.

She missed them too. At one time, those guys had made up a huge part of her world. "I heard Paul got married."

"Married with twins. Girls," Hunter said, and Mackenzie snorted. She couldn't help it. Paul, the band's playboy and self-proclaimed bachelor, was a daddy. Of girls. Oh, karma could be so cruel.

"What about Quinn?" she asked. "Don't tell me he's a dad too."

"No, but he's got a serious lady friend," he said with a heaviness to his voice that had Mackenzie hesitating on closing the last window. "They just bought a house out in Franklin and are talking about making it official after the next tour ends."

Mackenzie's eyes pricked at the realization that everyone had grown up and moved on. Found their place, their partner, and she was still stuck right where she'd been the day she'd walked away.

"But if I don't come up with a solid set, we lose it all, Mackenzie," Hunter said, and she could hear the raw truth in his tone. Gone was the easygoing charm and swagger, leaving behind nothing but desperation. And so much uncertainty that Mackenzie wondered if he was stuck too.

Sure, he'd been off traveling all around the country, living a large and vivid life, but that didn't mean that he'd found his place. And that was something she could relate to.

"This isn't just about me anymore," he added. "There are a lot of families counting on me to hit it out of the park, but all I keep scoring is singles."

She knew how that felt. Brody, Tia, and Muttley were counting on her to do things she wasn't entirely certain she could do. And while disappointing them was terrifying, facing all her demons at once seemed impossible. Especially since these were battles she had to fight alone.

"You have some really great writers at your disposal," she said. "Writers who have the talent to take you the distance."

"But I need someone who knows how much distance we can cover, because all they know is where it started," he said. "You know me better than anyone, Mackenzie. You and I are like one when we write."

That was what she was afraid of. Writing with Hunter was the most intimate and vulnerable position she could put herself in, and yet she couldn't stomach telling him no.

"There's no one else?" she asked.

"Just you, Trouble."

Sweet baby Jesus, he was good.

The man knew exactly what to say to make her feel all warm and gooey inside. Stronger women had fallen prey to that dimpled grin and lethal sweet talk. If Hunter turned up the charm, even half a notch, Mackenzie would be toast. Even if she couldn't see his dimples.

"Us working together is a bad idea," she allowed.

He made a sound as if he strongly disagreed. "No bullshit excuses. Give me your top three reasons."

Shoulders back, fake bravado dialed to *Dirty Harry,* she aimed her chin at the open window. "One—"

I kissed you.

"I'm writing a song for another artist who doesn't need me to go into a studio or hold her hand, because she understands I'm a writer not a band member."

"Sounds like BS to me."

Shoot.

With a dramatic sigh, she turned her head toward him. Even though she couldn't see, from the sound of his boot tapping the wood slats, she could sense where he was standing. "Two—"

You didn't kiss me back.

"It's been three years. We don't know each other that well anymore. And three—"

I'm pretty sure I still have the feels for you.

"It's hard to be creative when you're all up in my space."

She slammed the window closed, wanting to emphasize her point. Only, it got stuck halfway down. She struggled with it for another moment, ignoring the chuckle from the peanut gallery on the patio, before finally deciding that he was too big to crawl through the space.

"Now, if you'll excuse me, I have to get back to work." Chin high enough to reach the ozone, she turned to strut off—and ran into a big, yummy wall of amused man.

"You might want to start with the sliding door next time," he said, his arms brushing past her, and around, until her heart was pounding so hard she was certain it was going to leap out of her chest. Close proximity to the world's sexiest man could do that to a girl.

"Most people knock," she said, barely able to breathe.

"I'm not most people." He clicked the last window shut. "And I didn't want to chance you shutting me out."

"I wasn't shutting you out." Even more pathetic, she was shutting herself in. Something that had to change immediately if she intended on building the life she was working so hard to resurrect. "I just wasn't ready."

"And now?"

He was back, his breath skating across her face. Mackenzie closed her eyes.

The air between them thickened. She moved to gain some space, but there was nowhere to go. Hunter was right there, standing between her and freedom, the heat from his closeness piercing her every pore.

She pressed her back against the wall. He moved closer. "Are you ready now?"

Heck no. More like out of time. And, after her talk with Tia, she was out of options. If Mackenzie didn't act now, she would regret it. And she carried enough regret to last a lifetime.

"I'm willing to put myself out there," she said, squaring her shoulders.

"That's a start." Instead of backing up, like she hoped he would, Hunter rested his hands against the closed window, caging her in. "Now, about those issues you seem so stuck on. One, you are a hell of a lot more than a writer to me, and I'm asking you to hold my hand. Not the other way around. Two . . ."

He scooted even closer. "Three years or thirty, this thing between us won't ever fade. And three . . ."

The tiny gap between them closed, until they were sharing the same air. "You like me all up in your space. Some of your most creative moments were when I was all up in your space."

Hunter was a told-you-so guy. A trait that Mackenzie found annoyingly adorable. Which was why she knew what was coming and told herself to run, not walk, to the nearest exit. Only as Hunter's lips hovered over hers, pausing to give her ample time to speak up, she found herself moving closer—until they had liftoff.

Hunter took his time, his mouth gently caressing hers in a kiss so hot Mackenzie forgot to breathe. Being hailed America's Sexiest Man wasn't enough for him. Nope, in typical Hunter fashion, overachiever that he was, he also had to go for World's Best Kisser.

And he won.

By the time he lifted his head, Mackenzie's hands were fisted in his shirt and she was rubbing up against him like he was catnip.

"What was that?" she asked, her lips tingling with aftershocks.

"If you have to ask, I did something wrong."

Before he could go in for a do-over, which would have ended with her crawling up his body, she took a step back. Only to find that she was still clutching his shirt. She let go. "I thought you didn't do complicated."

"I don't."

"Then, back to my original question. What was that?"

"That was me simplifying things." His smile was so big she could hear its smugness. And before she could ask what *that* meant, he said, "Now, unless you have any more concerns you need me to address—"

"Nope." She stepped under his arm and out of kissing range. "I'm good."

In fact, she felt better than she had in months. Being around Hunter was like living life with surround sound on high. Every note full and alive. An emotion that was hard to reach when playing acoustic.

If Mackenzie didn't find a way to survive outside her bubble, she'd lose Muttley. And she couldn't survive losing one more thing.

Hunter was right. When they were together, they moved as one. And if anyone could help her navigate her way into the seeing world, it was him.

"Fine. I can give you three weeks." Surely she could keep it professional for three weeks. To be safe, though, she added, "But there will be rules."

"I'm listening."

"Number one." She held up a finger. "No more kissing."

"If you say so," he mused, taking her hand.

"Or that." She jerked her hand back. "And yes, I say." She crossed her arms to prove it. "If I agree to this, then you must agree that after the three weeks are up, we go our own way and focus on our separate careers."

"No kissing, no sharing space, and no hand-holding. You have a lot of rules."

Rules were good. Rules kept people safe.

"I'll need daily rides to and from the studio," she said, pausing to gather the courage to state her next condition to their agreement. "And once a week, I'll need a ride to the community center over by the university."

A request he clearly wasn't expecting. His energy softened, and his voice gentled in question. "Community center?"

Mackenzie looked away—a habit left over from before. "They have a support group every other Thursday from five thirty to seven, and I haven't been in a while."

"Why not?"

She shrugged. "It's hard to navigate the bus system during rush hour, and Arthur can't take me at night." Hunter remained quiet for a long moment, and Mackenzie felt her cheeks heat with embarrassment. "If it's too much, you can always drop me off and I can catch an Uber home after."

"It's not too much," he said with a gentleness that turned her chest to mush. "Every other Thursday night from five thirty to seven. Anything else?"

Yes, there was a big something else, but asking him felt as if she were admitting she needed a keeper. Which she most certainly did not. "I may need some help at the market. Muttley and I know how to get there and back without any problem, but once we're inside, figuring out what aisle carries what can be . . . frustrating," she admitted, then forced a smile. "So do we have a deal?"

"Yeah, Trouble. We have a deal," he said in a sweet and under-standing way that was all Hunter Kane. The down-to-earth, sensitive barroom musician, the guy who stole her heart with his innate capacity to care, and the guy who could very easily steal it again.

"Good," she said, twining her fingers. "Well, it's almost suppertime, so why don't we start fresh, first thing tomorrow?"

"Supper is a great idea." Hunter closed the gap between them, placing his hands on her hips. Her stomach did flips at the contact. "What better way to get to know each other again than over a couple of steaks?"

Mackenzie's palms started to sweat. Supper followed by an evening with just the two of them sounded a heck of a lot cozier than a few car rides into downtown and afternoons with a bunch of foul-mouthed bandmates.

Nope, this stupid crush didn't need any more encouragement.

"That wasn't an invitation," she said breezily. "And I already have plans for supper."

"With Arthur?"

"Not tonight." Tonight, her plans involved pizza, a cold root beer, and a bubble bath. For one. "But if you tell me what time you'll be by in the morning, I'll be ready."

"And leave you with nothing but pizza?" he said, and she must have expressed her surprise. "I saw the coupon on the fridge with a folded twenty and it's takeout Tuesday."

"Then why break tradition?"

"Because we can do better than that. And we've only got three weeks to get this record down and you market-ready, so I'm going to need an all-access pass."

Mackenzie's palms began to sweat. "What does that mean?"

"That after we go to the market, I'll stop by and grab my stuff," he said smoothly. "I'm moving in."

CHAPTER 11

Hunter took one look at Mackenzie in the produce section and knew this was a bad idea.

Stiff posture. Plastic smile. Nose so high in the air he was surprised she wasn't suffering from oxygen depletion. Mackenzie was working overtime to keep a brave face while navigating her way through the swarm of people. Sure, Muttley was taking the lead, and Hunter was close at her back, but people still managed to bump into her. Like the douche in the designer loafers who was too busy perusing the wine selection to notice Mackenzie. It was as if he didn't bother to look where he was going.

Normally Hunter would say, "Hello? What part of a lady with a Seeing Eye dog are you missing?" and then give the guy a little bump of his own, until he got the fucking point. But he didn't think that would inspire Mackenzie's confidence in his teaching abilities.

This "quick" shopping excursion had pushed past suppertime—and there were only ten items on the list. Three in the bag.

The sun had disappeared, the crowd was multiplying by the second, and Hunter was pretty sure the girl working checkout stand three recognized him. Based on the not-so-stealthy glances and lightning-quick swipes to her phone, she was likely posting, tweeting, and snapping Hunter Kane's current location.

Pulling his ball cap even lower, he stood back and watched as Mackenzie took her time selecting a cantaloupe. She'd squeeze one, lift it for a quick sniff, then place it back. On the fourth one in, her nose crinkled. "Does this smell ripe to you?"

"Are you asking me to smell your melons?" he asked, loving how her cheeks flushed.

"I'm asking you to be my eyes," she said, holding it out. "If I get one, I want it to be ripe. Firm but not too firm. Oh, and more tan than green."

"Firm but not too firm. Got it." Hunter took the melon and gave it a little squeeze, then casually broached the subject of her limitations. He'd done some reading online, researching her condition and ways to make her life a little easier. Give her some of her independence back. "I read about an app online that helps visually impaired people with shopping."

"They have an app for everything. Before I left rehab they showed me some technology for the blind," she said, but he noticed she didn't reach for her phone. "Like I have an app that tells me what an item is, another that tells me what color something is, and even one that reads the ingredients or price tag to me. But three apps to find the perfect melon feels like overkill."

It's probably frustrating as well, he thought.

She gave a shrug. "At some point it just became easier to order online and let someone else do the picking for me."

"But now you're interested in venturing out?"

"My sponsor reminded me that there won't always be someone around, and the more I master on my own, the faster my recovery process will go," she admitted, and damn if that didn't make his chest pinch a little.

"It wasn't until I knew I could stand on my own that I finally left home and moved in with Big Daddy." The words left his lips as if of their own accord. Hunter never talked about his dad. Ever. Yet there he was, standing in the produce aisle, squeezing melons and talking about the one topic he avoided at all costs.

"You never told me how old you were when you ran away."

"Eleven," he said, and then because he couldn't seem to shut the fuck up, he went on. "I'd spent the entire summer mowing lawns around town. Managed to squirrel away a hundred and seventy-three bucks without my dad knowing. The day before school started, I went to my uncle and asked him how much he'd charge to rent out the room above his garage."

Hunter remembered standing outside his uncle's bar with nothing more than a sleeping bag, a backpack full of worn clothes, a wad of ones in his boots. His hands had been shaking so badly he was afraid he'd drop the money, so he'd stuffed the bills into his cowboy boots.

He knew that if Big Daddy turned him away, he didn't have anywhere else to go. He also knew that anywhere had to be better than going back to Buddy and admitting failure.

Hunter knew his uncle's rules: no boys allowed in the bar during working hours. But Hunter wasn't going to him as a boy—he was a man with a job looking for boarding. Jesus, he'd been scared. Had thrown up twice before getting the balls to enter the bar. But eventually he had, and he'd said he'd like a meeting with the owner.

Big Daddy took one look at the pack on his slim shoulders and told someone to cover the bar, that he had business to conduct in his office. Then he'd walked Hunter back.

"He sat down behind that big desk of his, and I sat across from him as he made a big deal out of scribbling some numbers down, before he told me he'd take twenty bucks a month for the room in the attic, but nightly suppers would cost extra."

"He charged you for meals?" she asked, sounding horrified.

Hunter laughed. "You sound exactly like my aunt did. She said Big Daddy was talking nonsense, and that I could stay for free and she'd feed me all the food I wanted. But Big Daddy stayed firm on his offer."

"You were eleven!"

He'd also been a head shorter and a leg lighter than other kids his age, but what he'd lacked in size, he made up for in spit. Then again, one had to be tough as nails to make it eleven years with Buddy Kane as his father.

Not that *father* adequately described Buddy. One had to be sober enough to hold down a job to be considered a father. And since Hunter did most of the parenting in their relationship, he worked hard to keep what was left of his tattered family together—which meant hiding the worst of it from his aunt and uncle.

"I needed to know I could be my own man, that I could handle alone whatever came my way, because there was always the fear that's where I'd end up. And he knew that."

"Hunter," she said, placing a hand on his arm, and he had a better sense of how she felt when people offered her sympathy. It didn't feel like understanding. It felt more like a sentence. "Did he really make you pay him for the room?"

"Twenty bucks. First of every month. And I had to help him stock the bar every morning before school for my meals." He laughed when her jaw dropped. "But before you get all pissy on my behalf, Big Daddy saved every penny in a bank account that he gave me when I turned eighteen."

Hunter went back to the melons, while Mackenzie silently held his hand. After a long moment, she gave his free hand a squeeze. "I miss him."

"I do too." He picked up one more melon and gave it a squeeze. "Found one." He handed it to her. "And it feels like a perfect ten to me." He lowered his voice. "And I'm an expert when it comes to melons."

She knew he was changing the subject, but she allowed it, even giving him an eye roll over his lame joke while placing the fruit in the canvas bag on her shoulder. He'd offered to carry the bag when they'd entered the store, but she'd argued that if she was going to learn to shop on her own, she needed to do it *on her own*.

"I need some peaches for breakfast."

He leaned in to whisper in her ear. "If you thought I was good with melons, you should know I'm even better with peaches."

She ignored this and pointed. "Can you pick three from the bin over there?"

And damn if her "over there" wasn't spot-on with the peach display. In fact, he was confident that if it weren't so crowded, Mackenzie could have navigated her way around without any trouble.

She just needed to know she was capable. And he made it his top priority to help her realize how strong she really was.

Before they left, he was going to ask the clerk what time the store was the least crowded and schedule their next trip accordingly. Mackenzie's problem wasn't her blindness—it was the unpredictable nature of others.

"Normally, you'd have me at peaches. However, I promised a hands-on experience," he said, sliding the bag off her shoulder, sure to get his hand on some of that silky skin of hers in the process. "And, Trouble, I always come through on my promises."

"Rule number three. No touching," she said, but he noticed she didn't back away.

"I guess that means I can't inspect your peach." He gave a disappointed sigh. "But rules are rules, so I'll wait here with the bag while *you* inspect the peaches."

Mackenzie seemed to curl in on herself, holding tightly to Muttley's harness. When he got to her soft expression, Hunter knew he was fucked. It wasn't the adorable way she worried her lower lip that got to him or even the raw vulnerability he saw swimming deep down in those green pools.

Nope, what drew him in, like a moth to the flame, was the warm smile she gave when she reached her hand out in search of his and said, "Where are the peaches?"

Hunter's chest softened, which was the exact opposite of what happened south of his belt buckle, when she found his hand and twined their fingers together. "What happened to rule number three?"

That smile of hers grew. "What's a little hand-holding when you already sniffed my melons?" she asked. "Plus, the aisles here are narrow, and it sounds crowded."

"Or you just wanted to hold my hand." And before she could argue, he said, "Peaches are the third row back on your left."

He indicated the initial direction but let Mackenzie take the lead, making a temporary truce with Muttley as he herded her toward the middle of the aisle and away from the carts and other objects. The mutt gave anything that held potential danger the same stern look that he gave Hunter.

Without incident, they approached the display. Hunter placed her hands on the first grouping, slowly moving it over the fruit. "These are white peaches. And next to them"—he gently moved her hand—"are yellow peaches."

"I like white peaches." She picked one of each variety and held them, thoroughly inspecting each. Her brow crinkled in concentration. With a huff, she set them back down. "They feel the same."

Hunter was starting to understand how complicated small things could become, and that pissed him off. She had enough to worry about. Picking the wrong peach shouldn't be one of them. Hunter moved behind her and picked up a peach. "If you want to make sure you get a white one, then let me introduce you to the donut peach. It's flat and round."

He placed one in her hand, noticing that, while she was exploring the fruit with her fingers, her body was ever so slowly pressing back into his.

She brought the peach to her nose. "It smells sweet," she breathed, her lashes lifting toward him and—*holy Christ.*

Sweet didn't even cut it. In fact, a whole lot of words rushed to mind, and *sweet* wasn't one of them. Because she was looking at him like she was ripe for another kiss. And damn if he didn't want to be the guy to give it to her.

But he'd promised no more kissing. And no matter how tempting those lips looked, he was determined to follow through on his promises. Then again, she'd also said no touching, and her backside was touching a whole lot of his front side.

"Are you changing the rules on me, Trouble?" he whispered.

"I'm not sure," she whispered back.

The only thing Hunter was sure about was that he wasn't going to blow this. "Then until you are, why don't we agree on a fun trip to the store followed by a friendly supper?"

"With vanilla ice cream and white peaches for dessert," she said with a smile. "Arthur always gets the yellow ones because they're cheaper."

"Boring, gardener, and cheap?" Hunter tsked. "Sounds like an accountant."

"He's a music teacher," she said, casually selecting a peach.

"Like piano?"

"Like played at Carnegie Hall." She gave it a squeeze and set it back down. "Then he became a professor of music at the university." It was Hunter's turn to roll his eyes. "And I said he was sweet, not boring."

"Tomato, tomahto." Hunter took the peach back and slid it into the bag, then followed her to the bin of corn. "You play music together and he does your shopping. When did that start?"

"The music was from nearly day one, and he started shopping for me when . . ." She paused, as if flipping through her mental calendar, then smiled, big and warm and—

"Oh, when I moved in with him."

Hunter choked. "You live with him?"

Jesus, he hadn't seen that coming. Besides the flowers and note, there hadn't been a single sign of a male presence in her house. Normally, competition wouldn't faze Hunter.

This guy was different. He had everything going for him that Hunter had, except he was sweet, a gardener, and knew braille. Hell, the fucker had probably minored in braille while studying the different species of flora.

"Lived," she clarified. "Then I bought the house next door."

Because that made it *so* much better. She'd decided it was safer to move in with a practical stranger than confide in Hunter. A strange sense of, well . . . *Shit*. He was pretty sure it was jealousy overtaking him.

Hunter, the king of confident-casual, was jealous. Over an average Arthur—who didn't sound so average.

"Why did you move out?" he asked, not sure if he wanted to know the answer but desperate to get some insight into what Mackenzie had gone through. Help him fill in the gaps he'd missed.

"Because I needed to stand on my own two feet. And I got tired of losing at poker." She grinned. "Did I mention Arthur is a Vietnam vet who runs high-stakes poker games out of his garage?"

Which made the guy at least seventy.

"I think you forgot that part," he said drily.

"Sorry, it must have slipped my mind," she said, not sorry at all. "Arthur helps me out around the house, does my shopping, and transcribes my music. In return, I raise the house's odds by wearing my mirrored blind-girl glasses to poker night."

Hunter laughed. So did Mackenzie. And, *man oh man*, he didn't know if it was the sexy grin that lit him up or the fact that she wasn't shacking up with some guy named Arthur, but suddenly Hunter's shoulders felt a whole hell of a lot lighter.

"I think I get more out of the deal than him. But he likes to cook for someone, and I like to eat," she said as she put corn in the bag.

Hunter wanted to point out that while she had a wide spread of produce and dog treats, she didn't have a single ingredient in there to make an actual meal. But he held his tongue. "It sounds like a good trade-off."

"It is." Her smile faded, and Hunter's heart pinched.

"Except?"

"Arthur wants to move to Florida," she explained. "His house is too big for one person, and his older brother lives there. They've talked about living closer to each other, even consolidating to a bachelor pad like they had when they were younger."

"You're afraid he's staying here for you?" Hunter guessed.

"It isn't the Tennessee winters keeping him here," she said, her bravery breaking his heart. "If I can show him I'll be fine on my own, I know he'll feel better about moving."

"And who will be with you?" Hunter asked.

"I've always got Muttley," she said, those big fathomless eyes looking up at him. "And for the next few weeks, I have you."

He wanted to tell her that she'd always have him but knew that in a few months he'd be driving through some big-city USA and Mackenzie would be here. Alone in her little suburb of Nashville, relying on some punk behind the counter to give her fair change.

"Mackenzie—"

"Pity isn't on tonight's menu." She took the bag back. "So why don't you go find some of that fancy coffee you brag about, while Muttley and I locate the potatoes? They're on the next row at the end, right?"

"Right," Hunter said, unable to stop looking at her.

With a brave smile in place, she walked down the aisle, careful of the other customers, letting Muttley do his thing. And God bless her, she located the potatoes. Hunter told himself to go get the coffee, but he couldn't move. He was frozen in place by the delicate, feminine scent that lingered behind her.

Mackenzie worked her way through the potatoes, distinguishing the russet from the yams. She weighed one in her hand, then went in search of another. With two winners selected, she turned around to put them in her bag.

Only Loafer-Wearing Douche was back, and instead of heading to a less crowded row, he pressed forward, clearly oblivious to the fact that between the other carts, Mackenzie, and a guide dog with a white harness and fluorescent yellow vest, there wasn't enough room.

"Excuse me," he said. "You're blocking the aisle."

"Oh, I'm sorry," Mackenzie said, the comment clearly hitting a soft spot. Hunter found himself holding his breath as she plastered her body against the potato bin, tugging Muttley closer. But not close enough.

Loafer-Wearing Douche made a big deal of giving her a wide berth and clipped another cart, sending his cart careening into Mackenzie's space. Muttley was on it like King Kong to his Ann Darrow, charging the cart and putting himself between it and his woman.

The abrupt motion yanked the harness, sending Mackenzie's arm in one direction and the potatoes in the other. Thankfully, the cart didn't make contact, but Mackenzie grabbed the bin for balance, sending an avalanche of yams crashing to the floor.

Muttley barked and people vacated the aisle, including Loafer-Wearing Douche, leaving Mackenzie in the middle of an epic disaster zone. Surrounded by walking hazards. With nowhere to go.

Hunter rushed to her side, sure to clip Loafer-Wearing Douche on his way. "You okay?" he asked her.

"Coming to the market at rush hour wasn't such a great idea." Mackenzie knelt, her hands searching the ground, trying her best to clear the aisle.

Hunter crouched down to help her, but she shooed his hands away. Hers were trembling.

"I've got it." She struggled to place the potatoes back in the bin, then went for another handful.

"And I've got you," he said, gently taking the potatoes from her.

"For how long?" she asked, then immediately shook her head. "Sorry," she said, her voice going soft. So soft he barely heard her. "It's just if I'm going to learn how to do this, then I need to do it on my own."

Hunter wanted to argue but knew that it would only back her further into the corner. Instead, he silently helped, watching as the fierce determination beat out the humiliation.

Mackenzie was used to going it alone. She'd been forced down that path her entire life. And here she was again, having the rug ripped out from under her. But instead of complaining, she faced her situation head-on.

She might claim she wasn't the same girl he knew. And Hunter would agree. She was even more impressive.

When the last of the potatoes was cleared from the aisle, she gave him a sad smile. "I bet you wish you'd taken me up on the pizza. It would have been a whole lot easier."

"Where's the excitement in easy?" he asked. "Plus, cleaning up produce keeps me humble." Hunter helped her to her feet and then whispered, "It's also the perfect cover for checking out your melons."

CHAPTER 12

"I don't care how good you are with melons or peaches. You, Hunter Kane, are not charming your way into my kitchen. Or anywhere else, for that matter," Mackenzie said sternly—to her closed bathroom door.

It was the only quiet place she could find to think, since after their impromptu shopping excursion Hunter had set up shop in the kitchen—where he was currently cooking up a cozy supper for two.

Muttley gave a little whimper, and Mackenzie stroked his head. "I smell it too, buddy."

The tempting scent of Hunter's aunt's famous corn bread baking in the oven wafted under the door. Mackenzie's mouth watered at the thought of a home-cooked meal. Her stomach fluttered with nerves, and a few irritating butterflies, at the idea of Hunter doing something so domestic in her space.

"That is what you should have said to him when he strolled into your house as if he owned the place." With a frustrated huff, she slipped off her jeans, still damp from the rain, and pulled on a pair of leggings and a sweatshirt. "Stop being a pushover and start taking charge of your life."

Attitude thoroughly readjusted, Mackenzie stepped into her fuzzy pink house boots and opened the door. But when she bent down to pick up her dirty clothes, she noticed one of her tennis shoes was missing.

"Muttley," she groaned, but she could already hear him jingling his thieving little butt across the bedroom. "Give," she said and marched over to his doggy bed. It took less than a second before she felt a wet nose and shoelaces nudge her hand.

"Good boy. Now lie down." She gave Muttley the sign to sit in his bed and think about what he'd done. He gave an argumentative little huff but curled up as told.

That wasn't so hard, she thought as she leaned down to give him a good-boy ruffle of the ears. Except instead of his soft fur, her hand met leather. Drool-coated leather.

While she'd been giving herself a pep talk, it seemed Muttley had made short order of a cowboy boot, turning it into his own personal chew toy. An expensive, leather, Kane-size cowboy boot. Which Hunter had left by the front door when they'd arrived back at her house.

She gave a disapproving tsk at the canine-size holes in the buttery leather, but this time Muttley didn't back down.

Nope, he barked, proud protector pride strong in his tone.

"No steak bone for you tonight," she chided while searching for the other boot—which stubbornly stood at the foot of her bed, next to a duffel bag. A big, manly duffel bag that had no business being in her bedroom.

Sitting pretty, as if it belonged.

"Oh hell no." She threw her hair in a ponytail, snatched the boots and duffel, and headed down the hallway—his crap in tow.

One overbearing male dealt with, one to go.

Feeling all kinds of confident, she entered the kitchen and tossed his duffel across the floor. It skidded to a stop. "I found that in my room."

"I am sensing a pattern here," Hunter said casually. "Next time you're going to throw something at me, could it be silk or lace?"

"You're lucky I didn't throw these." She held up the offensive boots.

"What did those boots ever do to you?" he asked, taking them from her, injury in his voice as, she assumed, he inspected the bite marks.

"They crawled under my bed."

"They didn't crawl," he explained. "Everything around here seems to have its own place, and I wasn't sure where you wanted my stuff, so I set it in your room to make sure it was out of the way until I could ask."

That had her pausing, long and hard.

"Wow, uh, that was incredibly"—*thoughtful*—"observant." A complete one-eighty from the guy who used to simply leave his things wherever they landed.

"You don't need to sound so surprised. I may have gotten a bit caught up with all the hype back then, but I wasn't a complete asshat."

"I didn't say that."

"Yes, you did, and it was probably warranted." He didn't sound hurt, more accepting of the statement. "But I'll have you know, when I traded in my bachelor status for something more domestic, it was because I was done with life in the fast lane. In fact, when we're on tour, I usually opt for a condo over a hotel suite, so I can spend my downtime someplace grounding. Like a kitchen."

"I'm glad you found your big-boy pants, but I'm not sure your staying here is going to work." He hadn't even been there an hour and already her carefully crafted schedule had been abandoned.

"All I'm asking is for you to give this a chance," he said.

"This is my sanctuary, Hunter." She pressed her palm to her chest, noticing how fast her heart was racing. "The only place I have where I don't need Muttley to guide me, where I don't have to worry about tripping over someone's bag, and where I don't have to wonder if I remembered my pants."

"I understand how important your space is, Trouble." He took her hand between his much larger ones. "Just like I understand how much you are giving up by letting me stay here, which is why I will mind my p's and q's." He pressed her hand to his chest, and she could feel the steady beat of his heart when he whispered, "Scout's honor."

"You were never a scout." Mackenzie slipped her hand from between his, because it was impossible to think clearly while he was touching her. Reason enough to back out of this entire deal. "And minding your p's and q's means you sleep on the couch, your things sleep in the office closet, and your boots never sleep under my bed."

"Trouble, when we're not working, I'm going to be so stealth you won't even know I'm here." She could hear his victorious smile.

Hunter didn't have a stealthy bone in his body. In fact, the guy was so potent he could charm an entire stadium full of people with a single grin. There was no way she was getting through this unaffected.

Her disbelief must have been visible, because he chuckled. "I see I'm going to have to prove it to you."

Hunter led her to the table, and something about the strong, confident way he took her hand made her smile. A genuine smile that came from somewhere long forgotten and warmed her from the inside out.

"I'd like to be proven wrong."

This time he all-out laughed. "Trouble, if you were ever to get a tattoo, it would say, 'Told you so' in big bold letters. Right across your backside."

He had her there. As much as Mackenzie hated to admit it, she could come off as a know-it-all. But going blind had a way of changing one's perspective—on everything. Now it didn't matter so much if she was in the right . . . It was the consequences of being wrong that kept her awake at night.

Every situation, every encounter, was an exhausting game of sink or swim. And after three years of treading water, Mackenzie was too damn tired to argue about which direction land was.

"Maybe I've changed too," she offered quietly.

Hunter squatted beside her chair as if he was quietly studying her—something that usually caused her to shy away, but this moment called for honesty, so she let him look his fill. Let him see the discomfort his presence in her house caused, the embarrassment over the potato disaster, even allowed him a glimpse of just how incredibly lost she felt in her new world.

He'd come to her in search of that adventurous, take-no-prisoners spitfire from his past and found a struggling but determined songwriter whose inspiration came from long-ago memories.

"Then how about we start from the beginning," he said gently, taking her hand between his once again—and her heart pounded at the simple contact. Although a good part of the thump-thumps came from the thrill of what his offer would entail. "Hi, ma'am. I couldn't help but notice you sitting here all by your lonesome. I'm Hunter, and as fate would have it, I've got a batch of my aunt's famous corn bread in the oven and two of the best steaks you'll ever eat grilling outside."

"Those are some mighty big words."

"Only big if you don't have the goods to back it up," he said and—*oh boy, did he just turn up the broiler?* Suddenly she was feeling a little flushed.

"I also have some potatoes cooking in there as well."

"Potatoes and I aren't really getting along these days."

"Which is why they will be smashed, the way all unruly potatoes should be treated, with roasted garlic and a lot of butter," he teased, and just like that the embarrassment from the day evaporated. "And it would be a shame for even a bite of them to go to waste. So I was wondering if you would do me the honor of having dinner with me."

A shy smile made its way across her face, but Mackenzie let him see that too. "Is there honey butter to go with that corn bread?"

"Does Georgia grow the prettiest peaches?" His words were laced with a warm humor that brought her right back to how things used to be between them. Fun, easy, so incredibly right a lump formed in her throat.

"Well then, I'm Mackenzie," she said, that lump growing in size and intensity. "It's nice to meet you."

"The pleasure's mine." He gave her hand a gentle squeeze, which she felt all the way to her toes. "Now can I get you a beer to go with those steaks?"

"I tried that the other night and it didn't work out so well for me," she informed him. "I got a little tipsy, shared a few too many secrets, then passed out."

"Sweet tea, then," he said and stood, releasing her hand, and walked to the fridge. "What kind of assholes have you been hanging around? Plying a woman with liquor?" He gave a teasing whistle. "I hope the guy at least made sure you got home safely."

"Oh, he did." She pulled her feet up and hugged her arms around her knees. "But when I woke up the next morning, he was still here. Making himself right at home."

"Of all the dick moves!" Hunter sounded completely outraged, and she could almost picture him standing with his hands on his hips, shaking his head like he was all piss and vinegar, but his eyes would be full of laughter. "I mean, what kind of jerk makes sure the girl gets to bed safely, then sleeps on the couch with an attack dog eyeing his jewels all night?"

"Even worse, he didn't leave." Even though it was all a part of his game, flirting with Hunter felt good. "Then he tried to sneak his boots under my bed."

"Well, you won't have that problem with me, Miss Mackenzie. No, ma'am, I am a gentleman to the core."

"Good to know."

As if to prove the point, Hunter walked over and set a glass of sweet tea on the table, then placed his hands on her shoulders, pulling her back against his big, strong, I-can-shoulder-the-world chest. And when he spoke, the only contact they had was when his breath skated along her neck. "Because, Trouble, when my boots end up under your bed, there won't be any sneaking involved. It will be your call, your timing, and one hundred percent your decision. And that's a promise."

◆ ◆ ◆

"No, too Johnny Cash. I want more of a 'Jack and Diane' feel."

"The great Hunter Kane wants to record a ditty?" Mackenzie asked, stifling a yawn.

"A pretty lady once told me that just because the music is simple, it doesn't mean that the song can't be powerful," he said. "That song became my first number one."

It was also the first song they'd written together. Oh, they'd written several since that time, including a few over the past week, but none of them meant as much as the first.

Mackenzie laid the guitar down and rested her head against the sofa. Her fingers were sore from playing, her mind nearing creative meltdown, and her body ached from being locked in such close proximity for a week with a man who made her motor hum.

And her more delicate parts tingle.

True to his word, Hunter hadn't kissed her again. That didn't mean that he hadn't done his fair share of flirting and touching. And touching and flirting. Sometimes together, sometimes individually, but always potent enough to make her toes curl.

Today had been the worst. Hunter had started with breakfast in bed. Meaning he'd picked up chocolate doughnuts—her favorite—and eaten them while lying against her headboard. He'd just lounged there, sipping his fancy coffee, while Mackenzie figured out how to decently get to the bathroom without anything on but an old T-shirt and red undies.

He'd offered to help her get dressed, even volunteered to assist with lathering her up. Mackenzie had ignored him, shoving him off the bed and taking all the sheets with her. Hunter had chuckled, and her body had sizzled.

They'd worked through lunch and had supper in the studio, Hunter scooting in closer beside her as they worked on a song titled "Tangled Up." He grazed her thigh with his, his breath tickling her shoulder as the song grew—along with the tension—until she was certain she'd implode with a single touch.

"I think we should take a break," she said. And by "take a break" she specifically meant "get some space that doesn't smell of sexual frustration."

Not that Hunter got the memo.

Nope. Instead of backing down, he amped things up, taking her right hand in his. "And break the momentum?"

Yes. And maybe break the magnetic force that is drawing me to you.

"We can pick it up later." Only when Mackenzie went to stand, Hunter's fingers started a slow and delicious path up her arm to her shoulders to her neck, continuing to work his way back down. Her brain turned off and her body went tingly at the sensation of his ever-so-talented fingers strumming all the right chords until every girlie part she owned gave a breathy *oh my.*

She was entering dangerous territory. Her warning bells were blaring, *Get out before it's too late!* Her body was saying, *Enjoy the connection, what's the worst that can happen?*

And her heart? She didn't even want to acknowledge what *it* was saying, only that she was afraid it was already too late.

"We should call it a night," she said. Which was exactly what she was going to do—as soon as Hunter finished tinkering with the song's verse.

After all, his fingers were moving along her shoulders in rhythm to the song, and it would be rude to interrupt his creative process. So

Mackenzie closed her eyes and listened to the sound of his voice in her studio as he worked with the lyrics.

The melody led her mind to summers as a teenager. Inspired emotions and images, not from her own life but from the ones she had stored while watching other kids her age lift their wings. Cruising with your girlfriends, the windows low, Tim McGraw on high. Summers at the lake. Bonfires. First kisses on the tailgate of a green '55 Chevy. A feeling of floating freely through time.

She closed her eyes and a grin formed on her lips. "Like living every moment with no sense of time."

"Exactly," he said excitedly, his thumb tapping a steady beat against her palm. He hummed a few chords, then absently tapped, and the next line came to Mackenzie. The perfect words to match his melody, as if they'd been created simultaneously.

Man, was she ever in trouble. Mackenzie was in the fast lane to heartbreak ridge.

With Hunter, everything moved at a lightning speed. They'd written four songs in six days, and every moment together added to the sexual tension until it was electric. One spark and she was going to go up in flames.

Not ready to get burned, Mackenzie straightened and reached for her guitar. Placing the instrument and as much space as she could get between them without falling off the couch, she started playing the song from the beginning.

She worked her way to the chorus, and away from the fire, when something strong and heated moved closer.

"Hang on, go back and play that again," Hunter said. Without another word, he moved in behind her, eating up all that space she'd created. His hands slowly slid around her to rest on the guitar.

A little too close for comfort. Mackenzie tried to hand him the guitar. Instead of taking it, he scooted closer, not bothering to stop until he was completely up in her space. His body curled around hers until all she could smell was the smooth scent of leather and testosterone. Feel the heat of his body seeping through the cotton of her shirt.

"This feels right," Hunter whispered.

Sweet baby Jesus. It felt too right.

"Um, Hunter—"

"Don't move." Without even breaking his stride, Hunter moved so he cradled her body fully and rested the guitar on her hip. "I almost have it."

His fingers picked up pace—in perfect sync with her heart—and the song poured out of him.

Almost turned into a minute, then three, and then—*oh God*—the next thing Mackenzie knew, Hunter was fiddling to get it perfect, and she realized she didn't want to move.

Surrounded by a confident, yummy man was tempting. Being surrounded by Hunter while he was in the zone was a religious experience, one that she was sure would take her to the promised land. Every note pulled her further into his vortex of sexy, which made *her* feel sexy and feminine—and connected. Three things she'd never thought to feel again.

He'd found the heart of the song, raw and nostalgic and tender.

A few lines in and already a hit—she could tell.

Yup, Hunter Kane, the big badass musician, was back. His confidence and swagger were so mouthwateringly male she let herself imagine, for just a moment, what it would be like to have more than just his hands on her.

Suddenly, the music stopped, and Mackenzie felt the energy in the room shift—become more intimate and personal.

"You got it," she said, sounding ridiculously breathless.

"I think I finally did," he said. "In fact, if I got it any more right, you're going to have to amend your first rule."

"First rule?" she said through the sexual haze.

"No kissing, because I'm pretty sure we're one breath from contact," he said, and she was pretty sure he was smiling. "And even though we did share breakfast in bed this morning, I'm more of a second-date-kiss kind of guy."

Mackenzie straightened and pulled back. "This is work, not a date."

"Seems like you're working hard not to kiss me." He set the guitar down and leaned back on the sofa. "Don't get me wrong, I'm flattered, but that almost-kiss will have to wait until we're standing under the porch light and I'm walking you to the door."

"There was no almost-kiss."

"Sure there was, but don't worry, next time that almost will be a slam dunk, you have my word. In fact, I was thinking tomorrow night, you and me. I even know the perfect front porch."

"I know you're used to women who swoon when you wink, but you're going to have to try harder than that," she lied.

"To clarify, you're saying no to the date but yes to the kiss," he mused.

"Yes. I mean no."

"No need to get flustered. It's a simple question."

Simple, my ass. Hunter was the most complicated straightforward person she'd ever encountered. And this was the most complicated situation she'd been in since his rehearsal dinner.

"We're coworkers, and coworkers don't date," she rushed out, more for herself than him. "Last time I let it become about more than the music for me. I can't do that again. Not when I need to learn to stand on my own two feet."

"I'm not down on one knee." He sounded so sincere her heart pounded as if he were. "I'm just asking you to give this a chance to see where it goes."

"We both know exactly where this would lead." Mackenzie had been there, bought and buried the T-shirt.

"Why don't you explain it to me, just to make sure you and I are on the same page? I want a clear image," he said, suddenly in front of her. This time she was certain he was smiling. And it was his charming smile. The one with the double dimples she could never resist.

"*See where it goes* implies there's room for this to go somewhere," she said primly. "And there's not."

"Why is that?"

"My life is in these few square blocks. Yours is on the road." And if she wasn't careful, he'd take her heart with him when he left.

"Yet we always manage to find each other," he said.

She snorted. "Because we've never let it go too far. If we did, it would be over, just like that."

"Trouble, with me it goes on and on. And that's a promise."

Her nipples believed him. "When it comes to women, you burn hot and fast. And while I'm sure it would be an incredible night, it's not worth getting burned."

"Oh, I'm worth it," he whispered. "And let's be real, sex between us wouldn't just be hot, it would be a slow, scorching heat that would light you up from the inside out and last long into the next day."

She was afraid it would last forever.

"It's a work night, and we are on a tight timeline," she said, and as far as excuses went, it was about as lame as washing her hair, but she was desperate for an out.

"How about this weekend?" he asked, and she was tempted to say yes. How many times had she dreamed of the perfect date with the perfect man? "Wait, scratch that, I have plans."

"Is this the weekend you have to go to LA to meet with the label?" she asked.

"No. That's next weekend," he corrected. "And I thought you were going with me. They want to know how the album is progressing, and what better way than to bring along the talent behind the music."

"I'm sure your talent will be enough to fill the room," Mackenzie teased. "Plus, Muttley isn't air-travel confident yet." And neither was she.

"Which makes it the perfect trip to practice. I'll be there, so if anything—"

She rested a gentle hand on his cheek. "We're not there yet."

His jaw tensed beneath her touch, as if he had more to say on the subject but was holding back. His chest rose and fell, then a smile tugged at his mouth. "Well then, this is your lucky weekend. As I am spending two nights and three days in the countryside outside Nashville and am in need of a travel companion."

She rolled her eyes. "Of course you are."

"No planes or trains required. Just a simple yes, Trouble." He rested his hand over hers and her nipples perked up, giving her the A-OK to accept.

She laughed. "The yes might be simple, but the aftermath, I'm not so sure."

"Oh, did I forget to mention that this weekend comes with a two-foot-tall, live-in chaperone?" I promised to babysit Caroline so Brody and Savannah can have a little adult fun." He linked their fingers and slid her hand to his lips, pressing an openmouthed kiss to her palm. "And after the rugrat goes to bed, we can have our own adult fun."

She could hear the smile in his words; hers was ready to shatter. While three days of adult fun with Hunter away from the security of work was beyond tempting, it was also a colossally bad idea. Spending it with an adorable but unpredictable toddler was a disaster in the making.

She closed her eyes and reminded herself to breathe.

Hunter with his niece would absolutely melt her heart in so many ways she couldn't even comprehend. Hunter with his niece would also be an aching reminder of just how far apart their worlds actually were. Something that was easy to ignore when cocooned in the security of her house.

There was no doubt that Hunter was born to be a father. And she was equally as confident that parenthood was not in her future.

"Muttley and I meet with our sponsor on Saturdays." She pulled her hand back. "Plus, I need to get some things done around the house this weekend."

He was silent for a long while, and she could feel his scrutiny, as if trying to figure out if she was telling the truth. "Well, if you change your mind I can come get you."

"I won't." She untangled herself from his lap and stood. "How long will you be gone?"

"Why, Trouble? Are you going to miss me?" His tone was teasing, but she could feel his disappointment.

"I was just thinking through my weekend plans." And how, if she was going to fulfill her goal of hitting the market every day, she'd have to go it alone.

At least peaches are in season, she assured herself.

"It's a short trip." He stood too. "They leave Friday and get back Sunday night."

Three days seemed like an eternity to her—and that had her warning bells ringing. She'd made it three years without his help. So why did three days make the pit of her stomach churn?

Because you've gotten comfortable having him around.

And comfort was one step closer to dependence. Maybe this weekend would help her regain some much-needed perspective.

"Have fun," she said lightly. "As for the date, you're going to have to try harder than co-babysitting to sweet-talk your way into my bedroom."

"No sweet-talking necessary when it's the real deal. And this . . ." he said, reaching for her hand when she was about to walk away, "this is the real deal."

Oh, he was the real deal all right. So impressive that the air whooshed out of her lungs on first contact. Mackenzie had to cling to those biceps to remain upright, getting a hands-on inspection of each and every ripple and curve. The man redefined *chiseled*, and all that swagger somehow redefined where the line was. Moving it right past no-kissing and dangerously into sharing more than just personal space, making it easy for Mackenzie to get that much closer without actually crossing it.

"I'm going to prove it to you," he said, sculpting his hands around her sides, his fingers splaying low on her backside. "And, Trouble, when it comes to creative, I'm world-class, so be careful what you ask for."

CHAPTER 13

Hunter made it through a weekend of babysitting like uncle of the freaking year. He went back to being large and in charge, a guy totally on top of his game. Back to being *the Man*. Until he walked through Mackenzie's front door Sunday night and glimpsed her sitting in the sunroom eating a bowl of peaches and wearing the sweetest of smiles on her lips.

Jesus, those smiles. More of them appeared as the days went on, sometimes accompanied by comforting encouragement, other times with a gentle brush of her hand over his. Every time, though, they knocked him off balance.

So it was no surprise that by the time Thursday rolled around, Hunter was a complete goner.

Spending a week engaged in a never-ending battle of look-but-don't-touch with Mackenzie had only increased the tension between them. Not to mention the heat. Which was edging closer and closer to surface-of-the-fucking-sun, taking Hunter closer and closer to the point of no return.

Bottom line, Mackenzie slayed him. Mind, body, and soul—she had completely captivated him. He spent his days watching her spin words into magic and his evenings uncovering all the nuances that made her tick. In fact, the more he learned about Mackenzie, the harder it became to keep his distance. Even when he was sleeping, she consumed his thoughts.

Not that sleeping was an accurate description. Nope, with Mackenzie only two rooms away, lying in what he could only imagine were tangled sheets and some bright-colored lace, sleep was impossible.

Focusing was impossible. Hell, he'd spent his days distracted by her voice, her scent, intoxicated by the way she moved. Nights were no better, since he replayed that kiss of theirs until the taste was so real it lingered like a fine wine on his tongue.

Hunter was in a bad way.

Which was the only reason he didn't notice the set of serious fuck-me eyes aimed his way until it was too late.

And they weren't the warm, melt-your-soul variety he'd been hoping to see emerge from the community center. These were mascara-rimmed and intense—and headed his way.

Not wanting to engage with a fan right then, Hunter pulled his ball cap lower and rested his forearms on his thighs, pretending to be sending an email on his phone, when in reality he was playing Candy Crush.

The sun was nearly set. Mackenzie was about to come out from her meeting any minute, and he was anxious to hear how her class had gone.

When they'd arrived earlier, he'd planned on dropping her off and heading downtown to Big Daddy's, but she'd paused at the front door to the building, staring at it instead of going in. He'd offered to go in with her, or at least walk her to her classroom, but she'd given him a hard no, explaining that she didn't want his fame to cause a riot, then reminded him he was her driver—not her keeper.

He'd pointed out that it was a support group for the blind, so unless he started singing they should be fine, but she said his smugness was a dead giveaway, and blind or not, the other members would be distracted by him. No escort needed. She'd call him when she needed to be picked up.

Hunter had watched her swish that heart-shaped ass of hers before hopping back in his car and driving out of the parking lot, only to circle the block twice and go back to make sure she went inside the building. Then he'd turned off his car and waited patiently for her to call while doing his best not to attract any attention.

He'd failed at both.

His patience had vanished the second she'd disappeared into the brick building with the wheelchair ramp and motion-activated doors. The attention he'd attracted was from a tall, fiery redhead who was staring at him as if trying to figure out why he looked so familiar.

This kind of thing happened all the time. It was the downside to making it in his industry. A fan would spot him, ask for a selfie, then before he knew it he'd be surrounded by dozens of people all wanting something.

Normally, he was more than happy to visit, sign a few autographs, even pose for the camera. But since Mackenzie had looked close to calling it a night even before she'd exited his car, Hunter crouched down on the bench, tugging his ball cap lower.

Thankfully, the woman hadn't made the connection yet. In about two seconds, Mackenzie was going to exit the building, and he didn't want to give her another reason to close up on him.

He meant what he'd said about that all-night-long kiss under the porch lights. It had been a week of playing by her rules, and they were no closer to figuring out this thing between them.

Time for a different approach. One that included proving just how great things between them could be. The only thing he knew for sure was that she'd be hungry—and he was going to use that to his benefit.

Sure, there were some steaks in her fridge, but he wanted tonight to be special.

Going to support group had been a huge step out of her comfort zone, and he wanted to celebrate that. Over the past week, they'd gotten into a routine. Out of bed and in the studio by dawn, they'd work on the album until noon, then walk down to the grocery store and buy a couple of sandwiches and all the fixings for supper. After Mackenzie put another aisle to memory, they'd walk back home to her sunroom and share the sandwiches before hitting the studio for another few hours.

Supper would be in the kitchen. Last night, they had enjoyed Hunter's homemade chili while sitting on the back porch, which was a nice change. But tonight needed to be different. He was determined to get her away from the comfort of home in hopes they'd share other, more personal things.

Mackenzie liked talking about herself almost as much as she liked going out in public, so it would take some serious convincing on his part. But he'd already gotten over the biggest hurdle—getting her downtown. It wouldn't be that hard to get her to agree to supper at Big Daddy's. Once he got her to the bar and she reconnected with all her old friends, she'd remember how easy it could be.

"Excuse me," the redhead said, pulling up on a bike. Not the kind with a motor but the pedal kind. It was light blue, with a white basket attached to the front. Inside, riding shotgun, sat a pocket-size powder puff with wet black doggy eyes and paws bigger than his head.

Both driver and dog wore fitted pink tees that said BITCHES WITH A BITE, and while the dog was shoeless, the woman had on black boots—steel toed by the looks. She was an interesting combination of Dr. Dolittle meets GI Jane. "Are you Hunter?"

And here we go . . .

Adopting his best cover-of-*Rolling-Stone* grin, he stuck out his hand. "Yes, ma'am." When she just looked at it as if unsure he'd washed his hands after using the little boys' room, he flipped his ball cap around and said, "I bet you want an autograph or a picture."

Her eyes went wide and her cheeks pinked with nervousness. He'd seen it a million times. The woman was starstruck and needed some direction. Or in about three seconds, she was going to squeal and draw the attention of everyone in the area.

"A swift kick to the nuts sounds more my speed," she said, and wow, she wasn't giving him fuck-me eyes—she was sending him a clear fuck-off-and-die glare.

"Do I know you?"

"No, but that you had to ask reconfirms everything I've read about you." Hunter got the distinct feeling that she hadn't meant it as a compliment.

The dog barked several times, and that's when Hunter noticed his red "Dog in Training" vest. Combat Boots shushed him and then faced Hunter. "This is Puddles. He's trying to figure out playtime from work time still, so if you can ignore him when he asks for attention, that would be great."

"Is he yours?" he asked, wondering if she was in Mackenzie's support group.

"I'm training him," she said. "Now turn around."

When he didn't move, she gestured for him to get turning, and the dog went ballistic. With a gentle shush, the dog was staring up at his mistress, completely silent. Taking a cue from the dog, Hunter got out of the car and did a slow circle.

When he was done, she rolled her eyes. "Not bad, but I still think the best-buns title should have gone to that Captain America guy."

"Okay, show's over." He crossed his arms over his chest. He'd dealt with enough paparazzi to be wary of Santa himself. "Who are you?"

"Someone who cares for Mackenzie," she said, then hesitantly stuck out her hand. "Tia Flynn. I'm Mackenzie's sponsor. More important, I'm her friend."

He took her hand, noticing how fragile it was when compared to the big chip on her shoulder. "Sounds like we have something in common, then."

"That's what I'm counting on." She looked more hopeful than convinced. "She mentioned you guys were working on a project, and that you'd taken her to the store a few times."

"I've gone with her, yes," he said vaguely, and Puddles started barking so fiercely each low *yap* vibrated his little body.

Tia looked from the dog back to Hunter and gave the pup a good-job ruffle of the ears. "Puddles is an alert dog, trained to detect changes in body chemistry to signal an anxiety attack. He's also excellent at detecting bullshitters."

"Not bullshit, just cautious." Sponsor or not, Mackenzie was a private person, and it wasn't his place to share what she'd confided in him. If Mackenzie wanted Tia to know she was working on being more independent, Mackenzie could tell her.

"Huh," was all she said. "And did you drive her here?"

"Yup."

Tia studied him for a long moment, trying to get a read on him. Good thing for Hunter, he was used to people sniffing around in his business. So he upped that grin wattage and waited. Unlike most people, silence didn't bother him.

It didn't appear to bother Tia either, because instead of filling it, she used it to her advantage, taking the time to study him further, decide just how much she was willing to share. "Did she tell you why she needed the ride?"

"Yup. Did she tell *you*?"

"Yup."

It was clear the woman was as suspicious as he was and protective of Mackenzie. The way Hunter saw it, they could stand there all day and get nowhere, or they could help each other out and maybe gain deeper insight into what Mackenzie had gone through. She could fill in the gaps he'd missed out on.

"She said her usual ride was on vacation," he offered. See, he could be forthcoming.

"Arthur is on a fishing trip," Tia said. "Leaving Mackenzie to fend for herself."

"Not as long as I'm around."

"Great, a superhero complex as well." She rolled her eyes, then glared at him. Hard. "Did you know you're one of six visitors she's had since she left the hospital?"

"One of six?" Was she serious? Brody told him she'd lost her sight not long after he and Hadley had married.

She ticked off a finger. "Me. Her agent's family." She ticked off three more. "Arthur. And here's you." She wiggled the pointer finger on her free hand.

Hunter had a finger he wanted to wiggle at the universe. "I thought she got out of rehab a year ago."

Tia bit her lip, no doubt wondering just how much to share. "Eleven months, and transitioning back into the seeing world is difficult enough. And Mackenzie did nearly all of it on her own."

"She's stubborn." Hunter smiled.

Tia did not. "She's scared."

She was that too, but few people took the time to see past the tough exterior to the vulnerable woman beneath. Tia had, and that meant she could be an ally. And right then, he needed an ally.

"She's both," Hunter said, and Tia nodded.

"Which is why I'm going to ask you to stop helping her."

Scratch that. They were not on the same side. "She asked for my help, nothing will stop me from doing that."

He'd blown it the first time around, being so wrapped up in his own problems and plans that he hadn't noticed the signs that she was in trouble. He wasn't about to make that mistake again.

"I'm not saying don't support her, but there's a difference between helping and handicapping." She held up a hand when Hunter went to argue. "Transitioning into the seeing world is rough. Things that were as simple as routine become huge obstacles to overcome. It's not just adapting, it's reinventing your life, and Mackenzie's had a harder time than most. She's hit a wall and can't seem to get over it."

"She's gotten over worse and she'll get over this too. She just needs time," he said, knowing it was the truth. "Nothing will get in her way once she decides to go after something."

"If you're not careful, *you* will," she explained quietly. "It will be well intentioned, but if you give her an out, she'll take it."

A fact Hunter knew firsthand. It was how he'd lost her the first time around.

He'd known something serious was going on with Mackenzie leading up to his wedding, but when pressed, she'd only clam up tighter, and he'd let her. Had he taken the time to find out what was really going on, let her know she was a priority, things may have gone differently.

For both of them.

"What are you suggesting?"

"That you encourage her to entertain new experiences but stand back and let her fail."

"Mackenzie isn't big on change."

"I know," Tia said. "I don't think I've ever had a client so afraid to fail."

"Not around me." He laughed. "Hell, the woman is too busy pretending to have it all together to worry about failing."

"And when you're gone, how will she be then?"

If the sweat forming on his forehead wasn't an indicator of his increasing anxiety over what was to come when his time was up, then Puddles's yapping was.

In Mackenzie's experience, failing had dire consequences. And it was left up to her to push through the aftermath. But pushing forward was a part of her core makeup. However, taking care of others, was ingrained in Hunter's DNA. Which was going to make for one hell of a fun few weeks.

"Muttley was a hard dog to place because he has needs that go beyond a normal guide dog. If something doesn't change, Mackenzie might lose him. And that would crush her," Tia said.

Crushed was an understatement. Losing Muttley would be another loss in a list of many.

"I had no idea." He cupped the bill of his ball cap in his palm and resituated it. "This changes things." Because *this* was no longer just about the music or the two of them. If she was as distracted by him as he was by her, she might accidentally sacrifice her own needs and goals.

Even worse, Mackenzie was stubborn enough to lose it all rather than ask for help.

"I'll let her do things on her own, but I refuse to allow her to feel alone, and that means finding a way to get her excited about the change."

Tia gave him a genuine smile. "Maybe I had you pegged all wrong."

"What did you think?"

"That you were some narcissistic tater-dick who believes he knows what's best for everyone and everything, and is under the delusion that the world runs on his schedule." She shrugged. "Pretty much that you were a typical guy."

"I don't know what kind of assholes you've met—"

"Some pretty spectacular ones." Tia lifted a brow. "And even though Mackenzie says you're one of the nice ones, I've learned not to trust the nice-guy package."

"When it comes to Mackenzie, you can trust me." Even as he said it, his chest became uncomfortably tight—and the freaking lie detector went off again.

Yap yap yap.

Hunter had been honest when he said Tia could trust him. There wasn't much he wouldn't do to ensure Mackenzie's safety and happiness.

Suddenly, an overwhelming sense of uncertainty and helplessness slammed through him, twisting and churning until it created one hell of a complicated knot of emotions in his chest.

He could almost picture Hadley in front of him, shaking her head at his Superman complex. Reminding him that stunts like this were one of the main reasons their marriage hadn't worked.

Christ. The knot tightened until he could barely breathe.

Mackenzie had given an almost identical reason for why she'd kept her condition a secret in the first place. Yet he'd just planned an evening for her that she'd never willingly attend. After what was going to be a trying night.

Shit. It was as if he hadn't gotten a fucking clue over the past few years—the past few weeks.

He looked up at the universe and took a breath. *Got it. Message heard loud and clear.*

Hunter might have been slow on the uptake, but he was tuned in and listening now. First step: he needed a new plan.

"When it comes to Mackenzie, you can trust that I will annihilate you if you hurt her," she said, and just like that the dog stopped barking, highlighting just how serious Tia was.

Hunter was serious too. He was going to make sure no one ever hurt Mackenzie again—even Mackenzie. And especially not him.

All he needed was to find the perfect opportunity to get her to de-compartmentalize, expand her world, and prove to her that life could still be fun. And he would make sure that she could explore it on her terms. Not his.

He looked at Tia, a walking encyclopedia of solutions. "What's the next step in her therapy? And how can I be supportive and not suffocating?"

Tia smiled. "And here I thought men were all untrainable."

CHAPTER 14

Friday morning, Mackenzie found herself in the kitchen, listening to a YouTube tutorial on how to bake simple strawberry cupcakes with whipped-cream frosting in five easy steps. Cupcakes with whipped-cream frosting hadn't exactly been her goal when she'd awoken, but since it seemed less threatening than navigating downtown—or saying goodbye to Hunter when he'd left for the airport—she'd chosen the easy way out.

Yup, Cowardly Lion decision-making in full effect, she'd stuck to her not air-travel-qualified story—which suddenly seemed less terrifying than what would happen if she went to LA—then waited for Hunter to hop in the shower. The second she heard the water flick on she'd bolted for the nearest exit, under the guise of getting a jump on the homework she'd been assigned at support group.

Even more embarrassing, the focus of support group had been "Expanding Your World," which had highlighted the importance of stepping out of her comfort zone and venturing into situations that challenged her.

Mackenzie decided to take a literal approach, avoiding the emotional and going straight for a physical location. Except the only public places she felt comfortable going were Bark 'N' Bean and the market. Option one wouldn't work, because Tia would call her a cheater before she even entered the café. Which left the market.

Sure, she'd been there before, several times, in fact, with Hunter. But she'd never been down aisle five. So technically, it was a new place for her. Sneaking out the door to avoid a goodbye? Not so much.

In her defense, she had left a note. Placed it on top of his duffel bag, which had been sitting by the door, packed and ready for his trip.

So Mackenzie packed what she and Muttley would need for *their* trip and expanded their world by fifty-five feet of chips and salsa.

To ensure that she'd explored every inch of her newly expanded world—and to give Hunter enough time to depart for the airport—Mackenzie strolled through aisle five three times, even asking a passerby to help her add a few new chip flavors to her collection.

It was on her final lap when she remembered some of the outings the other patients in her support group were going to take. When compared to navigating an ATM solo or taking in a concert on Broadway Street, a trip down aisle five sounded particularly lame, so she added aisles six, seven, and eight to the adventure, even grabbing a box of cupcake mix in aisle nine.

Surely a fresh batch of homemade cupcakes would deflect attention from the fact that her idea of branching out had consisted of picking salt and vinegar chips over honey barbecue. She'd hit the dairy section on the way to the counter and grabbed a carton of heavy cream, because no self-respecting cupcake baker could forgo the frosting.

Her therapist stressed the importance of using family to help navigate the new world, but Mackenzie didn't have any family. And in a week Hunter would be gone. Not just for a meeting but for good. Which was why she'd decided to venture out alone. Well, that and the fact that she was terrible at goodbyes.

Only now she was home from the market, Hunter was well on his way to the airport, and she was regretting her decision. Note or not, sneaking out while he was in the shower hadn't been cool.

In fact, it was a move straight out of the old Mackenzie's handbook. She wasn't sure what a bold Mackenzie move would have been, but she imagined it would have involved a goodbye kiss.

"You blew that," she grumbled, adding some heavy cream to the blender. While it was too late for a kiss, she could still make his return trip special. Which was where the batch of homemade cupcakes came in.

A good portion of the cupcake batter didn't make it in the tray, but thankfully a dozen or so of the cupcakes were salvageable. Hunter's sweatshirt—the one he'd left behind and she'd slipped on, not because it smelled of him but because she was cold—was another story.

She added a teaspoon of vanilla and started the hand blender.

"Damn it!" Cold liquid splattered everywhere.

She turned the mixer off, wiping her face on the shoulder of the sweatshirt—the last clean space she could find. She didn't even want to ponder the current state of the kitchen. She'd have to call her cleaning lady to swing by before Monday.

Maybe for an extra twenty, she'd stop by the bakery on the way.

"Simple, my ass," she mumbled, setting the bowl aside. Muttley, who'd benefited from her earlier screwups, panted with anticipation.

Mackenzie was stuck on the last step: whipping the frosting. She'd carefully measured out the cream, vanilla, and sugar. Even used a chilled bowl. But instead of light and smooth whipped frosting, it came out more like melted ice cream.

"*Simple* isn't the *S* word I'd use when it comes to you," Hunter said from behind her.

His voice came from the doorway, but the scent of aftershave and damp skin filled the entire space from across the room. He smelled fresh, as if he'd just stepped out of the shower, and the sound of his bare feet moving across the floor made her heart flip. It also made her wonder what else of his was bare.

An image that created enough heat to melt the polar ice caps.

"More like *stubborn*." He moved closer, all that charm and easy swagger from yesterday gone. "*Sneaky,*" he whispered—and he was directly behind her. "As for your ass, *smackable* comes to mind."

Mackenzie dropped her hands over her butt. "Don't even think about it."

"I'm way past thinking." Coming up behind her, he placed his palms on the counter, effectively caging her in.

Oh my . . .

"Nice sweatshirt."

She tugged at the hem and played it cool. "I thought it was mine."

"Funny, me too."

She ignored that. "I thought you were on your way to the airport."

"My flight was delayed, and so I came out to tell you, but you were gone," he said, his breath whispering past her ear. "And so was my sweatshirt."

"I went to the market. And I left a note," she said, as if that was a sufficient answer.

"I found it," he said, and even though there wasn't any anger in his tone, she could detect a slight hint of disappointment. It was buried beneath his amusement and a gentle understanding that made her feel even worse.

Because had the roles been reversed and Mackenzie had come out of the shower to find an empty house and a two-sentence note, she would have been hurt. Especially after how close they'd grown over the past couple of weeks.

She turned to face him, only he didn't move, so she found herself sandwiched between the counter and his rippling chest. "Leaving a note was a pretty shitty move and I'm sorry."

"It *was* a shitty move," he agreed, flattening his palms on the counter to lean in even closer. "You want to tell me why?"

"Not really," she said, and he chuckled.

"Okay, well then, apology accepted."

She blinked. "Just like that?"

"You seemed to be as upset about my leaving for the weekend as I was about going," he said. "And while I would have rather talked it through, I get it. So yeah, just like that."

No argument, no demands. Hunter accepted what she could give in the moment and forgave the rest.

A small smile touched her lips. "You might want to hold out a little longer, there is a bribe part of the apology."

"I can see." He tugged at the bottom of the sweatshirt and let go—expelling a cloud of flour. "Did you have fun at the market?"

"I don't know about fun, but today was good practice," she said, doing her best to ignore the feel of his body surrounding hers. It didn't matter that he wasn't touching her. He was close enough that his heat seeped into her pores.

"Practice makes perfect," he said, not surprised one bit that she'd gone and lived to tell the story. And something about his confidence in her made her smile. "Now tell me about this bribe?"

"I'm making cupcakes," she said, as if it were something she did often.

"Need any help?"

"Nope, I'm almost done." She paused, her shoulders slumping at the lie. "Actually, you could come back Sunday and I'd be standing right here, still trying to figure out how to make whipped-cream frosting. I'd just have more sugar on my apron."

He leaned past her and stuck his finger in the bowl, then licked it off. "Tastes good to me. What's the problem?"

"It's supposed to be light and fluffy. I whipped the first batch too long and it came out like butter. The second time I turned the blender on high and it went everywhere." She pointed to the disaster on the front of his sweatshirt.

He gave a low whistle. "Impressive."

"I know. Now it's just a runny mess." She sighed. "The video says beat until it looks like stiff white peaks, but since I can't see what it looks like, I don't know when to stop. I don't want to stick my hand in when the beaters are going, so I can't test it without stopping the blender. And all the pausing lets the bowl get too warm. For all I know I'm using buttermilk instead of whipping cream."

She set the mixer down and dropped her head to his chest. "Maybe we should just eat the cupcake."

As if knowing exactly what she needed, Hunter pulled her into him. "Trouble, there is no point of cake without frosting."

"Says the man whose life exists in the frosting."

"If only I could find the right cupcake," he whispered. "Now what can I do to help?"

"You can make the frosting," she said and gave him a bat of the lashes.

"Tempting. But I think we can be more creative than that." A moment later, she felt his finger brush her lips. "Taste."

When she didn't open, he ran his finger along her lower lip, waiting for her to lick it off. "That taste like buttermilk to you?"

"No." It tasted like foreplay, and suddenly all she could think about was that all-night-long kiss he'd promised but never delivered on. "It still doesn't solve the consistency problem."

"One thing at a time," he teased. "All we need is a pro to tell us how long to set the timer."

"The video said to do it by sight," she explained. "So why don't you just tell me when it's ready?"

"You've got everything you need right here," Hunter said, pressing forward, his hands slowly working their way around her waist, his nose burying itself in her hair, and it felt like a solution she could get on board with.

In fact, this was an adventure she was more than ready to take. Sex with Hunter would be more exciting than cupcakes, frosting, and a trip around the world. Talk about expanding her horizons.

"What are you doing?" she whispered.

He whispered back, low and sexy in her ear. "Looking for something. Be patient."

She didn't do patience. Even better, she had a map she could give him that would lead to all her somethings. But his fingers seemed to have internal GPS, because they were on a direct path to her big something and Mackenzie held her breath. They slid lower and lower, until—

"Found it."

Mackenzie wanted to argue that "it" was a few inches lower and dead center, but his fingers were back on the move, headed north, away from the promised land, and—he grabbed her cell.

Then—*poof*—his fingers were gone. Leaving nothing but a wave of quivers and need in their wake. "What are you doing?"

"Being supportive," he said, sounding way too amused. "Now stand still. I needed your phone to download this new app. It's still in the beta phase, but it is supposed to replace all the apps you have in one convenient, voice-activated bundle.

"Just tell me what you want it to call you." He snapped his fingers. "Oh, I know: Sweater Cupcakes."

"Sweater Cupcakes?" she asked.

"First thing that popped into my head." More fiddling, and then he spoke slowly. "How long does it take to whip cream?"

A computer-generated voice filled the room. "Here is what I found, Sweater Cupcakes. It will take approximately four minutes to whip cream using a hand mixer, ten minutes using a whisk."

"That's incredible," she said, taking her phone.

"It's a search engine that will convert any text to speech, and if you take a photo of an object, it will tell you what it is. You just have to push the center button on your cell. Like this."

The camera-phone shutter sounded, followed by, "Lucerne heavy whipping cream. Half gallon."

"It will also tell you the difference between a yellow peach and a white peach, so you don't have to rely on the produce guy to know where things are," he said. "All you have to do is take a photo of the sign in the bin and it will read it to you."

He pushed the button again, and her phone recited the brand and flavor of cake mix.

A warm zing flittered through her body over his thoughtfulness.

"Wow," she said, completely touched. "Where did you find this?"

"I know a guy."

"You know a guy who told you about it? Or you know a guy who built it?"

"I know a guy," was all he said, as if what he'd done was nothing more than make a phone call. "I was testing out some of the tools for the visually impaired. Some are okay, but most of them sucked, so I asked a buddy for help. He says this has every function you'll ever want. It can tell the difference between a five-dollar bill and a hundred, gets up-to-the-minute bus routes, and can even tell you when your bus is arriving."

"Hunter, this is . . ." She trailed off, the emotion too thick to continue.

"Useful?" he asked, sounding hopeful. "I looked at the apps you had and figured this could be more useful. I say give it a shot. If you don't like it, no biggie, we can just try something else."

"It's perfect," she said, beyond moved.

One of the many reasons she'd fallen in love with Hunter was the way he cared for the people in his life. He had a compassionate and nurturing way about him that always left her in awe. It was what made him such a great musician—and friend. But this, this brought on all kinds of crazy feels.

Feels that made her heart roll over and show its soft underside.

"Thank you."

"You're welcome," he whispered. Taking her finger, he gently wiped it off on a towel, then rested it over the button. "Go ahead. Press here and then set a four-minute timer."

Mackenzie did, and Hunter handed her the mixer, guiding her hand to the bowl. He didn't do it for her, but he didn't walk away either. Just stood behind her, a strong, supportive force at her back.

Four minutes and a few emotional swallows later, she had white peaks in her bowl. It wasn't as stiff as she wanted, but it was fluffy enough to top her cupcakes.

"I did it," she said, bouncing on her toes with excitement. She turned around and slid her arms around Hunter. "I made whipped cream!"

He held her for a moment before pulling back. "I never had any doubt."

"I did!" She dipped the tip of her finger into the bowl and licked it off. "But now I have frosting, which after my first few attempts seemed impossible. I didn't lose a finger or destroy the kitchen, and . . . taste?"

She reached in again and held it out for Hunter to try.

He gave a small groan of male appreciation, his mouth covering her finger.

Gently—and oh so thoroughly—he sucked until there was nothing left but the sensation of his tongue on her skin. He didn't stop there. Oh no, Hunter lifted her hand to his lips, the light scruff rubbing her palm as he kissed each and every fingertip until they were clean and throbbing—and her legs had turned to melted ice cream.

"Perfectly sweet," he said against her palm.

"So are you," she whispered, desperately wishing she could see his face. "Today was turning out to be a complete disaster, but you managed to save the day and make it fun."

"It wasn't a disaster."

"It was about to be, then you showed me that app, and . . ." She held up her finger.

"You made the cupcakes and the frosting. I just provided some technical support at the end."

"You provided more than that, Hunter." She smiled a big goofy grin. "Thank you."

"Any time, Trouble," he said, his voice a low timbre.

"You were right," she began slowly. "I left this morning without telling you because I didn't want you to leave."

"You don't owe me an explanation," he said softly.

"But I do," she admitted. "Only when I grabbed Muttley's harness to leave, I hesitated because suddenly I felt as if I *needed* you to go too. And that scared me, almost as much as how much I was going to miss you this weekend, so I went to the market to prove to myself that I could do it alone."

"And you did, and I am beyond impressed at the courage it took, but being independent and being alone are two very different things." She went to comment on that, when he added, "Just like I'm understanding the difference between being responsible for someone and being responsible to them."

"And what's that?" she asked, having a hard time hearing anything over the pounding of her heart.

Mackenzie had spent most of her adult life securely stuck in the first category and wasn't convinced she could ever live in the second. People either protected her or pitied her. There were very few who believed in her enough to push her. Her heart ached to hear where Hunter fell on that scale.

"One comes from a place of ego. The other a place of respect," he said, gently brushing his knuckles against the back of her hand. "I have so many people depending on me to make things happen, I forgot what it felt like to just let things happen."

"Oh, Hunter," she said, for the first time seeing things from his perspective.

"I didn't want to go with you because I think you need me to hold your hand," he admitted. "But because I want you to want to hold mine."

She was moved by the idea that this big, badass guy who carried the financial futures of more than a hundred families was looking for support. From her. Even if it was just to hold his hand.

He'd helped her with her project. Maybe there was still time to help him with his before he left for the weekend.

"When do you leave for the airport?" she asked, wiping her hands on her apron.

"I don't," he said, and Mackenzie's stomach took flight. "I bumped it until Tuesday."

"You bumped it?" she asked. "Why did you do that?"

"I wanted to," he said. "It gives me more time to prepare for the meeting, and it gives me more time with you. This way they can come to me, which they are. They're flying up to meet us Monday."

"They're coming here?" she asked, wondering how he'd pulled that off. The label put so many travel demands on Hunter he'd spent most of the beginning of his career commuting among LA, Nashville, and New York. It had gotten so bad he ended up with a car and apartment in all three cities.

"I told them I couldn't travel to them, so they're traveling to us. Don't look so surprised." He laughed. "My life is more flexible than you think. In fact, unless we're on tour, I'm in Nashville most of the year."

She gently turned her body to face him. "If I had known you were going to stay the weekend, I wouldn't have snuck out."

"If we're being honest," he said, scooting closer, "sure, I bumped it so we had time to hammer out the last song, but my ego bumped it because it was under the delusion that you'd need my help."

"On the whole honesty thing"—she reached out to touch his arm—"I stole your sweatshirt because it smells like you."

His nose nudged her neck. "Now it smells like vanilla. And you."

"Since you don't have a flight to catch, do you want to help me?" she asked, toying with his fingers.

"Trouble, are you asking me to frost your cupcakes?"

"What if I am?"

"Which cupcakes are we talking about?"

Warm flutters filled her belly, the rest of her body humming with desire over the possibility of what the night could bring. Mackenzie had always been a star student, and she was about to ace this assignment.

"Depends on how good you are with your hands," she said, placing hers on his pecs.

"It's not my hands you need to be watchful of." Something soft brushed over her lips and down her bare neck. "It's my mouth that gets me in trouble."

"A little trouble can be fun."

"When it comes to trouble, I want all of you," he said against her skin, replacing his lips with something soft and voluminous. "Which is why I got these."

Curious, she turned his hand over and found what felt like two movie tickets, only longer. She brought them to her nose, grimacing at the metallic smell. "What are they?"

Hunter feathered them over her lips. "Tickets to Keller Auditorium for Tuesday night."

"That's opening night for the Philharmonic." She held them against her chest, to keep it from exploding. "They're doing a tribute to John Williams and it's been sold out for months."

Not that she had considered going, but she'd been tempted. The chance to hear his scores played by an orchestra would have been hard to pass up.

"Yup." He rocked back on his heels, his voice all smiles. "Tia told me your homework included venturing into the unknown."

Mackenzie froze. "You talked to Tia?"

"More like she talked at me," he said. "Wanted to point out that my car didn't count as public transportation."

"Yeah, well, public transportation is scary," she said sternly.

"So is Tia," he said, and Mackenzie wondered what else they'd talked about.

"She'll be happy to know that I visited aisle five," she said, and, yup, it sounded lame.

"Aisle five? Impressive—we hadn't hit that aisle yet," he said, not an ounce of mockery in his tone. Just a deep sense of understanding that shook her to the core. "But I think the assignment had to do with something a little more challenging than potato chips and salsa."

"I whizzed through the frozen section, didn't even run into a single display door. That takes skill."

"Then the concert should be a breeze."

She thought about the suffocating amount of perfume and sardined bodies she'd have to push through. The deafening sounds of thousands of people conversing at once. "Or a disaster."

"Nope, when it comes to music, you are in your zone," he said so confidently she began to believe him. "The setting might be a little bigger than your sunroom, but the music will distract you from the surroundings and create an environment where you'll feel comfortable enough to try new things."

"You really thought this through," she said, stunned. Not at the thoughtfulness behind the surprise—Hunter was one of the most thoughtful people she knew—but at the time he'd spent, planning an evening that would push her as much as it would soothe her nerves.

"I called a buddy of mine who manages the hall."

"Schermerhorn Symphony Center is more than a hall, and on opening night it will be more like Disneyland for music aficionados," she said. "Muttley would get trampled." And she would have a panic attack. In fact, she was pretty sure she felt one coming on.

He linked his hand with hers, then rested them against his chest, right over the steady beat of his heart. "We'll enter through the VIP entrance. And the second we get to the box seats, it will feel like a cozy night at home with you, me, Muttley, and the Philharmonic."

The Philharmonic.

One of her bucket-list items she'd given up on ever crossing off. But Hunter was giving her the chance to experience it. All she had to do was say yes.

"What if someone recognizes you or we get separated?" she asked, scooting closer.

Hunter lifted her hand to his face. A soft and sculpted beard replaced his usual scruff. It was rugged and sophisticated—and damn sexy. "I don't think anyone would recognize me like this."

"I would," she said, running her fingers over his jaw, his lashes fluttering shut beneath her touch. She'd never been into beards, but she was into Hunter—and he made it hot.

"Because you're you," he said quietly. "And I want your first big fun activity to reflect that."

"I may need you to hold my hand," she admitted—sliding her fingers through the hair at the back of his neck and going up on her toes until their lips were lined up. All it would take was one of them to breathe too hard and they'd be kissing.

A sensory activity she could get behind.

"Only if you hold mine back," he murmured.

"A little hard to do, since they're holding my bottom."

He gave a squeeze and she smiled. "Are you trying to kiss me, Trouble? Because I already told you, I'm a front-porch kind of guy."

"Why don't we discuss that while you frost my cupcakes?" she said, sticking her finger in the frosting and trailing it across her lips. "I'll supply the whipped cream."

CHAPTER 15

This was going to be the best fucking tasting of his life.

Mackenzie was standing there in his sweatshirt, covered in flour, and looking like a sexy cupcake begging to be licked, so his brain was having a hard time figuring out if this was harmless flirting—which he hoped to God it wasn't—or if he'd just won the lady lottery.

Then she'd gone all seductive baker on him, offering a new and tempting option on tonight's menu, and he sent up a silent thank-you to the universe. Because what she was offering broke rule one and, he was pretty sure, obliterated rule two, making him the luckiest SOB on the planet.

The heat from the oven hung thick in the air, adding to the hot ball of fire already raging. Nothing between them but fabric, a few inches, and frosting made for a whole hell of a lot of chemistry. Because it was a lip full of frosting, right there for the taking. And he wanted to be the guy to take it, he really did, but beneath the sexy offer of hers lay a hint of uncertainty that had him pausing.

Mackenzie had made it more than clear that when this was over, they'd go back to their separate lives. It was no secret she'd been stuck in a revolving door of disappointment, and he refused to be another person who let her down.

Blowing this wasn't an option. If they went there—neither was walking away.

"Be sure, Mackenzie, because this is a game changer. Once this happens, there's no going back." He gave her a moment to weigh the outcome. A moment to make sure this was really what she wanted.

Because he knew what *he* wanted. And it was more than one night.

Hunter had taken the past few weeks to slowly uncover the many different shades of Mackenzie, and he wouldn't stop until he'd uncovered them all. Which could take a lifetime. Something he was okay with.

In fact, he preferred it.

Mackenzie wasn't a burn-hot-and-fast kind of woman. Nope, she was beautifully complex, an intoxicating mix of sweetness and fire meant to be savored. And he wanted to be the guy lucky enough to experience each and every nuance of Mackenzie. The new, the old, and everything in between.

"I've spent most of my life looking back. When I'm with you, all I want to do is move forward." Threading her fingers in his hair, she gave him a taste of what was to come. And if her tongue in his mouth wasn't a clear affirmation of just how far tonight was going to take them, then the way her body shrink-wrapped to his sure was.

Proving to her that she wasn't in this alone, Hunter did his part, eating off every inch of frosting, going back for a second pass just to be sure. And when her head tilted back, he trailed little kisses down her throat, tugging at the collar of the sweatshirt to get a hint of the creamy cleavage he'd been dreaming about.

Christ, she looked good in his shirt.

Feels even better, he thought as he walked her backward and up against the counter. Soft and curvy and so fucking perfect his hands shook as he molded them over her body. She didn't seem to mind, since those talented fingers of hers were doing a little molding of their own.

Down his chest to his abs, carefully exploring his stomach before dipping under the hem of his shirt. Her warm skin on his sent one hell of a thrill through his body that settled right behind his button fly.

"I want to feel you," she said, her hands tugging at his shirt.

Always the gentleman, Hunter gave her what she wanted. Scooping her up, he sat her spectacularly stubborn and sexy ass right there on the counter, then pressed himself between her legs. Making sure she felt all of him.

Front and center.

"I meant lose the shirt, but that works too," she said with a sweet smile.

"You're right," he said. "Where are my manners? Shirt first. *That* second." Hunter eased his thumbs under the hem of her sweatshirt and slowly tugged it up, his thumbs reaching the underside of her breasts when she stopped him.

"*Your* shirt," she clarified.

"Sorry, where I come from, it's always ladies first." With a final tug, it was over her head and on the floor and—*a-fucking-men*—what a sight.

There weren't enough words in the dictionary to accurately describe the view. In fact, he was pretty sure it qualified as the eighth wonder of the world. Her pink lace showed just enough peaks and valleys to officially blow his mind.

"Well, where I come from, it's ladies' choice," she whispered and gave his shirt a hard tug. "Lose the clothes, Hunter."

"Lucky for you I'm a compromising man." He yanked his shirt off with one hand as the other went for the frosting. "How about ladies' choice *and* ladies first?"

"I've always had a secret love of duets," she admitted.

"Well then, it seems we're perfectly matched." And man, that sounded good. "With so many interesting options, what do you choose first? Here?" His finger, thoroughly frosted, traced her lower lip. Next came the valley between those perfect tens. "Or here?"

Mackenzie let loose a surprised but sexy little moan that drove him crazy, so he decided to take a little detour and frost one pink-laced peak, then the other, loving how ragged her breathing became with each stroke.

"And don't forget, we also have here." He painted a sugary trail down her stomach, watching her muscles contract and ripple as the frosting disappeared beneath the waistband of her shorts. "What will it be, Trouble?"

"Most songwriters would start from the top. But I find it more creative when you start from the hook and work your way backward." She rested her palms behind her on the counter. "Hook me, Hunter."

"Who am I to argue with a lady?" Hands back on her ass, he slid her forward to the edge of the counter until her cupcakes were eye level, puckered, and frosted for his tasting pleasure.

"It's hotter down south," she said, even as her breath caught.

"You said the hook, not the climax. And trust me, you're about to be hooked."

Hunter considered himself a man of action who always delivered on his promises, so when he pulled her into his mouth, he took extra care in teasing and licking off the frosting, making sure he didn't miss even a drop before giving her nipple a gentle bite.

"So hooked." She sighed, her hands tracing his face, his jaw, his shoulders. Everywhere they could reach. They never stopped exploring, even as her head fell back, giving him an all-access pass to explore, which, of course, he took.

His mouth moved down into the valley, where he noticed a few spots that he couldn't reach.

"I'm a big fan of pink lace," he whispered against her skin. "But this has to go."

"Don't worry," she assured him as she unlatched her bra and slid it down her arms. "There's more." And that's when the show part of show-and-tell started.

And what a show it was.

Mackenzie undid the top button of her shorts and lowered the zipper, just enough so that—

"Holy Christ," he breathed. Because there, beneath her cutoffs, was the ninth wonder of the world: the teeniest, tiniest pink thong ever created. Powerful enough to render a man speechless and sexy enough to stop his heart.

"I did warn you that it was hotter down there."

"The temperature is about to climb, Trouble." Hunter placed her hands on his face, letting her trace his jaw as he trailed long, hot kisses along her rib cage and across her belly button. Her fingers shook, and her stomach quivered the farther south he ventured.

When he got to the lace edging of her panties, the frosting ran out, but Hunter didn't stop, because why the hell would he? This close to heaven? There was no way.

Not that it mattered because, when he pressed an openmouthed kiss right beneath the waistband, her skin was sweeter than any frosting or dessert he'd ever tasted. To be sure, he sank to his knees while pressing her legs wider, desperate to get a better taste—right in the middle of her cotton shorts.

Her body came off the counter, and Hunter's breath caught at the pressure against the back of his fly.

"So sweet," he groaned, making a second pass. And Mackenzie, always the helper, pressed up into him, giving him a taste that rocked his world. By the third, he slowly slid her shorts down her legs, leaving her in nothing but the thong—which he tugged to the side and—

"There," she moaned. "I choose there!"

He seconded that motion. Deciding he could stay right fucking there all night. It was like the sweet spot of a song, where he'd fall into the pocket and never want to leave. She clung to him as if she was on board with that idea, so Hunter settled in for the long haul.

He used his tongue, his teeth, playing her body until she was gasping his name. Until her body climbed so high it vibrated. She drew tighter and tighter, until he felt her clench. Felt her body go from fire, to molten lava, to nuclear-fucking-explosion.

"Now for that climax we talked about," he said right before he took the entire thing from the top again, adding more pressure and giving her so much heat that her body melted back on the counter.

Panties now on the floor, he pressed her legs farther apart with his broad shoulders and frosted her up the center. She gasped at the sensation of cold on slick heat, then moaned low and long as his tongue soothed her. Over and over again, steadily making his way home.

He slid one finger inside, loving how her legs squeezed him as if to hold him there. Like he was going anywhere.

Her hips pressed forward to deepen the friction, so he added a second finger, slowly and deliberately driving her right to the edge. All she needed was the perfect stroke, and she was going to fly apart.

He wanted to savor her all night but knew she was holding on by a thread. So was he.

With one well-placed kiss, he had her shuddering, and then came the stroke, right over her swollen, wet flesh, and she exploded. Just like he knew she would. Her release was so forceful he felt it radiate through his own body, until it shredded what was left of his control.

Mackenzie seemed to be in the same boat, because even as she was vibrating with aftershocks, her hands were on his jeans, unbuttoning and yanking.

"I want *that*," she said, and he had just enough time to grab the condom from his back pocket before she freed him and sent his jeans around his ankles.

Getting the condom on was a little more difficult, since Mackenzie insisted on lending her hand to the cause. Only she was doing more touching than helping, and Hunter's eyes rolled to the back of his head.

Her hands made a path from base to tip and back again, curving around him and exploring with a gentle curiosity that slayed him.

"Slow down, Trouble," he said. "This is still ladies' choice."

"Good, because I want to see all of you."

Placing his hand on hers, he stilled her movement. "You're going to see us right through to the finish line at that pace. And I want to finish with you around me."

"Like this?" she asked, wrapping her legs around his waist.

"Good choice," he groaned, covering himself and sliding home in one desperate stroke.

She gasped. He didn't move. Just stood there, holding on tightly and welcoming the feeling of finally being inside her, being with her. Drinking in the sight of her.

Head thrown back, those long curls of hers spilling around her bare body and flirting with his forearms. But it was her expression that got to him. Full of warmth and wonder, not resignation.

This, he thought. This right here was the Mackenzie he remembered.

Free, passionate, so bright with life she shone. And so incredibly in the moment, her body wrapped around his, squeezing tighter and tighter until he was sure he'd suffocate.

What a hell of a way to go.

"If it's my choice," she whispered against his neck, "I choose you."

◆ ◆ ◆

The silence after Mackenzie's announcement was so thick she was afraid to breathe.

Maybe because Hunter had sucked in a breath big enough to deplete the room of oxygen at her confession. It was as if those three little words had leveled the moment. As if she'd said the other three little words instead. And she was afraid that if she let it settle too long, the night would be ruined. But if she loosened her hold, it would all slip away.

And she'd start crying.

She hadn't meant for it to come out. But she'd never been chosen. Had gone her entire life choosing people who were unable to really choose her back, to put her needs first. Not that they wouldn't, but they couldn't.

Her solution had been to go it alone.

That was before she'd understood how powerful she could feel with someone by her side. Giving as much as they took.

Hunter was an easy choice. He was genuine and brave and had this amazing capacity to love.

Mackenzie was a harder choice. She understood that. So it was okay if he didn't choose her back.

At least that's what she told herself. Because while making this work for the long term would require sacrifice on both sides, Hunter would be the one who'd sacrifice the most. Which was why she decided to pretend, for the moment, that it would work—that they worked—and fell heart first into his embrace.

Only she didn't crash. Hunter was right there, holding her tightly. His strong arms came around to cradle her to him as he took her mouth in a kiss that was as sweet as it was drugging. Slow and languid and tender, one fading into the next.

The franticness from earlier was replaced by a warm confidence that moved between them, connecting them in a way that was breathtaking.

He slid one palm up her side, cradling the back of her head. The other drifted south to caress her butt, rocking her toward him, against him, until she felt full and complete—as if she'd finally found what she'd been missing.

She didn't know how else to explain it. The hollowness inside warmed and spilled over, filling her in a way that was healing. It was the way he touched her, she decided, the way he held her as if she were enough.

"You feel perfect," he breathed against her mouth.

And just like that, Mackenzie fell. Fast and completely. The truthfulness in his words shook her entire being, and *oh boy*, this didn't feel like pretend anymore.

Nope, his kisses were so achingly gentle she felt delicate, feminine, and utterly adored. They melted Mackenzie's heart as he pressed them slowly down her neck to her shoulder until the past three years fell away, and Mackenzie had no choice but to let go of the what-ifs and open herself up to the possibility of more. A feeling she had missed, and now that she'd found it again, she desperately wanted to cling to it with everything that she had.

Afraid she really was going to cry—or admit something even more embarrassing, like she still loved him—Mackenzie focused on the pleasure. Gave herself over to the slow withdrawals and even slower thrusts. Loved that he couldn't be rushed. That he wanted her to enjoy every moment and wanted to enjoy the moment with her.

"Mackenzie." He whispered her name as if to start a confession she wasn't sure she wanted to hear. Not right then. So she silenced him with her mouth.

Cupping his face, letting the soft stubble of his beard slide through her fingers, she poured everything she felt but was afraid to say into that kiss. He got on board immediately, cupping her butt and lifting her up, only to slide her back down the length of him.

"So good," she said at the sensation.

"I was aiming for fucking perfect," he corrected, lifting her and letting her fall back down. Only this time he rose to meet her and . . . perfect indeed.

"Again," she begged, tightening her arms around his neck.

Always the overachiever, Hunter did it several times, and the combination of the friction and pressure had them both groaning in pleasure. Before long, their bodies were slick with heat, sliding against each other, ramping up the anticipation of what was to come until she thought she'd die from the pleasure.

"There," she moaned. "Right there!"

And there they went, finding their perfect rhythm. So in tune with each other, it pushed her up, and up, and up.

And ladies' choice was now her first choice because the anticipation didn't even come close to preparing her for the sensation that followed, rocking her world and sending her over the edge into a Hunter-induced explosion of bliss.

Hunter continued to pump, sending more little tremors through her. Continued to harden inside her until he followed her over with an explosion of his own, his entire body shaking around hers as he reached his release.

"God, Trouble," he groaned, his head arching back before coming to rest on her shoulder.

Her body wrapped limply around his. Both breathing hard, they held on until she felt the cool spring air roll over her heated skin, leaving goose bumps.

He lifted his head and kissed her forehead. "You okay?"

"Yeah," she said with a goofy grin on her face.

"Then you want to repeat what you said back there?" he asked, and her smile vanished.

"It's not polite to ask a lady what she says in bed," Mackenzie said, letting go and sliding to the floor.

"Good thing we aren't in bed." He took her hands, preventing her escape. "And I wasn't talking about your dirty talk, although the 'God, Hunter' part was pretty hot and will play in my head for years to come. I was more interested in what you chose."

She remained silent, and he lifted her hand to kiss the inside of her wrist. "No going back, remember?"

Oh, she remembered. And now that she wasn't in a lust-driven state, she didn't know what she'd been thinking.

"I'm pretty sure you said you choose me."

"I can't remember, I wasn't thinking clearly." Had she been, she never would have admitted that. Not to the guy who needed to be everyone's personal hero.

"Well, I hope you're listening clearly," he said, placing her hands on his face, encouraging her to feel. Instead of the shocked horror she expected, he wore a genuine smile that gave life to the bead of hope she'd buried deep inside. "Because I choose you back, Mackenzie Hart. Freely and willingly, I choose us."

CHAPTER 16

It's damn good to be Hunter Kane these days, he thought with a goofy-as-shit grin plastered to his face.

It had been more than twenty-four hours since he'd last helped Mackenzie, twenty-four hours since he'd kissed her as he headed out to meet with the label, and he could still taste her on his lips. He'd been so punch-drunk he'd had a hard time focusing on the negotiations at hand.

"Un-fucking-believable," Paul said, enough hero worship in his tone that he had Brody rolling his eyes. "They walked in here ready to dump our asses, and in one conversation, you convinced them to send us on a world tour."

It had taken more than one conversation. In fact, the negotiations had begun early the previous morning in Brody's office and lasted well into the night. Hunter had undergone a long succession of tedious meetings, beginning with the tour sponsors and ending with Lionel Drake, the head of the label.

The sponsors had anted up enough dough to add additional cities to the Hunter Kane Band's upcoming tour. More important, Lionel was on board with the band's new direction. It had taken a lot of convincing on Hunter's part, but the second Lionel had heard the new tracks, the man had been sold.

The problem with labels was that it was a hurry-up-and-wait kind of relationship—where the label refused to do any of the waiting. They'd taken their sweet-ass time finalizing the tour schedule, using it as leverage to get Hunter into the studio. Now the label was finally on board and wanted the band to sign off on the dates before Lionel went back to LA the next morning.

Which was how Hunter found himself at Big Daddy's during Tini Tuesday, sitting in a booth with his band and staring down a round of *man*tinis. They'd specifically ordered a round of Lone Star, but since it was also guest-bartender night and Brody's talented wife was in charge of the shakers, Brody accepted the round with a stupid-ass grin. The fucker.

Otherwise, Hunter would already be back at Mackenzie's, helping her get ready for their date tonight. He'd seen the black strapless number hanging on the front of the closet when he left the previous morning, and he couldn't wait to help her into it—then help her out of it. It was the single image that had kept him focused throughout all the posturing and positioning.

But if they didn't speed things along, there wouldn't be any show before the show. And Hunter enjoyed a little pre-party almost as much as he enjoyed an encore.

"A tour this size is a good sign that the label is finally ready to put the money behind us that we'll need to hit the next level," Quinn said, rubbing his fingers together in the universal sign for *Show me the Benjamins*.

"It's also a huge commitment," Brody pointed out.

"Jesus, man. You sound like my ex-girlfriend," Quinn said. "I haven't even lowered the zipper, and already you're talking about commitments."

"Because signing on that line is as binding as a paternity test, so I want to make sure you're all aware of what you're agreeing to," Brody added.

"Are you shitting us?" Quinn asked, then looked at Hunter. "He's shitting us, right?"

"I have no idea what he's doing, but I think we should order him another princess drink." Hunter held a hand up to flag down the bartender.

Brody held up a hand of his own. Only his was sporting a single finger. "I'm not saying don't sign it. This is a huge opportunity. But it comes with a shit ton of appearances, most of them back-to-back."

"It's also a shit ton of money," Quinn said. "We are signing the biggest deal of our career. What is there to think through?"

"Seventy-two cities, nine countries, and eleven months. That's already triple the dates of your last tour," Brody said to the group, but his eyes were focused on Hunter. "Then tack on the additional travel for the overseas shows, the radio tour for the album, and don't forget the press tour."

"If we want to stick to the timeline for the next album, we need to go all-in on this tour," Quinn stated. "Dragging out the dates will only cut into the studio time."

Jesus! They hadn't even recorded *this* album, and already he was feeling the pressure to deliver big on the next.

"Exactly my point. Working nonstop doesn't give the downtime needed to start thinking about the next album." Brody addressed Quinn, but his eyes met Hunter's. A squirrelly feeling settled in Hunter's chest just thinking of exactly what that kind of scheduling would entail. "We're talking months at a time on the road, away from home. From people who count on you."

Hunter knew how hard it was to make a relationship work when living in different time zones. At first the hype of the tour overshadows the time apart. But eventually the adrenaline wears off, the long nights and missed phone calls get old, and that's when everything starts to unravel.

He'd been torn when Hadley hadn't wanted to start a family. Looking back, she'd been smart not to want to bring kids into that.

And now Hunter had Mackenzie to think about. He knew that this thing between them was strong. But it was also new.

Hunter looked at Paul. "He has a point. Have you thought about how Bethany will feel with you being away from home for long stretches like that? You've got one kid and one on the way."

Paul and Quinn looked at him as if he'd grown a third testicle.

"Are you kidding? Bethany has been waiting for this moment as long as we have," Paul said. "Will it be different? Sure, probably even difficult. Which is why we talked about the possibility of her joining us on the road when we started trying to get pregnant again." Paul gave a casual wave, which was in direct opposition to how Hunter was suddenly feeling. "We hoped it would happen when the kids were small, so the timing couldn't be more perfect."

The dreamer in Hunter, who had been working toward this moment for more than a decade, couldn't have agreed more. Unfortunately, the realist in him wasn't so sure. His marriage hadn't been able to withstand a four-month tour with only nineteen shows. Mackenzie had said she was all-in, but that didn't include eleven months apart just when things were heating up.

Shit.

"What about Libby?" he asked Quinn.

Quinn sipped his girlie drink. "Libby will be on board with whatever. She telecommutes, so joining me for a few weeks at a time won't be a problem with her boss. Plus, we're talking about a world fucking tour." He high-fived Paul.

Two seconds ago, Hunter had been ready to join in on that high five. Hell, he would have raised it with a round for the entire bar. It would have been an all-night-long, caution-to-the-wind kind of celebration that would require a taxi ride home and two days to sleep off the hangover.

Only the satisfaction that should have come with the gold-plated icing on this cake of a deal, playing sold-out stadiums and securing their spot in the spotlight, eluded him. And damn if that didn't leave him confused.

"A world fucking tour doesn't require any thinking, it requires action," Quinn added.

"It also requires a real round," Paul said, standing and heading to the bar. Quinn followed.

Brody waited until the two were gone before he spoke. But when he did, his expression was an annoying combination of all-business and brother-knows-best. "What about you? Have you thought about what this will mean?"

Hunter sat back. "Which part are you talking about? The extra exposure that bands dream of? Or checking off one of my biggest career goals? Or how the hell I'm going to make this work with Mackenzie?"

"All of it," Brody said quietly. "Have you considered that you would be putting yourself in the same position you were in with the last album? This kind of schedule doesn't leave a whole lot of time for anything else. I just don't want you to come back to find the rest of your life a disaster."

Like last time.

Hunter remembered the empty house he'd come home to, the paralyzing guilt he'd carried from failing at the two things his father had botched: family and love. Not to mention that while Hunter had been nursing his wounds and throwing the pity party of the century, he'd nearly cost the band their future. It took him months after Hadley to process what had happened. A year before he could even begin to piece things back together.

That was a place Hunter never wanted to revisit.

"I won't let that happen again," he vowed. "I know I put everyone in a bad situation. You, the label, the band. But it all worked out. I mean, our ass was to the fire, but we pulled through."

"For the record, *we* didn't pull through. Mackenzie did." Brody went from serious to shit-just-got-real. "And without her, we wouldn't be here toasting to our future successes. How does Mackenzie feel about you being gone for eleven months on the road?"

"I'm not sure if she could do the full eleven months, but we'll work it out," he said, wondering who he was trying to convince. Hell, he hadn't even been able to get her to come with him to the bar tonight.

"You're not sure she could do the whole eleven months?" Brody repeated, his eyes wide in disbelief. "You're actually considering asking her to come on the road with the band?"

"I don't know, man. I just signed the contract and haven't had the chance to tell her."

"Yeah, well, maybe you should have talked to her before telling the guys you're all good with the plan, even though it's clear you aren't."

"This tour is great for the band, and I'm not going to screw this up for everyone because I can't figure out my personal life. After the show tonight I'll talk with Mackenzie, and I'm sure we'll find a way to make it work. Because that's what people who respect each other do," he said, feeling all kinds of mature man in a mature relationship. "They talk it through."

"And just how will that talk go?" When Hunter didn't answer, Brody shook his head. "Mackenzie will hear 'world tour' and put her needs behind yours. Which will leave her with two options: let you go or suffer through a revolving door of venues and hotel rooms, each with different obstacles and a different floor plan."

And each with a different aisle five. Frustration began to build, along with something a hell of a lot scarier: uncertainty that, in doing the right thing, he'd somehow screwed everything up.

"I hear you, man. I didn't say I had a solution. I just said I know that between her and me, we can figure one out." They had to, because this was too important to screw up. "I need to call her," Hunter said, fishing his cell from his pocket. He dialed Mackenzie, and the second her voice came through the earpiece, he found himself smiling. It was that big, stupid-ass grin again. "Hey."

"Hey," Mackenzie said, her voice shy and sexy as hell. "How did the meeting go?"

Hunter looked at Brody, and Brody was looking back—as concerned and overwhelmed as Hunter felt.

"Amazing." He excused himself from the table and walked toward Cash's office before saying, "What are you wearing? Part of me is hoping you're in that black number I saw hanging in the closet. The other part is praying you're in nothing but lace and those sexy little house boots you always strut around in."

There was a long, tense silence, followed by a breathy little giggle that had him prepared for a little world domination of his own. *Her* world, to be exact.

"Have I told you how much I've come to love those boots?" he asked.

They were pink suede with pink fur around the calf and little rhinestones on the cuff. More crazy cat lady than sex kitten, but on Mackenzie he found them, oddly, a turn-on. It was what she wore when they were home and relaxed. What she let him remove when she felt safe.

He heard her clear her throat through the phone, and he rested a shoulder against the wall. "You're wearing the boots, aren't you?"

"Yes," she said, a strain in her voice he couldn't decipher. "And I'm sitting at the kitchen table with your cousin, who says he's here to pick me up for the symphony."

Hunter closed his eyes and took a deep breath. "Which one?"

"The good-looking one," a familiar male voice said in the distance, and Hunter could almost hear Wade's smug-ass grin. "And before you go asking me what *I* have on beneath *my* outfit, you should know you're on speakerphone."

Ah, Christ.

Wade might be four years younger and wear loafers and a suit to bed, but once he grabbed hold of a story, he was like a toddler with a Binky—a good thing, since he made his living ferreting out potential problems. Tonight, however, the only problem Wade was supposed to solve was how Hunter was going to get two adults and a full-size dog to the symphony. Which was why Hunter had asked to trade his pickup truck for Wade's sedan.

"I told you to call when you were on your way."

"I did call. Three times," Wade said. "Then I was afraid I was beginning to sound desperate."

Hunter looked at his phone and, yup, three missed calls. "So you arrive an hour early? Don't you know it's rude to show up on a lady's doorstep unannounced?"

"What I know is a lady this beautiful deserves to arrive before the second act starts. And since the address you gave me is on the wrong side of a ten-car pileup, and I have supper at six thirty, I decided to be proactive and have a car service meet me here. That way you get the car, and I keep everything moving smooth and easy."

"They have a pill for that."

"For being considerate?"

"No, for confusing on time with uptight."

"And yet I'm the one sharing a drink with the pretty lady."

Wade had a point. Hunter glanced out the front window of the bar, toward the east side of town. A steady drizzle had already turned the streets slick, and he could see a solid line of red lights in the distance. "Where's the accident?"

"That would be between your *man*tini and here," Wade said.

Hunter rolled his eyes. "Brody told you?"

"Cash posted a picture on Instagram. It shows you in one of those white undershirts you are always mistaking for outerwear, sipping from a dainty glass."

"It already has twenty thousand likes," Mackenzie added, ever so sweetly.

"The little 'Nothing says celebration like a Big Daddy's *man*tini' talk bubble over your head really makes the meme," Wade pointed out. "In fact, people are lining up to throw back a celebratory tini with the famous front man of the Hunter Kane Band."

Hunter looked around the bar and swore. It had gone to standing room only thanks to a sea of fans toting pink drinks and album covers. He looked at his watch and swore again.

He was going to kill Cash. Slowly and painfully.

There was zero chance of his going across town to pick up Mackenzie and arriving back in time for the show. Which meant that Wade was right.

Closing his eyes, he said, "Mackenzie, I am so sorry. I don't think I have time to get to you and then get us back on this side of the city with traffic."

"That's okay," she said, but he could hear the disappointment in her voice. "We can go another time."

Hell no. Tonight was a big step for Mackenzie in proving her independence. And a big night for Hunter to prove their lives could work together. He just wasn't sure who he was so set on convincing anymore.

"I'm not canceling. We are switching gears, which is why I always have a plan B." Then to Wade, he said, "How long would it take to get Mackenzie to Schermerhorn Symphony Center?"

"If I avoid Vanderbilt, probably a half an hour. Maybe a little less. But I have dinner plans at six-thirty."

"Tell her you have a meeting with your boss and will be a little late," Hunter said. "That always works."

"Not when you're meeting with your boss."

"Shit."

"Seriously, it's not a big deal," Mackenzie said quietly, so much understanding in her tone it broke Hunter's heart.

"Her dress says differently, man," Wade said, and it sounded as if there was a struggle for the phone. Clearly Wade won, because when the muffled fight ceased, the phone was no longer on speaker, and Wade was on the line. "We're talking red silk and tiny straps. Definitely not a reschedule type of dress."

Mackenzie wasn't a reschedule type of woman. She was the kind of woman you dropped everything for, a fact he somehow had overlooked the first time around—and would never miss again.

"I have no intention of rescheduling." This was nothing more than a simple problem with a simple solution, one that all couples face, and one he could easily resolve. So Mackenzie couldn't just jump in the car and meet him at the venue. So what? That just meant they'd have to get creative. And if there was one thing Hunter loved, it was getting creative with Mackenzie. "Could you drive your boss and have the company car take Mackenzie and Muttley to the venue?"

"The driver is a total tool. Says he's hired to drive the CEO and only the CEO. So unless you want Walter Chapple to join you on this date, it's a no go," Wade said.

"Tell him I'll pay him under the table. Give him front-row seats and VIP passes to my next concert. Even hire a driver for him and his lady friend. Whatever floats his boat."

Wade breathed heavily into the phone, and Hunter could hear him considering his options. And the only reason his cousin wasn't telling him to go fuck himself was because Mackenzie was in the room, arguing that it wasn't a big deal. That she was tired anyway and could use a quiet night at home.

"Come on, man. I need this."

"It will cost you," Wade said quietly into the phone. Then in a loud voice for all to hear, he added, "Mike always likes an early night and he'd be waiting on the mayor until midnight. I don't see a problem."

"Thank you, Wade." It would take Hunter twenty minutes, tops. Which gave him enough time to stop by his tailor and change into something more appropriate for a date night with the perfect woman.

"I'm sorry, I didn't catch that," Wade said with a grin so loud Hunter's head throbbed. "Was that a thank-you?"

Hunter snorted. "I said 'Fuck you,' but I can see how you'd mistake the two."

"Are you sure? It sounded more like a 'Thank you for being such a forward thinker, Wade. Nobody is as great as you.' But I couldn't be positive."

"Nobody likes a smart-ass," Hunter said, then explained the exact location for the driver to meet him. It was the entrance the talent used, which Hunter had asked the venue's security for access to ahead of time. He wasn't worried about Mackenzie and Muttley making it through the mash of symphony goers. He was worried about being stopped for an autograph—or ten.

Tonight was about him and Mackenzie, a normal couple simply going for a relaxing night on the town. Their talk about the future could wait.

"I'll have her there by six," Wade said.

"Great, I'll meet her there." He disconnected, and even before he turned around, he knew Brody was behind him. The loud huffing gave him away.

"Please tell me that wasn't a hired car," Brody said.

"No," Hunter said. "That was Wade. And before you go lecturing me, I got it handled."

Brody gave an amused laugh. "The fact that you can say that and not break out into a sweat tells me you have no idea how close to drowning you are." Brody leaned against the doorjamb, ankles crossed, *man*tini in his hand. "Just do me a favor—when you realize you're drowning, don't pull Mackenzie under with you."

"When did you become such a Debbie Downer?" Hunter asked. "No wonder it took you a decade to win over Savannah."

"It took me as long as it did because I wasn't ready to be the man Savannah deserved." Brody pushed off the wall, not stopping until he was in Hunter's face—and Hunter could see the whites of his eyes. "Are you ready to be that kind of man, Hunter?"

"I'm not the one drinking a fucking mantini."

"Exactly. I'm drinking this mantini because my wife made it for me. And, even though it tastes like pineapple and ass, I'm going to go order another because it makes my wife smile. That's what people in love do, Hunter. They put the other person's happiness first." Brody downed it in one sip. "Mackenzie needs stability, not a last-minute plan B."

"Plan B is often better than plan A," Hunter argued.

"Yeah, but you can move from plan B to plan C, D, E, and F all before lunch," Brody said. "And if you hadn't been so busy figuring out the next plan, you'd realize that Mackenzie likes to know what's coming, since she can't see it. She can't wake up and hop on a plane like Savannah can and meet us on the road. And you won't always have someone sitting around to pick her up when plan A goes to shit. If you're late to meet her at the airport, she can't just hail a cab." Brody took a breath. "The other option is for her to sit back and wait another year for you. And you can't ask her to do that."

The truth of the statement was like an arrow through his chest. "I can't let her go."

"Holding on isn't the same as letting go," Brody said.

Hunter knew that, just like he *knew* seeing Mackenzie a day or two a month wasn't an option. He wanted more time with her. Lots of time. Time that didn't have an expiration date. This past weekend had cemented that.

Brody was right about one thing. Mackenzie needed a steady place in Hunter's life. And it was up to Hunter to figure out how to make that happen.

CHAPTER 17

If the past few weeks had taught Mackenzie anything, it was that taking on one Kane was difficult.

Taking on two? *Heck no!*

The sheer amount of charm and testosterone one Kane could put off was enough to send a girl's head spinning. Or maybe that was anxiety she felt at the thought of two Kanes in her house.

Everything had changed so quickly, Mackenzie hadn't had a chance to catch her breath.

Which was the only reason she could come up with for why she'd agreed to this ridiculous situation. One minute she was adamant that Wade didn't need to change his dinner plans. The next, she was sliding into a waiting town car and being whisked down the interstate as if she were the queen of England.

If Hunter hadn't sounded so excited about how his meeting had gone, she wouldn't have agreed to the arrangement. But she was certain the label had loved the new direction, and she didn't want her nerves to ruin Hunter's big night.

Yet she couldn't control the growing uncertainty.

"I guess this is how the elite roll, Muttley," Mackenzie said, her voice disappearing into the vastness of the back seat.

Maybe that was the problem. Apart from Muttley, who had his butt on the leather seat and his face pressed to the window, Mackenzie had the entire back of the car all to herself. The driver, Mike, had even closed the privacy window.

Mike had been uneasy about the whole situation. She'd sensed it in the way his body tensed as he'd cupped her elbow to help her into the car. Then again in his tone when he'd asked if someone else would be accompanying her.

Mackenzie wasn't sure if the disappointment stemmed from her plus-one having four paws and the potential for drooling on the leather seats. Or if he was afraid his fare might need something he was incapable of providing. But Mike's rush to get her out of his hair made Mackenzie's stomach clench.

She was used to Arthur, who was a Titans fan and dog lover and drove an ancient El Camino. With Arthur, they'd chat about music, his brother, and what kind of fish was biting that day. He didn't care if Muttley got fur on the upholstery or that Mackenzie was blind.

Mike was young, too formal, and—like most guys—terrified of feeling inept. When she'd asked if she could sit in the front seat, the driver had been so flustered she'd laughed it off and graciously let him place her and Muttley in the back.

Hunter intended for her to arrive relaxed and pampered, but the whole ordeal had left her feeling vulnerable. She resisted the urge to call and cancel. She'd effectively canceled the past few years of her life, and she was determined to finally start living again.

"Rule number one," she mumbled to herself. "Life is unpredictable."

Things happen, plans change, but big girls keep on moving. Today, Mackenzie was a big girl. She even had on the panties to prove it.

The car slowed as the privacy window whirred down. "We're here, ma'am. Just hold tight for a second and I'll come around with an umbrella, so you arrive dry."

"Thank you," she said and took Muttley's harness. As promised, Mike came around and opened her door. "Is Hunter here?"

"I don't see him, but he might be waiting inside. It's really coming down." He took her elbow and assisted her out.

Rain splattered at her feet as they walked up on the curb. Three steps in and Muttley pressed firmly against her side, not guiding her forward but corralling her back.

"Nope, we're not going back in the car," she said.

A whine started low in Muttley's throat.

"Then stand under the umbrella."

Muttley wasn't having any of it. Not only did he step farther out from under the umbrella, but he tugged Mackenzie with him. Then barked, as if telling her that he was the one giving the directions today.

Muttley gave another bark. This one was loud and threatening and sent a wave of unease rolling down Mackenzie's spine. Before she could calm her dog, chaos exploded around her.

An army of shoes slapped against the wet surface, and a loud clicking surrounded her from all directions. Muttley sounded off, his barks echoing through the alley.

"What's your name?" a forceful voice shouted from her right.

"What is your relationship to Hunter Kane?" This question came from someone standing directly in front of her.

"Mike?" Mackenzie spun around to reach for her driver's arm.

He was gone.

"Is it true the Hunter Kane Band signed a twenty-million-dollar deal for their world tour?"

"I don't know," she said.

"Is Hunter inside the car?" A camera clicked behind her. "Hunter, are you in there?"

One after another, the questions fired. The voices got louder, became more forceful, and multiplied. An intense energy pressed closer, the heat of bodies surrounded her, making it difficult to navigate her surroundings—figure a way out.

Muttley pressed his body aggressively against her legs in a *Let's blow this joint, Mom* move.

Mackenzie wanted to leave, fast, but she was turned around. Didn't know which way the car was. Or where her driver had disappeared to. Or if the car was even still there.

"Mike?" She called out to him again, but she couldn't hear anything over the shouting. Or maybe it was the pounding of her heart, so loud and erratic she put her hand to her chest to keep it from bursting.

The smell of wet asphalt and hot breath made her stomach churn, and a dark wave of panic wrapped around her, making it hard to breathe. Out of habit, she widened her eyes over and over, praying that if she got them wide enough she'd suddenly be able to see again.

All that greeted her was blackness. And fear.

It was like she was back in the hospital, opening her eyes for the first time only to realize that darkness was her new reality.

"Back up," she demanded, putting an arm in front of her and swinging her purse at the reporters. "I need some space."

And air. God, she needed air. But the only thing she could seem to get was little bursts of oxygen.

Muttley's bark turned to low, guttural growls, as if he sensed her panic.

"It's okay, boy," she whispered, but it wasn't okay. Not by a long shot. Something Muttley was picking up on.

Circling her body protectively, he put himself between her and the press.

This was why she avoided crowded places. The unpredictability of it all was terrifying. There she was, stuck in the middle of a mob, unable to see what was happening or sense what was headed her way. Unable to soothe her dog.

This—right here—was her biggest nightmare.

"Back off! You're scaring my dog," she yelled and turned her head to aim it at the loudest voice. A hard object collided with her cheek. Bright lights flashed behind her eyelids, followed by an acute ache that wrapped its way around her.

Mackenzie gasped, and her handbag crashed to the ground. Muttley yanked on his harness, lunging toward and snarling at the reporters.

"Jesus," a male reporter yelled, followed by the sound of a camera crashing to the ground. "He nearly bit my hand off!"

"Only because you were shoving it in his face!" she yelled.

"You need to control him," he said, and Muttley let out another bark. She didn't have to see to know the reporter had leaped back.

Mackenzie was torn between praising Muttley and crying when camera shutters fired in rapid succession, no doubt getting a shot of Muttley foaming at the mouth and baring his teeth. She could already hear the headlines: KANE'S NEW WOMAN: AS RABID AS HER DOG.

Even worse, she could anticipate exactly what the guide dog foundation would do when they saw the pictures. And they would see them. Nothing said front-page gossip quite like a celebrity's crazy girlfriend assaulting the paparazzi with her attack dog.

"I should sue," the man said.

"Randy, if anyone has a complaint, it would be the lady you're harassing," a strong and commanding voice said from behind them.

Hunter.

Mackenzie's panic turned to relief as she felt all the energy turn from her to Hunter.

"Every judge in this town knows you have an issue with personal space," Hunter said and slid his arm around Mackenzie's waist. "Now give us some room or *I* will be pressing charges."

"This is public property," Randy argued, but his point was lost beneath the swell of questions coming Hunter's way.

He fired off "No comment" as fast as the questions came. With a final "good night" to the reporters, he guided her through the crowd and toward safety.

"Can he sue me?" Mackenzie asked, her voice shaking.

"I'll buy him a new camera and he'll be fine," Hunter said, leading her into a stairwell. The door shut behind them, drowning out the noise.

"How can you be sure?"

"Because he's done this kind of thing before. He's a known trespasser. No judge will side with him," he assured her. But Mackenzie didn't feel sure—about anything.

"Muttley will look like a vicious dog. I don't even want to know what the foundation will do if they hear about this."

"Hey." Hunter cupped her face. "They won't take Muttley away. I promise."

Mackenzie's chest caught on those last two words. They were two simple words. But when strung together, and delivered with so much conviction, it only stirred up doubt. A town car full of doubt.

"You can't make a promise like that," Mackenzie whispered, placing her hands over his.

"Why not?"

"Because you have no control over what happens to Muttley."

Or me.

"All I meant was that everything will work out," he said, bringing her hands to his lips.

Her heart slowed down until everything felt painfully surreal, the events of the day lying in direct contrast to the last three weeks.

Only the last three weeks had been nothing but the two of them, locked away in a protective bubble. Creating a false sense of safety. A fantasy that could never survive in Hunter's reality.

"How did they know you were coming?" she asked.

"I think the driver tipped them off." His voice shook too. But not from fear. Oh no, Hunter was pissed.

"Why would he do that?" she asked.

Hunter blew out a breath. "Money, to feel important, for a story to tell his buddies. Who knows."

If his answer was meant to reassure her, it did the opposite.

"That's the problem." She dropped her hands and took a step back. "*I* need to know. I need to know who and why, and if it will happen again. I mean, will that photographer come to my house? You said he's a notorious trespasser. Muttley is still learning his role, figuring out what his limits are. What if he actually bites him?"

"I can't tell you that," he said, taking her hands again. "But I can tell you that the driver won't have a job come tomorrow, and if Randy even tries to come near you, he'll have to deal with me."

"Which would only lead to more bad press. For you," she pointed out. "And what about when you're on this big world tour? What will happen then?"

As the silence built, so did the pressure in her throat until she was certain it would suffocate her. This wasn't a one-time situation. This would be an everyday thing.

"Who told you about the tour?"

"One of the reporters asked me about it. I didn't know what to say, because I didn't know about the deal."

"I was going to talk to you about it tonight."

"What is there to talk about?" she asked. "This is a huge opportunity for you and the band," she forced herself to say.

"It is. And I wanted to talk to you about joining me on the road," he said gently, and intense longing mixed with the harsh reality to create one complicated ball of emotion in her chest.

"You want me to go with you?" she asked, unsure why she felt like crying.

She'd waited her entire adult life to hear those words. From this man. Only, like their evening, things happened and plans changed. And Mackenzie's big-girl plan had included helping Hunter so she could find closure and move on with her life. Then a new door had been opened, and Mackenzie wasn't sure she had panties big enough to walk through it.

"You'll be working," she pointed out. "Late nights, long days, and I have my work. Which happens here. In Nashville."

"Your clients are everywhere. You can work from anywhere. And we can make this work," he said with an unwavering conviction that had Mackenzie wondering if they could.

But she knew better. Knew firsthand what it felt like to be trapped by someone else's limitations, and she refused to be that kind of burden.

So yeah, while that kind of conviction felt unbreakable in the moment, it would be their downfall in the end.

"I am so proud of you, and I know the tour will be everything you dreamed of. But . . ." Mackenzie slid her hands away. "I'm barely ready to navigate my own little suburbia of nine square blocks, let alone stadiums around the world."

"Then we find someone to be your tour guide," he said.

Everything inside Mackenzie stilled. "You mean like a keeper?"

"No, Trouble." His voice was soft. "More like an assistant."

"An assistant to get me from point A to point B without getting harassed? Or lost?" she clarified, knowing that, one, the interview would include questions on experience with special-needs clients. And, two, the first step toward freedom was admitting one's limitations. "Will they shop for me, drive me around, keep my hotel room picked up?"

"That's not what I meant." Hunter blew out a deep breath. "At least I'm looking for a solution to blend our worlds. You're looking for a way out."

"No, Hunter." For the first time, she was looking past her independence, past the fear, past the obstacles, and toward a future. A happy and free future.

She desperately wanted to believe they could be that for each other. That regardless of what happened or where life took them, if they were together, they could make it work. Or at least make each other's worlds fuller.

Mackenzie let out a shuddery breath. She'd been here before. Hopeful. Delusional. And so desperately in love it hurt.

"I'm looking at eleven months on the road. And the tour after that. And all the amazing things coming your way," she whispered. "But if I say yes and go with you, all of that will change. For both of us."

"It doesn't have to," he said gently, brushing away a stray drop of rainwater from her cheek with his thumb.

She closed her eyes and absorbed the feel of his skin on hers. Gave herself over to the sensation, memorized it, then resigned herself to what she had to do.

Following her heart meant giving up her freedom. And asking Hunter to give up his. Because if she said yes, she'd be placed in a situation where she'd be relying on him to be her connection to the outside world. That was a lot of pressure for any relationship, let alone one that was just beginning.

Swallowing hard, she steeled her voice. "But it will, Hunter. No matter what you believe now or how hard we try, our worlds won't ever blend. Yours will completely absorb mine."

At her words, Hunter didn't move, didn't even breathe. She could sense the frustration and anger rolling off him. Frustration at the situation, but the anger? She was pretty sure that was directed at her. And the longer he remained silent, the harder it became to hold the tears back.

"I call bullshit," he finally said. "A few years ago, sure, I would've accepted that. Would have even agreed that, yeah, in the past I lost track of what was important and didn't pull my head out of my ass until it was too late. But I'm not that guy anymore. Not with you," he said flatly. "Never with you."

"I know. That's my fear."

"My putting you first shouldn't scare you, Trouble." He gently cupped her hip, drawing her closer.

Darn it, if that didn't bring the first round of tears, then the conviction behind his words did. And as the first drop spilled over her lashes, she knew she'd never come back from this moment. Not in one whole piece anyway.

"It should scare you too, because eventually I'd end up doing the same, until our relationship was so full of compromises someone would end up losing," she said, her voice wobbling. "I knew the day we met you could never really be mine, not without a huge sacrifice on your part. For this to work, it would mean more than simple changes. For both of us."

"Changes we can get through together," he whispered, his voice as raw as her heart felt.

"That's just it," she pleaded as a familiar sense of despair rushed over him. "You don't need me to go onstage and sing. Just like you don't need me to write music or go on tour. You have everything you need in here." She rested a hand on his chest and realized she was shaking. "But for this to work, I'll need you."

"By *this* you're not talking about the tour anymore, are you?"

Even though she couldn't see the disappointment in his eyes, she didn't have a hard time imagining it.

"Jesus." Hunter dropped his hand and took a step back. "So what, we finish out our last twenty-four hours, then go back to how things were?"

"That's what we agreed on," she said. "You help me, I help you, and then we go back to our separate lives. Keep it simple. That was the promise."

"I don't give a shit about simple, I care about you, about making this work. So it might get complicated? So what? If life were simple, it'd be boring," he said, and she ignored the misery in his plea, because she was drowning in her own.

"Don't you get it? My world is simple. It has to be." She wiped angrily at her cheek. "Boring is a delicacy. I would kill for boring. For the day when I can go to the store, cook supper, and maybe catch a movie and have it be so boring I don't break out into a sweat. But that's going to take me time. The kind of time that will consume another person's life. I've lived that life, Hunter. I don't want that for you."

His voice went soft, so soft she felt her chest hollow out. "Have you ever considered what I want?"

"Hunter—"

"No." He cut her off. "You're so busy protecting this amazing life you think I have you've never once asked me what I want. Because if you had, I'd tell you that I want *you*, Mackenzie. I want you in my arms, my bed, in my life. Every fucking day." He reached up, his fingertips skimming her cheek as he cupped her face, catching a tear with his thumb. "How is that for simple?"

Nothing about her life or this situation was simple. She knew that, and there was nothing she could do to change it. "Love is never simple."

His voice softened, along with his touch. "No, it's not. I've also learned that it's not enough. But I've also learned that it's a good place to start." Hunter tilted her gaze toward his. "So the only question you need to be asking yourself is what do you want, Mackenzie?"

Another sob rose in her chest because she wanted everything.

To be happy and loved and unafraid. To be a part of something bigger than her limitations. She wanted to remember what it felt like to look forward to all the tomorrows. And look back on today feeling useful and strong.

And more than anything, she wanted her love to exist without conditions. And while Hunter's love would come with limitless possibilities, hers would always bring boundaries.

"I want to know what it feels like to stand on my own two feet. No, I *need* it," she said, choking on the pain of what she knew she was about to say. "I need to remember what it's like to be capable. Just like I need for you to look back in a few years and not regret today."

"Then don't run away again," he begged.

"I'm not running, Hunter. We're just headed in different directions," she said.

He was silent for so long Mackenzie's heart was racing. "And here I thought I made it clear I was headed toward you," he whispered. "You're so stuck on sacrificing yourself in the fight for me you've completely missed that I've been fighting for us. I love you, Mackenzie, exactly how you are. The question is, do you love me?"

Yes, she wanted to cry. Everything she'd done was for love. The easy choice would be to take what he was offering. But love never came easily for Mackenzie.

"Hunter, I—"

"Enough said." His hands fell away from her, and he took a step back—in more ways than one. "I guess you're right, Trouble, we do want different things," he said flatly. "You want to go back to the way things were. Problem is, I can't."

"So that's it?" Panic began to curl itself around her. "There is no middle ground?"

"Love doesn't work that way. It's an all-in kind of thing. And I think you're all-in, you're just too scared to admit it," he whispered, and she could sense his gaze on her face, lingering, memorizing. Then he pressed a heartbreakingly gentle kiss to her lips. "When you figure it out, I'll be waiting."

With that he headed toward the door. It slammed shut behind him, echoing through the empty stairwell. For a minute, she could hear him calling a ride for her, and then everything went quiet.

The silence was so final it resonated through her. Instinctually, her shoulders immediately straightened, back to the place where she could carry the weight of the world—only this time it felt heavier, as if she was going to buckle under the pressure.

She held strong to her decision, fighting the need to crumble. But she was so tired of fighting. For love, for her freedom, for life to finally go her way.

And suddenly, she was too tired to fight. A chill swept around her, clinging tighter with every second that passed. A sob worked its way out, racking her body, quickly followed by another, until her knees began to give way.

She reached back and found the handrail, lowering herself to the bottom step.

Muttley whimpered and pressed himself securely to her side.

Unable to hold back any longer, Mackenzie buried her face in his neck and let the emotion spill free.

The frustration, the longing, the anger, and the grief. Lots of grief. So devastatingly raw it ached to breathe.

If she thought she'd experienced pain all those years ago, it was nothing compared to the deep emptiness filling her chest now, the cold so severe her body was on the brink of shattering with each second that passed.

Mackenzie had survived her share of loss, had learned how to embrace it. She even knew how to put the pieces back together. This time, though, she was afraid she'd never find all the pieces to make herself whole again.

CHAPTER 18

"Man, I can smell the stench from here," Brody said to Hunter, waving a hand in front of his nose like he was in fucking middle school. Then the prick looked at Cash. "You smell that?"

Cash leaned across the bar top and took a whiff. "What, the self-loathing? Or the pile of Hunter-brewed shit he's been wallowing in all week?" Cash said, taking way too much joy in Hunter's current situation.

"Fuck you." Hunter placed a hand on Cash's face and gave a hard shove.

Had the situation been swapped, had Cash gotten himself in the middle of a shit sandwich with a woman, Hunter would have seen the humor. But things weren't swapped, and this wasn't just any woman. Mackenzie was *the* woman.

Always had been. He'd just been too stupid to see it. And now it had been thirteen long days of silence. Thirteen days since he'd seen her, held her, even spoken with her. She'd told him in no uncertain terms that they couldn't work, their lives were too different, and pursuing anything more would only end in further heartache.

Further heartache? Hunter fought back a grim chuckle.

He already ached. He didn't think his heart could ache any more if it stopped beating. Even that would be a welcomed change if it meant the pain would stop with it.

"You going to call her?" Brody asked.

Hunter looked out the front of the bar and watched the rain slide down the windowpanes. An early spring storm had blown in from the south, bringing with it tropical gusts strong enough to cause horizontal rain. Most of the shops had closed for the night, and patrons brave enough to battle the elements had headed home hours ago.

"I put the decision in her hands," he said, looking at his cousins. Oh, his cousins were looking back at him like he was a complete idiot. "What? From the beginning she made it clear she needed time, so I am going to give her what she wants."

"If you think that's what she wants, you're worse off than I thought," Brody said.

"Since when are you for me pursuing Mackenzie?"

"Since it became clear that the two of you were meant to be together, and on your own you're bound to screw this up. Again," Brody said bluntly.

"What do you mean, again?"

Brody laughed. "For the first time since your divorce, you have a shot at the real deal. Too bad you're so busy trying to uncomplicate everything for everyone that you're screwing over the one person who's had your best interests in mind the entire time."

"And now I'm putting her interests first."

"Explain how you running off to your big dog and pony show is putting her first," Cash said.

"I'm not running off. I don't run. I'm giving her space." Only he was afraid this space would eventually lead to breaking his heart. Today they would be friends, but tomorrow she would be sending him straight to voice mail. The next thing he knew, she'd cut ties completely.

Fuck.

"We've been asking for space for years, but you keep coming back and hounding us like the damn plague," Brody said.

"She's different." Of that he was certain.

"Exactly." Cash laughed. "And yet you're here. Wasting time with your bros, like some high school prick, waiting for her to make the next move, because you forced the ball into her court."

"Yeah, I fucked up. I had three weeks to convince her how perfect it could be. Three weeks! So I pushed too hard too fast." Hunter shoved back from the bar and stood. "Now I'm trying to fix it."

"You got it all wrong." Brody stood too, got in his way, and blocked his path. "You had forever." Brody's face softened. "Your plan, though? The perfect one where Mackenzie fits seamlessly into your already scheduled world tour? That plan had three weeks. Love doesn't submit to a concert tour."

"I told her I love her." And she'd told him she wanted out.

"Yeah, you also told her your love was conditional. That for it to work it had to be on your terms and your timeline."

"That's not what I said."

"You sure? Because when you get laser focused on making things happen, you don't leave a lot of room for input or error. And Mackenzie's continued success depends on a daily routine of trial and error," Brody said. "And at the first error, instead of reworking *your* world, you threw your hands up and walked."

Jesus, was his cousin right?

Hunter gripped the back of his neck and squeezed, trying to stop the panic that had been strangling him all week. It didn't help. Nothing seemed to help. With every minute that passed, the stranglehold became stronger, tighter, working its way around his neck until he was certain he would stop breathing.

He leaned against the counter, or maybe his lungs finally gave up the fight. He wasn't sure, but suddenly his vision dimmed and all he could see was the past few weeks—rushing at him with a force too staggering to remain upright.

He replayed how terrified she'd been about losing Muttley, how resigned she'd been about him going off to live this amazing life. A life that would mean nothing without her.

Without love.

"Simplifies everything, doesn't it?" Brody said with a smug smile.

Hunter couldn't find a goddamn thing to smile about. Mackenzie wasn't running. She'd given him her love—the only way she knew how. And what had he done? Said it wasn't enough. He'd never made enough room for them to even exist. Never made room for her love. And he knew exactly how that felt.

He'd been so desperate to make it work he hadn't taken the time to ask her what wasn't working. So afraid of losing out on love again, losing out on a life with her, he'd somehow missed the "with her" part.

She hadn't missed it. She'd seen exactly what life with him would be like. Her alone in a dark room and him surrounded by the house lights.

He stared at the storm raging outside, and a flash of light exploded over the city. He looked at his cousins, both of them smiling like idiots. "I gotta go."

Brody clapped him on the shoulder. "Figured as much."

CHAPTER 19

Rain beat down on the roof and hail pelted the windows, rattling the panes until Mackenzie feared one would shatter. The house moaned under the awesome force of the roaring wind.

The storm had raged for three days, flooding parts of town, knocking over trees, downing power lines, and shredding her already frazzled nerves. It had left her virtually housebound, not that she had anywhere she intended to go, but the thought that she couldn't left her feeling suffocated, out of control.

Muttley whimpered, his collar jingling, and fabric rustled as he turned in circles before nuzzling farther into his doggy bed.

"For such a big dog you sure can be a scaredy-cat," Mackenzie teased in a soothing voice.

Everything stilled. An eerie silence emerged a fraction of a moment before the crackle of lighting overhead. She counted the seconds, anticipating the thunderous clap to arrive.

One.

Tw—

A boom of thunder shook the entire house. Fear snapped in Mackenzie's heart and rattled beneath her ribs, making her breath stutter. Muttley yelped and darted to the foot of her bed, his wet nose seeking her hand. She felt small and weak beneath the onslaught of Mother Nature. As soon as the fear ebbed, the pain of losing Hunter crept in, followed by anger.

White-hot anger. With Hunter for holding on to the hope that things between them could be different—that their worlds could somehow coexist—and refusing to see that sometimes hope was nothing more than the inability to accept reality.

She was angry with herself too. Angry that she lacked the confidence and skill to adapt to change faster—to become the person he needed her to be for their relationship to work.

But mostly she was angry with the situation. The reason letting go was so incredibly painful was because it was the only choice—for them both.

Mackenzie fisted the soft flannel of Hunter's shirt and closed her eyes. And for just a moment she allowed herself to remember how he'd felt lying next to her. The comforting weight of his body, the smell of his skin, the stubborn superhero complex that drove her nuts.

And a strangled laugh escaped her lips, followed by a sob so small and so broken her chest ached at the sound.

"Gawd, you're pathetic," she said, lying on her back and flopping her hands to her sides.

Refusing to dissolve into more tears, Mackenzie pulled back the covers and swung her legs out of bed, hoping some tea would quiet the what-ifs that had haunted her for the past two weeks. Her limbs were leaden and trembled as she stood, not from fear now but from sheer fatigue.

Mackenzie had worked so hard to keep it together when saying goodbye to Hunter that the second she'd been left alone, the floodgates had opened. And she was still trying to plug all the little cracks—without much success.

At first, the only way she could get the tears to stop was to sleep. So she'd spent most of the first few days in her room, sleeping in Hunter's shorts and spooning her dog for dear life, which placed her on the corner of Pathetic and Dramatically Tragic.

Then on day four, Savannah had come over with a T-bone, an umbrella, and a dozen doughnuts. The steak was for Muttley, the umbrella was for their daily walks around town, and the doughnuts—those were for celebrating the end of Mackenzie's pity party.

A party Mackenzie was determined to end. Her heart was a little slow on the uptake, but she knew from experience that if she put on a brave face, the bravery would eventually come.

This time there was too much at stake. So every day she pulled out her umbrella and courage and walked a block farther than she had the day before.

Mackenzie found a numbing slice of solace in her daily routine. The tedious monotony kept her busy enough to avoid thinking about Hunter and forced her to rejoin the world of the living. Not that she could call barely eating, sleeping, or writing living, by any means. But every day got easier.

The nights were another story—a rather embarrassing one that still involved a little canine spooning and that damn shirt she'd hidden from Savannah, unable to let go of her last piece of Hunter.

She stroked the soft fabric now as she half shuffled through the kitchen to make herself a much-needed cup of chamomile tea. Just her, her panties, her sleep tank, and Hunter's shirt.

Oh, and an unharnessed Muttley, who was usually one step in front of her. Tonight, however, he was right at her heels, brushing his body against hers, not in a signal of danger but to offer comfort and request it in return.

Another clap of thunder shook the walls, knocking something to the floor, and a loud thud filled the air. Confused, Muttley shoved against Mackenzie's legs in a command to stop. She bent down and ran a soothing hand through his coat.

"It's okay, buddy," she said, tugging at his collar and directing him to his pillow in the corner. "You just stay here while I make some tea."

In a strange way Mackenzie felt an affinity with the storm, which had been labeled by the news as turbulent, violent, and angry. Mother Nature was PMSing, and Mackenzie could relate. Her emotions had been all over the map and would hit with such volatile force she'd been left at their mercy.

Five steps forward and two to the left, Mackenzie grabbed the teapot and filled it. After two more steps left, she placed it on the front burner and turned the switch to high. The familiar muffled click followed by the coil heating never came. Mackenzie moved the pot and held her hand over the burner, palm down, and waited.

Nothing. No heat rose up to meet her skin. She clicked it off and back on again.

"Oh, come on!" She slammed the pot down and looked up at the ceiling. "You've got to be kidding me."

Logically she knew it was only tea, but her logic seemed to set with the sun, and if Mother Nature expected her to make it through tonight, then she needed her damn tea.

The wind howled, and branches slammed against the glass of the sunroom. The doggy door flapped back and forth. Fearing the flap would rip off its hinge, Mackenzie dropped her head with a resigned sigh and shuffled against the cold tile to fasten it shut. It wasn't as if Muttley would venture out tonight. She couldn't even get him to enter the sunroom, let alone go out in the storm.

When Mackenzie secured the door, her toes settled on cold, wet tiles, and she cursed. In her woe-is-me tantrum, she'd forgotten to throw on not only pants but also her house boots.

Shaking her head, she turned back toward the kitchen to fetch her boots. An enormous crackle of energy filled the air, so close Mackenzie could feel the static build around her. Before she could move, thunder exploded directly overhead, rattling the glass walls.

Mackenzie's heart stuttered. The floor vibrated, sending violent tremors underfoot. She pressed a hand to the wall for balance. The cold glass fogged under her touch when, somewhere close, a transformer exploded, emitting a sharp, static-filled rumble. Directly overhead, another ominous quake of thunder shook the house.

Muttley let out one ferocious bark after another.

"Stay, Muttley," she commanded with a tone that demanded compliance.

She was about to join him when an ear-piercing crack pounded through the yard and ricocheted off the sunroom's glass walls, followed by a terrifying crash.

Instinctually, Mackenzie's hands flew over her head as she ducked, curling into a ball.

As if the room were possessed, a chaotic symphony of cracks and bursts erupted as the roof shattered. Her scream was cut short by a shower of glass. Razor-sharp shards rained down, pelting her arms and legs and slicing at her feet.

The chaos ended as quickly as it had begun. Mackenzie's ears rang through the still silence. Eventually the buzz gave way to Muttley's ferocious bark, the whistle of wind as it blew through the space with enough force to whip at her hair. She didn't need her sight to know that the house had been ripped open and was now exposed to the elements.

The groan of broken wood, the crackle of leaves, and the scent of sap settled around her, telling her the old oak tree had caused the crash, and she was extremely lucky she hadn't been in its path.

Breathing hard, her heart pounding against her ribs, Mackenzie slowly lowered her hands and straightened. She held her breath and shook her head, tiny bits of broken glass sprinkling to the floor.

Muttley continued to bark, his stress increasing with each cry.

"Okay, boy," she told him, "I'm fine. I'm coming." Mackenzie took a tentative step toward her distressed pup, and pain sliced through her foot. She sucked a breath at the sting of glass and pulled back.

The clack of Muttley's nails and the jingle of his dog tags shot fear through Mackenzie's heart. She thrust her hand out. "Stay," she ordered. But she was too late, and Muttley yelped in pain, then whined.

Now she wasn't the only one with glass in her foot. And there wasn't anyone around to help. She felt that familiar panic swell, fill her body with the leaden need to sit down until help came.

She shivered as a cold wind cut through the room. Taking a breath, she bent down to gingerly brush glass from the sole of her foot. When it was clean, she carefully set it down in the same place it had been when the roof caved in.

"You got this," she whispered, hoping when she said it, it would become truth.

Biting her lower lip, she balanced herself equally on both feet and crouched. She lightly patted the floor around her, testing the surface for debris. Glass scratched her palms and she gasped, drawing her hands back.

She so didn't have this. She was barefoot, alone, and surrounded by a sea of shattered glass.

"Holy shit."

Overwhelmed by the situation, she felt the words choke out of her. She wrapped her arms around her knees and pressed her forehead there. Her insides trembled, and her mind raced. What now? What the fuck now? Savannah was gone, Hunter was out of her life, and she had no way of calling out for help. She was trapped in her own worst nightmare.

And, God, she was tired. So tired of handling everything alone. A sob of utter anguish rocked her chest.

Muttley's barks had become shrill and scraped her nerves. A wave of white-hot, disgusted-with-herself fury swept through her, and she lifted her head and yelled, *"Muttley. No."*

His barks transitioned into whines, and Mackenzie put her head back down, wiping her face with Hunter's shirt.

Hunter. The thought of him made longing cut through her. God, she missed him. Missed the way he held her and the way he believed in her—even when she didn't know how to believe in herself.

And right then, she could use some of that unwavering belief of his. Needed his courage to take the leap without being able to clearly see the net.

Tears burned her eyes. Tears of frustration and pain and fear. And for one self-indulgent moment she thought about just giving up. Just sitting down in the glass until the storm passed. Until someone found her. But then she wouldn't be living independently, would she? Then she would have given up Hunter for nothing.

Another blast of frigid air wafted through the house, blowing across her wet body and racking a shiver through her.

She swore at the universe. And then she swallowed her fury and all her self-pity. No one was coming. At least not until tomorrow, and Muttley wouldn't wait that long. Not when rain splattered them with cold waves of droplets as trees swayed overhead and thunder continued to roll and rattle the house.

Using her most calm and confident tone, she said, "Muttley, sit." Then to herself she said, "You got this."

She didn't feel any more capable, but she moved into action anyway.

Lifting her head, she stretched out one arm at a time as far as she could without toppling over. She touched an end table. She could pull it over and get on top of it, but that was as far as the table would take her. Though it did give her another idea.

When she couldn't reach the sofa, Mackenzie pulled the sleeve of Hunter's flannel over her hand and gingerly swept a spot on the floor clear of glass. Shards pricked at her palm, and when she moved her knee to that spot, baby-fine slivers dug into her flesh. She gritted her teeth and growled through the pain, reaching toward the sofa again. Her fingertips brushed the velour of the arm, and hope sparked, lighting the darkness swamping her chest.

Shivering with cold, she covered her other hand and repeated the movement until she could reach over the arm of the sofa. Pushing herself upright forced glass deeper into her knees, and she whimpered at the pain. Sliding her hands down the side, she was able to get the piping of a cushion between her fingers and fought to pull the soaked fabric over the arm. The simple task made her arms and lungs burn.

Thankfully her fear had turned to anger—at her situation. And herself. Anger strong enough to haul the cushion the final few inches over the side.

Glass flew from the cushion, grazing her face. She flipped the cushion so the side protected from the glass turned up, and she dropped it on the floor. She painfully leaned into one knee while she brushed glass from the other and set it on the cushion. Then did the same with the first.

She rested there a minute, relishing the feel of a glass-free surface, even if it was squishy and cold with rainwater. Once the pain ebbed and she'd caught her breath, she straightened and used the arm of the sofa to help her stand.

Muttley encouraged her with a bark of excitement.

"I'm getting there, buddy."

With covered hands, she brushed glass from the arm and leaned over it, tentatively searching for more softness. She touched a blanket, got hold of a couple of throw pillows, and dragged them all to her, careful to set them down beyond the cushion where she stood with the glass-free side up.

Turning, she crouched again and positioned the blanket—the first ladder rung toward safety. Out of breath again, she paused before making her way across the protected floor.

She'd done it.

"Oh my God!" She'd actually done it. She could use these props to get her out of the glass and reach Muttley. Make sure he was okay. Then she could call 911.

There would be insurance, cleanup, repairs, and new furniture to deal with, but she'd done it. She'd survived an emergency on her own with only superficial scrapes.

She made her way across the glass to her dog, and this time when the tears came, they originated from someplace different. A complicated combination of relief and bitterness at the injustice of it all swirled together to make a giant knot in her stomach.

She'd pushed through, found her independence, and proved to herself she could do it. On her own terms. Yet the one person she wanted to share the moment with was gone.

Muttley used the pillows she'd thrown down as a bridge to meet her halfway, licking her face when she reached out.

She made it to his dog bed and swiveled, dropping her butt to the soft, dry surface. When she caught her breath, she could tend to her wounds, change into dry clothes, and call emergency crews to help with the house.

Yup, Mackenzie was officially self-reliant.

And she was heartbreakingly miserable.

◆　◆　◆

Hunter's stomach rolled as he turned onto Mackenzie's street.

The rain came down in sheets, filling the already-flooded streets of downtown and turning his usual fifteen-minute trip to Mackenzie's into an hour and change—an agonizing hour spent thinking about

Mackenzie and realizing that the guy lucky enough to spend his life with a woman like Mackenzie wouldn't hesitate to put her needs first.

And Hunter was going to be that guy. Was going to spend his life showing her just how special she was.

First, though, he had to convince her to give him another chance. And every second he wasted driving through puddles was another second she was left thinking she wasn't worth the trouble.

The darkened streets and downed poles only added to the stress. But when Hunter pulled into her driveway and saw the destruction, his heart went from pounding to thundering.

Branches littered the walkway, her front porch swing was hanging by one chair, and the giant oak behind her house was gone.

The truck was barely in park when Hunter leaped out and raced up to her front porch. Calling her name, he shoved through the front door, and his chest nearly exploded.

The old oak wasn't gone. It had torn through the sunroom's roof and obliterated the back wall. Twisted metal, sheet music, and pages from her journal littered the space. Shattered glass covered every horizontal surface. And her guitar, the one she'd used to create all her music, was in pieces beneath the tree trunk.

"Mackenzie," he yelled, dread spiraling through his veins as he strained to listen for her response. For any sound that would let him know she was okay.

Silence was his only answer.

He called out again and heard a bark coming from the back of the room. And that's when he saw her.

Mackenzie.

Sitting at the edge of the destruction among the debris, in the dog bed, with her arms wrapped around her knees and her head down. Muttley sat beside her, his tail wagging at the sight of Hunter. Relief and regret forced the air from Hunter's lungs.

"Mackenzie." He rushed toward her and crouched, scanning her body for injuries. She had cuts on her shins, blood streaks marring her skin. "Are you hurt?"

She lifted her head, her expression exhausted and confused. "Hunter?" A shiver rocked her wet body. "What are you doing here?"

What are you doing here?

Talk about an arrow straight through his heart.

He slipped off his jacket and wrapped it around her body, watchful of the scratches on her shoulders and arms and a little more alarmed when he saw the bloodstain near the hem of her shirt.

"You're bleeding." He tugged her shirt up slightly, looking for a wound.

"It's not all mine," she said, and—*thank Christ*—he pulled her carefully against him.

"I came here to tell you I was an idiot, but then I saw the tree, and I thought—"

He silently shook his head, not wanting to go where his thoughts had led him a moment ago.

He cut a look at the gaping hole in the sunroom, the spot on the sofa where Mackenzie usually sat now occupied by a thick branch of the old oak that had once been in her yard. Then he saw the trail of blankets and pillows highlighting her location at the time of the crash, and his blood turned to ice.

A foot to the right and he wouldn't be holding her right now.

"Were you in the sunroom when it came down?"

He hoped to God she'd say no, but the small nod of her head made him sick.

"I went to close the dog flap when the tree snapped," she said, and for a moment, he saw the event without eyes, the way she must have experienced it. The noise, the uncertainty, the struggle. "Thankfully Muttley was in the house somewhere when it came down. Only once things settled, he tried to get to me and stepped in glass, so I told him to stay put, that I'd come to him."

"Of course you did," he said, easing down next to her in the dog bed. There wasn't enough room, and his butt was hanging half-off, but he didn't care. She was all right.

She's all right, he realized, and a rough laugh escaped.

Okay, maybe it was closer to a cry, because—*Jesus*—most people in the same situation would have been too panicked to safely navigate themselves out of that disaster. Not Mackenzie.

Nope, in nothing but her nightshirt, bare feet, and the bravery of an army, she'd managed not only to get to safety but also to rescue her rescue dog.

"He actually stayed." She tilted her face toward his and flashed a small and tremulous smile. "He stayed put so I could come to him and get the glass out of his paw." She turned to Muttley and ruffled his ears. "Didn't you, boy?"

Muttley barked, then plopped half his body across Mackenzie.

"He trusts you." He gently lifted Mackenzie so she was on his lap, then pulled Muttley against Hunter's side, until all three of them were fully in the dog bed. "He's a smart dog."

With a nervous whine, Muttley rested his muzzle on Hunter's thigh.

"I'm really okay." She tried to get up, but he held her to him. "Most of the blood is from Muttley's paw."

"I may have been slow on the uptake, but I know you are," he said, resting his cheek on the top of her head. "I'm the one who needs a hug right now."

She wrapped her arms around him and held tight, and that's how they remained for a long moment. Silently holding each other, while Hunter breathed in her scent.

And sitting there with Mackenzie in his arms, he realized that his cousins were right. It didn't matter how long it took or how perfectly everything fit together, love wasn't a destination. It was a journey.

CHAPTER 20

"Seriously, I'm okay," Mackenzie said into the phone for what felt like the hundredth time, as they pulled into Hunter's garage. "Muttley's okay, and the house can be fixed."

Her relationship with Hunter? That was still up in the air.

He'd swooped in like some kind of superhero for hire, held her until she stopped shaking, bandaged her wounds, then packed her and Muttley safely into his truck and driven them to his place.

He'd been warm and caring and gentle—so incredibly gentle she'd nearly wept. But whenever she'd broached the topic of them, he'd squeezed her hand and said, "We'll get there."

Only now they were at his place and they were no closer to *there* than they'd been last week at the symphony.

"You sure, darlin'?" Arthur's concern came over the phone line loud and clear. "You sound like maybe you could use a strong shoulder, some tissues, and maybe some of my chili. Maybe I should come home. My chili always makes you feel better. Plus, there's going to be contractors to call, crews to orchestrate, and you'll need a place to sleep. You can't sleep with all that racket and chaos going on."

"Well, there's nothing to be done tonight, and I'm already staying at a friend's," she assured him. For how long she didn't know, but for tonight she had everything that mattered: her safety, her dog, and her man.

Without warning, the passenger-side door opened, and Hunter leaned in, slipping the phone from her hand.

"Hey, Arthur, this is Hunter. The friend," he said, and she didn't miss the humor in his voice. "Mackenzie is a little battered but holding strong. All she needs now is to get warmed up and a good night's sleep."

"And where will *you* be sleeping?" Arthur asked Hunter, and had Mackenzie not been so tired, she would have laughed at the parental tone.

"That's up to the lady," Hunter assured him.

"Don't say that." Mackenzie pressed her palm over the mouthpiece. "Now he'll think that we're—"

"What did you say, darlin'?" Arthur's voice was muffled but audible. Which meant he'd heard her.

She uncovered the phone. "That he's sleeping on the couch."

"Good girl. Now if you need anything before I get home or something changes and you need a place to stay, you have the spare key."

The wind howled, and a shiver swept through her body with some pretty serious force.

"Thanks for checking in, Arthur, but we've got to go," Hunter said, sliding the phone from her fingers and ending the call. Then he leaned all the way into the truck, one hand on her knee and the other on her shoulder, until all she could smell was the rain on his skin. "The shower is on the second floor. Do you want to hobble up there all by your lonesome, or can I carry you?"

Her answer was to wrap her arms around his neck.

"I'll take that as a yes," he mused, then whistled. Muttley jumped out of the back seat, and his claws tapped against the floor as he followed them inside the house and up the stairs.

She knew when they'd reached the living area because the air was warmer, the space cozier. The clanking of Muttley's tags was muffled, as if the room was filled with furniture and fabrics—things that made up Hunter's world.

When he finally set her down, it was on a bathroom counter. "I want to double-check your feet for glass shards."

He disappeared for a moment, and she heard the shower start. Within seconds a cloud of warm steam engulfed her, warming her skin as his thoughtfulness warmed her heart.

Then he was back.

His big hands settled around one ankle as he lifted her foot to inspect it. His fingers moved gently across the sole and around the heel before giving her a gentle squeeze and doing the same to the other foot. When he was satisfied, those nimble fingers settled on the zipper of her jacket and slowly tugged down.

"What are you doing?" she asked breathlessly.

"Checking the rest of you." Without further explanation, he slipped the jacket off and then went for the hem of her nightshirt.

Ever so slowly, he slid her shirt up and over her head, leaving her in nothing but her bra and panties.

She heard him suck in a breath, but when he touched her, it was to trace the scrapes and scratches on her arms, then her neck, and finally her cheek.

"After you shower, you'll want to put a Band-Aid on a few of these, but most are pretty shallow." He cupped her cheek in his palm. "Do you need help?"

"No." She needed to talk about what had happened between them, but she knew he'd say later. And for right now, she was okay with later.

So when he went to step back, she caught his hand in hers. "But I don't want to do it alone."

"God, me either," he said, pressing a kiss to her forehead.

Mackenzie wasn't sure if he meant he didn't want to leave her alone or if he didn't want to leave her side. Either way he helped her off the counter and led her to his shower. She removed her bra and panties and stepped into the hot spray.

Hunter came in behind her, running his soapy hands down her body in a gesture that was more tender than sexual in nature. He took his time, making sure there was no glass left in her hair, no scratch left untouched. And when she was finally warm, he shut off the water and wrapped her in a fluffy towel before tugging one of his T-shirts over her head.

"I'm never going to get this shirt back again, am I?" he asked, placing her on the bed and pulling the covers up around her.

She sniffed the soft and worn cotton and shook her head. "Nope. Sorry."

"Glad I didn't pull out my vintage Johnny Cash one, then."

She laughed, but the emotion quickly changed to something closer to an unbearable ache. "Hunter, about before—"

"Shhh," he said, feathering the lightest of kisses across her lips. "After you get some rest, we'll have plenty of time to talk. I promise."

She nodded, not because she was okay with waiting. She wasn't. But she nodded because she was close to losing it. Tears were already lining her lashes, just waiting for one more gentle touch or word to spill free.

"Muttley," Hunter said and gave a pat on the mattress.

Muttley wasted no time hopping up and sprawling himself across the width of the bed.

"Move over, you bed hog." She pushed, but Muttley went limp. "I know you're awake, now move."

A snoring sound came from the boulder of fur in the middle of the bed. "Seriously, just shove him over so you have room."

"I'm sleeping on the couch, remember?" She opened her mouth to argue, and he kissed her again. "Plus, if I don't call Brody and check in, my entire house will be flooded with family, and then no one gets any sleep," he said. "I put your phone on the nightstand in case you need to call me." He took her hand to show her. "And I kept Muttley's harness on in case you wanted to explore without me."

He was giving her the independence she'd asked for while reassuring her that he was there if she needed him. And for the first time, Mackenzie wondered if maybe she had it all wrong. She'd always associated love with sacrifice—with limits and boundaries. And to be happy, she thought she had to be self-sufficient.

But Hunter's love didn't feel like a burden. It felt a whole lot like freedom.

◆ ◆ ◆

"I get that there is no going back and that once we do it, it's done," Hunter said to Brody, who was sitting across the coffee table on the couch, his hand kneading small circles over his chest.

"Savannah's right. You're going to give me a heart attack. I'm going to die before Caroline graduates from Mommy and Me, and then my wife will hate me for leaving her, and it'll be all your fault." A small smile tugged at Brody's mouth. "But my brothers would have to step in for Savannah and deal with the teen years. Maybe it wouldn't be so bad."

Hunter sat back on the couch and laughed. And to be honest, after the night he'd had, it felt good.

He'd been with Brody for the past hour, trying to figure out the best way to change the band's tour without getting sued by everyone in Nashville. He didn't care if he lost everything as long as he had

Mackenzie, but ending this amicably with his sponsors and label would make it easier to pick back up if that's what they decided to do.

"Garth Brooks took a ten-year hiatus, all I'm asking for is some time for Mackenzie and me to get settled, then figure out together how we want to move forward."

"I agree," Brody said, stifling a yawn. "And I would have agreed with you tomorrow morning after the sun came up."

"Yeah, well, tomorrow I'll be busy asking Mackenzie to forgive my dumb ass, and you'll be talking with the band. The guys need to decide who among them is willing to man up and take over some of the heavy lifting. If they want a world tour and all the stuff that comes with it, then they need to start making room for the interviews and meet and greets and all the rest of the BS I handle."

"There's going to be some major pushback," Brody warned.

Hunter shrugged. He didn't care. Most guys never got a second chance with the right woman. He was lucky enough to get a third, and he didn't care what he had to give up, as long as it wasn't her.

"Convince the label you haven't lost your mind, renegotiate a hundred-million-dollar contract, and force a bunch of bros to man up." Brody stood, and that's when Hunter realized his cousin was in a raincoat, flannel pajama bottoms, and rain boots. "Got it, now can I go back to bed with my wife?"

"Thanks, Brody," Hunter said, and he meant it.

Hunter stood to show his cousin out when they heard dog paws at the end of the hallway.

"Hunter?" The soft and sleep-roughened voice also came from the end of the hallway.

He was about to tell her Brody was just leaving when she walked into the room and both men froze.

"Oh shit," Brody mouthed.

Oh shit, indeed. Because before either of them could move, Mackenzie padded in with her hair hanging loose down her back, his

T-shirt flirting with her thighs, and a very pink, very lacy, and very small pair of panties playing a game of peekaboo every time she stepped.

"Go," Hunter mouthed back, waving his hand at Brody to get out.

To which Brody gave a *How the fuck do you expect me to do that?* look, because between him and the door was a half-naked woman who would be mortified if she knew he was there.

Hunter held a finger to his lips, and Brody gave him a no-shit roll of the eyes.

"At least look away, man" was followed by the universal hand gesture for "cover your damn eyes."

"Hunter?" she said again, and both men looked back at her. Because this time the uncertainty was creeping in. Not to mention Muttley had taken one look at Brody and was going in for a doggy high five.

"Right here, Trouble."

She smiled at his voice and changed direction. Muttley was by her side, pressing against her leg, navigating her away from Brody and toward the couch.

"Did I wake you?" And, damn, that Georgian accent was even thicker when she was half-asleep.

"Nope, I was just finishing up and was going to come check on you."

"Funny, I was doing the same thing." She paused and wrinkled her nose. "Did you let Muttley out earlier?"

"No. Why?"

"I don't know, it smells like wet dog"—she sniffed again—"or wet hair or something."

Brody glared at Hunter. Hunter grinned.

"Nope, he was with you the whole time. But it looks like someone forgot their pants again?"

"Again?" mouthed the third wheel in flannel bottoms. *"What happened to taking it slow?"*

"What happened to leaving?" Hunter punctuated this with the finger, and Brody quietly headed down the stairs and to the door, presumably to let himself out.

"I didn't bring any." She reached her hand out, and he met her halfway. Taking her by the hand, he wove her around the coffee table and into his arms.

"Isn't that a damn shame," he said, brushing her hair behind her ear, noticing that her eyelids were still heavy with exhaustion. Her vulnerability hit him like a hard punch to the chest, powered by the guilt and the memories from a night he could never erase. "You didn't sleep very long."

"Too much going on in my head to sleep." She stepped into him and held his face in both hands. Her gentle touch, combined with the raw vulnerability in her voice, was his undoing. "I couldn't sleep until I told you how sorry I am for the other night. I was scared, and instead of facing it, I pushed you away."

"You're not the one who needs to apologize. That's all on me. You pushed because I didn't give you much of an option." He wanted to haul her in and kiss her breathless. But that would lead to touching and eventually amazing sex—and right now she needed support. So he pressed her hands to his lips. "But seeing you tonight, sitting there in that dog bed, knowing what you went through and how brave you were. How brave you had to be . . ." He swallowed hard. "I am so damn proud of you."

"I'm not."

"Nothing about the past few weeks has been on your terms. Nothing." A situation, sadly, that he'd played a huge role in. "But you never gave up. Not even tonight, when most people would have crumbled."

She lifted one slim shoulder and let it fall. "Sure, I figured it out by myself, but when the storm had passed, I was *all by myself.* I didn't have anyone to share the victory with."

"And that's my fault," he said, curling his hands even further around hers, loving the way she tightened her clasp. "I was so stuck on proving to you that we could work, I never slowed down enough to ask you what you needed to move forward. And what you pictured *us* looking like in the future."

"I would never want you to slow down," she said apologetically, and her words made him still. "Just like I would never want to be the person to hold you back. I'm not sure how to keep up, or if I even can, but I want to."

"That's where you got it wrong," he whispered against her fingers. "You don't slow me down, you remind me to live full in every moment. Experience things as if it was the first time. You are my reason, Mackenzie." His head listed forward, resting against hers. "I love you, Trouble. All of you."

Tears flooded her eyes and spilled over her lashes. "I loved you the first time I saw you. You were my best friend, and then my lover, and now you're my everything. I want all of you." Which worked for him, since every single cell in his body was overflowing with love for her.

She wrapped her arms around his waist and met his gaze, and—*holy Christ*—there it was. Shining on her beautiful face for the world to see. The one thing he'd spent his entire life looking for. Right there. His for the taking.

Love.

The pure, unconditional, no-strings-attached variety that he'd written about, dreamed about, and chased with abandon but feared he'd never find for himself.

"You've had me from the moment I saw you in my uncle's bar," he said, realizing it was true.

"I know I can take care of myself," she said, and the way her soft pink lips quivered nearly brought him to his knees. "But it doesn't mean anything if I don't have you to share my life with."

For the first time, Hunter felt as if he'd found his place. And it was right beside the woman who saw beneath the hype to the guy he'd kept hidden.

Hunter tipped his head to hers. "I love you today, tomorrow, and forever." Then he captured her lips in a kiss so raw it was what songs were written about.

EPILOGUE

Three months later . . .

Heart so full it felt as if it might burst, Mackenzie tightened her grip on Muttley's harness, and she heard the bus pull up.

Earlier that morning, Tia had stopped by with amazing news: Guide Dogs of Tennessee was so impressed with her and Muttley's progress, they'd made Muttley's placement permanent. To celebrate, Mackenzie decided to show off her new skills and head downtown to catch a bus.

Not just any bus, though, she thought with a grin.

The door swung open, and over the rush of air from the hydraulics, Mackenzie could make out enough distinct voices to tell her the bus was at full capacity.

"We got this," she told Muttley, who barked in agreement, then started up the steps with a confident stride.

Taking a deep breath, she followed his lead—and her heart—as they took one more step toward their happy place. Muttley stopped right inside the door. Before Mackenzie could say a word, the conversation on the bus came to an abrupt stop and the collective attention swung to Mackenzie.

"Hey, y'all," she said with a shyness that took her by surprise.

Her greeting was met with a few *Howdy*s and the occasional *Hey, darlin'*, but one voice stood out from the rest. A voice that made her lips curl into a big grin and her heart give an even bigger *thump-thump*.

"Trouble?" Hunter said, his pleased surprise at seeing her on his bus loud and clear. "What are you doing here?"

"I have good news," she said.

Two warm, strong hands slid around her waist as Hunter tugged her toward him. "I love good news. Almost as much as I love seeing you." He brushed a kiss across her lips, short and sweet but with plenty of promise for later.

Whoof, Muttley barked but kept his butt cemented to the floor.

"Hey to you too, buddy." Hunter gave him an ear ruffle, his other hand twining with Mackenzie's. "Now what's this news?"

"Tia called to say that the home study went amazing, and GDT doesn't see a reason to have another."

"I guess that means we're stuck together," he said to Muttley. Then, to her, he said, "I am so proud of you."

"It was all the trips to the market and around town that sealed the deal," she said, and no statement could have rung truer.

Hunter had been beyond amazing these past few months, helping her expand her world while showing her that love and independence didn't have to be mutually exclusive. Real love was as comforting as it was liberating.

"It was all you. I was just along for the ride," he said, giving her another kiss—this one a bit longer and a bit hotter.

Brody cleared his throat. "And we're all along for this ride with you, and I'd like to get off, so please tell me the meeting is over, because I'm about to see things I won't ever be able to unsee."

"I can come back," she offered.

"No way," Hunter whispered. "From this angle I can see a red piece of lace beneath that dress. Celebratory red." The gruff in his voice told her exactly what kind of celebration he was imagining. "Plus, these guys were all leaving anyway. Said something about throwing back a few brews at Big Daddy's. Right, guys?"

"It's been sprinkling all day and is supposed to really come down tonight, which is why I'm staying inside tonight," Quinn informed them. "Not to mention the bus leaves at oh-dark-hundred."

The band was heading out in the morning for New York, where in a week's time they would be hosting the listening party for their new album. To build some hype around the upcoming release, they had also scheduled a mini radio tour, hitting a select few stations on their way north. It was the first time the entire band would be required to be present at all the radio stops.

Not surprisingly, the band had agreed unanimously to limit the trip to just major-market stations.

"Then you'd better get going so you avoid the rain, get a jump on packing your things," Hunter said.

"My things are already packed," Quinn argued. "They're here. On the bus. Which is where I am planning on sleeping."

"Well, change of plans. Big Daddy's or head on home." When no one moved, Hunter added, "I can always text your women and see which they'd prefer."

There were a few grumbles, but one by one the band members told Mackenzie goodbye, except for Quinn—who hugged her while telling Hunter to go fuck himself.

"Night, darlin'," Brody said, giving Mackenzie's hand a warm squeeze.

She squeezed back. "Can you tell Savannah that she doesn't need to bring anything tomorrow? I went to the store already." Her chest filled with pride. "We're having a tea party at my place."

"I heard," Brody said. "I asked if I could come, but Caroline informed me it was a girls-only event." Brody paused. "Glad to have you back, Mack."

"Glad to be back."

"And I'm glad to see you go," Hunter said, and this time he did kick Brody off the bus. Only as Brody passed by her, she caught a whiff of something that smelled a whole lot like—

Wet dog?

"Oh my God. Your jacket, it smells like wet dog. You were at Hunter's that night."

"Good luck with that, cuz," Brody said as the door whooshed closed behind him.

"The night of the storm. When I walked out in my panties—oh God!" Her hands flew to her mouth in horror.

Hunter's hands? They were back on her, molding to her hips as if she weren't freaking out.

"Brody was at your house. I was in my panties. And you didn't say a word!" She batted at his hands, but he just moved them lower. "Hunter, I'm serious."

"You said *panties*. It doesn't get much more serious than panties." He walked around until he was behind her, and his lips grazed the outer rim of her ear. "Red panties."

"You know I never sleep in pajama bottoms. You should have warned me," she chided, but his body felt so delicious pressing into hers she couldn't resist melting back into him and resting her head against his chest.

He slid his arms around her waist and pressed a kiss to her shoulder. "It was only Brody."

"Only Brody? He's never going to let me live this down."

"Trouble, he was so uncomfortable I thought he was going to stroke out." He nuzzled the back of her neck and made her shiver—in the best possible way. "I doubt he will ever want to relive that particular moment. I think it was kind of like hitting on a chick at a bar only to realize she's your first cousin and you aren't in Arkansas."

"Is that supposed to make me happy?" she asked, turning to face him. "Because it doesn't."

"How about this, then?" He leaned down and kissed her. Not softly either. It was one of those lay-it-on-the-line, blow-your-mind kind of kisses, where she had to wrap her arms around his neck just to stay standing. When he finally pulled back, they were both breathless—and she was feeling *much* happier.

In fact, she couldn't remember what they'd been discussing.

"Getting closer," she teased, threading her fingers through the hair at the back of his neck.

"When it comes to your happiness, Trouble, close doesn't cut it." Hunter slid his talented fingers down, over her hips and lower, and that's when her heart gave one last *thump* before stopping altogether.

Because Hunter Kane, Sexiest Man Alive, was slowly unbuttoning her dress. She knew when he got to the bottom button, because her dress fell open and he sucked in a breath.

"Let me go on record as saying I am one hundred percent committed to your happy place." He feathered kisses down her neck and across her collarbone.

"You *are* my happy place, Hunter," she said, capturing his face between her hands so he could see how serious she was. "You always were, and you always will be. But promise me something."

"Anything," he whispered. "And everything."

Those three words were spoken with so much conviction any reservations that may have been lingering deep inside her completely vanished— and she was filled with a warm blast of love and adoration.

"Next time we have visitors, you'll give me a heads-up," she said.

"Done." He rested his forehead against hers. "And since we're making promises, I need *you* to promise *me* something, Trouble."

"What?"

"Promise me you," he said before delivering a soul-melting kiss to her lips. "Every day, every second, every moment—promise me all of you."

ABOUT THE AUTHOR

Photo © 2010 Tosh Tanaka

Marina Adair is a #1 national bestselling author and holds a master of fine arts in creative writing. Along with the Kane series, she is also the author of the St. Helena Vineyard series, the Heroes of St. Helena series, and the Sequoia Lake series. She currently lives with her husband, daughter, and two neurotic cats in Northern California. As a writer, Marina is devoted to giving her readers contemporary romance where the towns are small, the personalities are large, and the romances are explosive. She also loves to interact with readers. Check her out on Facebook, or visit her at www.MarinaAdair.com. Keep up with Marina by signing up for her newsletter at www.MarinaAdair.com/newsletter.